MAKING
· ROOM ·

MAKING
· ROOM ·

Michel Tremblay

Translated by Sheila Fischman

SERPENT'S
TAIL

My warmest thanks to Paquerette Villeneuve and Jacques Godbout, for their illuminating advice.

– M.T.

I am grateful to Lawrence Boyle of Librairie l'Androgyne for his encouragement and for his sensitive reading of this translation, and to Anne-Marie Bourdouxhe for once again unlocking the final doors.

– S.F.

BRITISH LIBRARY CATALOGUING IN PUBLICATION DATA

Tremblay, Michel
Making Room
I. Title
843 [F]

ISBN 1-85242-162-2

Originally published 1986 as *Le coeur découvert* by Les Editions
Leméac, Ottawa, Canada
Copyright © 1986 by Michel Tremblay

First published in English 1989 by
McLelland & Stewart Inc., Toronto, Canada

Translation copyright © 1989 by Sheila Fischman

This edition first published 1990 by
Serpent's Tail, 4 Blackstock Mews, London N4

Printed on acid-free paper by
Nørhaven A/S, Viborg, Denmark

To Jonathan, with the hope that one day he will understand how important he has become in my life.

Jean-Marc

I've always hated the bars. The simpatico spots where the regulars, tired of seeing the same faces bent over their glasses of lukewarm beer, turn towards the door with anxious optimism whenever a new silhouette appears, as well as those big trendy clubs, often ear-splittingly loud and crawling with the latest version of what passes for a smart set – dressed to kill and constantly on display and most of them as dull as white icing. One night when I was feeling especially down, a guy told me, as I tried to fan a spark of conversation: "If talk's what you want, you're in the wrong place. Nobody listens here."

So then I had a choice between, God help us, taking part yet again in a dialogue I know by heart, one I could recite with all its twists and turns and slightest variations, or watching the contortions of gorgeous perfect bodies who use as admiring mirrors the eyes of the other dancers and of the drinkers who circle the dance floor.

Now this isn't the bitterness of a man of thirty-nine who senses that he's getting old, less desirable, less quick to please, no, really, I've never liked the bars, not even in the days when all I wanted was seduction at any cost.

Still, I used to hang around them, a lot. In the early sixties, cruising in the streets of Montreal was difficult. So in spite of myself I'd known the golden era of the Hawaiian Lounge, the birth of PJ's, the years of glory of the Taureau d'or. I won't actually deny that I enjoyed myself, I'd be lying, but I've always maintained certain reservations, a coolness even,

1

towards those long evenings spent watching La Monroe or Belinda Lee make a spectacle of themselves, while keeping an eye out for who was coming, who was going, who was cruising who and how.

Nowadays, the streets are the best place for cruising. And the easiest. The meat's there, up for grabs and obvious, showing plenty of skin, even in winter. It rules over Ste-Catherine and St-Denis, day and night, though it's seldom very happy. On the contrary: cruising's become quite a serious business, one to be undertaken with furrowed brow. Now that the butch look is back, you just have to deck yourself out in workers' drag and a snarl, then watch the heads turn, even if, like me, you aren't all that pretty. So I take advantage of it. The French prof that I really am has a good laugh, though, at what's really pretty silly dressing-up: in my tight jeans, shirt open down to here and scuffed sandals I don't bear the slightest resemblance to myself, but look more like an extra on a street where everybody's playing a role that's not his real one either. It's a communal game played by a community that's always attracted by fun-house mirrors and fantasy come-ons.

But in this dank August heat that sticks to your skin and drains your energy, the street was out of the question. It was too hot to walk and I kept looking for any place with air-conditioning, especially late at night when I should have been home, asleep, but when the mere thought of my bed made me gasp. I sleep with the window open, winter and summer, and the arrival of Montreal's annual heatwaves always makes me slightly sick. Those nights of tossing and turning, throwing off the sheets and punching the pillow, wear me out.

So I kept going back to the Paradise, a bar that's unchanged because it's unchangeable, but I just sank deeper and earlier into the blues, so then I started asking around about the new hot spots, emphasizing that I wasn't interested in any discos that were too "young." The bartenders at the Paradise mentioned what they'd heard was a civilized spot, where the young university crowd that wanted to avoid the sound and fury of the gay mad nights of Montreal had been going for a few months now.

I went to boulevard St-Laurent just north of Prince-Arthur, a neighbourhood, where I seldom stop, except for the really good bookstore, and I was amazed to find a gay bar there.

Like most establishments of the sort, which are quick to open, quick to close and quick to be forgotten, La Cachette didn't look like much: black walls on which you could barely make out some pseudo-erotic posters so crude and poorly executed they wouldn't be a turn-on for a guy who hadn't had it off for years, lighting that aimed at discretion but achieved near-invisibility, scanty furnishings, and staff that seemed a little lost. The music, too loud for my liking but well-chosen, came from an excellent brand-new sound system that must have cost a fortune, that would survive only as long as this place was à la mode. The lack of personality was painfully obvious but it had one tremendous advantage: it wasn't hot and it wasn't freezing cold.

So I ordered a beer from a passing youth in a cunningly revealing get-up, then took a seat at the bar that gave me a good view of the huge rectangular room that must have served until recently as a rehearsal hall or a dry goods warehouse.

Two things struck me right away: the absence of queens and the presence of a number of young girls who seemed to be enjoying themselves. Both sights pleased me. Queens can be the death of a pleasant place and I've always been in favour of gay bars that accept women. Ghettos scare me: I prefer mixtures, even the most heterodox, to wall-to-wall homogeneous crowds that shun diversity and reek of exclusivity.

3

I'd been warned that La Cachette was a hangout for university students, but I didn't know that nobody else went there ... It didn't take me long to realize that I was the oldest person in the place and I was getting sardonic little grins that seemed to say: "Came to the wrong place, eh, grandpa? You're stuck here now ... " And in fact I did feel pretty uncomfortable. I even caught myself looking around to see if any of my students were among the animated groups that kept staring at me. Was that the paranoia of a teacher who doesn't want to mix his private and professional lives? Probably. But there were no familiar faces.

Beside me, slouching on their stools in a way that made me want to warn them about curvature of the spine (the teacher again), two guys with terrified expressions were talking about AIDS. They were citing indiscriminately newspapers, TV, conversations they'd had or heard, articles in American magazines, their mothers who "knew" and were tearing their hair out, their fathers who didn't know and called it "divine punishment" ... I could sense from the tone of their remarks some genuine fear, even terror, the kind that stops you cold and prevents you from functioning. One said he hadn't had sex for weeks now, claiming he was constantly obsessed by the thought of making love and having the most erotic dreams he'd ever experienced. The other said he'd gone to see some porno films at the Cinéma du Village to remind himself of the good old days of anything goes, when the only dangers waiting for you were benign gonorrhea and boring old syphilis.

When I caught my first dose I'd nearly died of shame but then, at the sight of the lewd smirk on the doctor who treated me, one that said "Look at this little stud, so young and already going with women," I decided I wouldn't let it ruin my life, otherwise the experiences that were coming my way would be nothing but anxiety and terror. I've had my share of minor venereal disorders, but nothing too dramatic.

4

AIDS, of course, is something else. As long as the disease was foreign to us, a strange condition that only struck a few super-specialized ghettos in New York or San Francisco, I didn't give it too much thought. It was something like herpes a few years ago: everybody was talking about it, everybody was afraid of it, but nobody in Montreal knew of a really serious case, and we ended up treating it as a joke. Whereas AIDS ... Slowly, guys were dying, even in Montreal: a couple of acquaintances, a former journalist at *Le Devoir* ...

I finished my beer in one gulp as I do when I'm preoccupied or when I'm naive enough to think that alcohol will bring forgetfulness. I'm terrified of AIDS too, but I've resolved to think about it as little as possible. I'm not hiding my head in the sand, I just want to get on with my life. The chances of catching it are still negligible and I refuse to turn my life upside down for such a hypothetical risk. At least that's what I tell myself on nights like the one in question, when I'm on the lookout in a bar or on the street, my manner convincingly laid-back, my smile winning.

At La Cachette, however, my smile wasn't winning at all, quite the contrary: I felt more like burying my nose in my glass so nobody would know I was there. Another evening down the drain. In a few hours I'd be in the depths of a muggy August night, alone and anxious, perhaps even condemned to roam the streets until dawn, until fatigue overcame me. Then I realized that it was too hot for sex anyway, which was a relief. I ordered another beer, promising myself I'd make it last as long as possible, and then I started to relax. I left my seat at the bar and headed for the dance floor, which was packed, noisy and better lit. People weren't thrashing around the way I've often seen in other places, where the dancing seems like a more aggressive form of cruising; no, the dancers were energetic but not excessively so; they moved about with laboured ease (after all, weren't they the show?), but nonchalantly, as if it wasn't all that important, while the dance floors in other places seem like the site of military operations.

I concealed myself behind a cluster of motionless spectators silently sipping their beer as they eyed the spectacle of these moving bodies, all aware and grateful that someone was watching them.

It was as I was watching the movements of a dancer who was very inspired and surprisingly oblivious to what was going on around him that I first noticed the dark eyes staring at me from the other side of the floor with near-comical solemnity. A former student? No, he seemed much too young and I was sure I didn't recognize him. A very good-looking guy actually, his features fine without being feminine, like a local model sure of his effect but not ostentatious about it. Of course it happened just when I'd decided to stop cruising.

I didn't feel like crossing the dance floor or walking around the bystanders to join him, so I decided just to let things develop, then we'd see. I even moved discreetly towards the big window that looked out on boulevard St-Laurent.

I'm not attracted to any one type of guy in particular. I've always taken what came along, and anyhow, I think specialties are a little suspect. It strikes me as impossible always to want the same thing – the same build, the same look, the same atmosphere. It reeks of fixation, which grates on my nerves. Men who chase after child-women, for instance – I know a few, my department at the CEGEP's full of them – always make me uncomfortable, just like my friends at the Paradise who only get off on bulging muscles and a sadistic military look. Unless you're married and faithful, I don't see the practicality of always being lured by the same carrot. So, I've got nothing against guys a lot younger than I am, though I'm not an out-and-out pedophile, another annoying disease that's fairly widespread in my circle.

I stood for a while leaning against the window of the bar, looking out at the few passers-by who were strolling down the street. Most of them turned onto Prince-Arthur, looking for a reasonably-priced restaurant. In the end I forgot about the guy who'd been observing me earlier, and once I'd downed my beer I made my way to the door.

He had moved towards the bar so he'd be able to see the entire establishment. Now he was deep in conversation with a guy his own age who seemed to be very interested in him, but he still kept looking in my direction, as if he hadn't taken his eyes off me all this time. I was very flattered, so flattered in fact that I decided to hang around a little longer.

When he saw me hesitate at the door, he gave me a tentative little smile. The other fellow who was talking to him noticed and with an inane look that spelled out eloquently his I.Q., slipped away discreetly, probably claiming he had to pee.

Should I move in now? No, I decided to leave the decisions to him, all the way. I went back to the dance floor, now livelier than ever. He followed. But he didn't approach me. He was still staring, but seemed too shy to speak. Only his eyes, piercing, almost feverish, were impudent.

It kills me to come up with the opening remark. I exhausted them ages ago, at least all the ones that aren't embarrassingly dumb, and the ones that occurred to me that evening were so trite they made me blush.

He had a Université de Montréal sweatshirt knotted around his neck. The pretext wasn't the most original but I had to start somewhere, since he obviously wasn't going to.

"You're at the university?"

He seemed surprised.

"No . . . Why do you ask?"

"Your sweatshirt ... "

"Oh, that! ... It's a guy ... a friend lent it to me ... I put it on because of the air-conditioning."

He raised an eyebrow at my own sweatshirt.

"I won't ask if you went to the University of Wisconsin ... "

And then I remembered the big yellow letters emblazoned across my chest.

I was very surprised to find out that he was twenty-four years old. I'd imagined he was nineteen or twenty at most. I was relieved, but also a little annoyed with myself: I'm usually quite good at guessing ages, especially the young people with whom I spend ten months of the year and whose tricks for looking older or younger I've caught on to. Most of my students fall into one of two categories: the larger one, those who claim to be older so they'll appear more confident, and those who are already lopping years off their age. Why do that at seventeen? I've never understood. Maybe it's a form of blackmail to conceal character flaws: I'm younger and weaker than the rest of them, have pity on me . . .

When he said his name was Mathieu I didn't believe him. In 1960 you didn't call your child Mathieu.

"Your mother was avant-garde! Why didn't she call you François or Michel like everybody else?"

"She wasn't avant-garde at all, she was crazy about Québécois music . . . She and my father used to go to La butte à Mathieu, that boîte à chansons in the Laurentians . . . You must've been there . . . "

"Come on, I may be older than you but I'm not old enough to be your father."

"How old are you?"

It came out just like that before I had time to think:

"Thirty-five."

Like spitting in the air . . . I almost caught myself and told him no, listen, that's wrong, I just turned thirty-nine, but he broke in.

"You never went to La butte à Mathieu?"

9

"Hardly . . . I was born in 1950 . . . " (Another lie. Now I was in too deep to get out.)

"You don't look it."

"What?"

"You don't look thirty-five . . . I figured you were maybe thirty, thirty-two . . . "

I could have kissed him on the spot. For some time now I've been feeling run-down and ancient, and suddenly here's a kid with piercing eyes who slices almost ten years off my age. But you have to be wary of compliments exchanged in a dimly-lit bar where bags and wrinkles disappear. That sort of flattering lighting has so often led to disappointment: young men picked up after too many beers who turn out to be not so young after all; peaches-and-cream complexions that change to melon rind on the street; spiritual flashing eyes that turn out to reflect nothing but advanced alcoholism . . .

"You haven't seen me in natural light yet . . . You might be disappointed."

He smiled. It was so beautiful, so genuine I wanted to tell him stay like that, don't move, I haven't seen such a glorious smile for so long. But you don't say such things, they sound tacky . . .

He laid his hand on my arm.

"You can't hear yourself think in here . . . Want to go out?"

And there we were in the midst of the curious fauna you find on la rue Prince-Arthur. The restaurants were just letting out; meals were being slowly digested, at the same rhythm as the after-dinner strolls. The street was packed with little pastel outfits casually dawdling in the post-prandial silence or necking with an obvious lack of urgency. The benches were occupied by tottering rubbies or by golden-agers ending their evening watching the passing scene, the lucky people who could afford restaurant meals. A crowd

10

had gathered around a fire-eater with an English accent, and they were letting out perfunctory little Oh's when an exceptionally brilliant flame shot out of his mouth.

The crowd was so dense, Mathieu had got up on tiptoe for a better look. He leaned his head towards me until his cheek was almost resting on my shoulder.

"Whenever I see a fire-eater I wonder what his breath's like ... "

The air around us smelled of sweat, cheap perfume and garlic snails. The *artiste* had finished his show, to feeble applause. A few coins began to clink on the newly reconstructed "olde-style" sidewalk. Montreal isn't just rediscovering its past: for the past few years it's been inventing one. The city's passion for the old is almost hysterical; everywhere, the goal of renovations is to make it old. I know, I've fallen into the trap myself. The work on my house isn't even finished and I'm already sick of exposed beams and stripped woodwork.

The crowd dispersed with unfeigned haste and there we were, almost alone, watching the *artiste* gather up his things. Scraps of half-charred wood, little containers of gasoline, boxes of Eddy matches. He looked at us in amusement.

"If you missed the start of the show you'll have to wait half an hour ... I don't fire myself up till after my break."

His accent was very funny and he knew it; I'd seen him playing on it during his performance, using it to get a laugh from the crowd. I even heard a particularly gross pig tell his girl-friend: "*Maudits Anglais!* They'll do anything so they can stay here!"

We gave him some change and moved on. Mathieu seemed uncomfortable.

"It's weird, but I'm always embarrassed giving money to somebody on the street. I didn't have much myself for a while, but I was too uptight to ask for anything. I don't know how they do it . . . I'm not criticizing them, I guess it's my problem."

We managed to get a seat on the terrace of the P'tit Café. Some people had just vacated a table in the front row, an amazing stroke of luck at that hour of the night. Two coffees, half-drunk and half-spilled, were cooling on the painted tin table. The ashtray was full of butts that turned my stomach. I'm a non-smoker, not quite a fascist but fairly intolerant. During the seventies I stopped smoking even my trademark pipe, and I've felt so much better ever since that I find myself a little too often hoping to persuade other people to give it up. But I restrain myself. I was a smoker long enough to know how tiresome a non-smoker with an acute case of proselytism can be. So I merely pushed the ashtray away, discreetly I hoped.

Mathieu, who had just taken a package of cigarettes from his pocket, hesitated.

"Will it bother you if I smoke?"

"Not unless you blow it in my face."

He frowned, then put them back in his pocket.

"I was kidding, Mathieu. Smoke all you want."

We had left a crowded place in search of peace and here we were in the midst of a crowd that wasn't too noisy but was still very much there. Since we were at the front, handbags kept brushing against us and we could overhear scraps of conversation that sounded very silly out of context: "So I said, I said . . . ," "so big it wouldn't go in . . . ," "American Express cheques. It hit her so hard she came straight home," and I could see the moment approaching when some rubby was going to come over and bum a cigarette, or change "for the Métro."

The waiter appeared, starchy and unctuous. I hadn't even looked at the menu. I ordered a mineral water, to make a good impression but also because I knew I'd had enough to drink. Then the waiter recognized Mathieu and suddenly he was all smiles, batting his eyelashes like a twenties starlet.

"Mathieu! Haven't seen you around for a while."

Mathieu seemed reluctant to talk to him, as if he didn't want me to know they were acquainted.

"I'm hardly ever in this part of town . . . I wasn't even intending to go to La Cachette tonight . . . "

"Your friend, you know, the one that's on TV . . . He was in a while ago . . . Seemed to be looking for somebody."

Mathieu was visibly annoyed at the waiter's familiarity. I found it amusing.

"It wasn't me . . . I don't see him any more . . . Once was enough, thank you very much!"

"Anyway, he didn't even open his mouth to say hi! Stuck-up bastard. They're all alike, those actors! They cruise you once, then they don't even *know* you! I mean really, sometimes you feel like a used Kleenex . . . That really gets under my nails. I feel like a bottle of Dom Pérignon that's about to pop a cork . . . Sorry. What'll you have?"

"Lemon pie and a glass of milk. And listen François, don't waste your tears . . . He wasn't worth it."

"It's not him I'm talking about. He's stuck up, but I never slept with him . . . It's the other one, the comedian, you know . . . "

From the rather cavalier way Mathieu had cut him off I concluded they must be close friends.

"François, you've got customers waiting. Us, for instance."

He walked away with a look like an offended virgin. A customer at the next table who'd been waiting for his bill since our arrival swore in exasperation. I leaned towards Mathieu.

"Your friend's going to be out of a job . . . "

"Don't worry about that one. He's one of the best waiters

13

in Montreal when he wants to be. Everybody fights over him: he's reliable and funny and he works hard and never bitches about working double shifts ... He's just got one fault: he says what he thinks. But for a waiter, that can be an advantage. Because believe me, he won't let anybody walk on him ... When I was a waiter, if a customer gave me a hard time I'd let it get to me – and I'd still lose my job ... "

"That reminds me, I didn't even ask you what you do."

"Unofficially, a salesman at Eaton's; officially, I'm an unemployed actor."

He registered my reaction at once. I hadn't budged but something in my face must have changed.

"You don't like actors? Like François?"

I assumed an innocent look that can't have been very convincing, because Mathieu smiled.

"Why'd you ask?"

"I don't know. You looked ... well, skeptical ... No, not skeptical. Irritated maybe. Unless it's Eaton's salesmen you don't like ... "

"Where'd you get that idea?"

A perceptive one, young Mathieu. I've met so many of those actors or pseudo-actors, megalomaniacs most of them, who string you a line about their so-called career or their hypothetical future, that now I really can't take any of them. Suddenly, I wanted to be far away. I was looking him straight in the eye as he spoke and I wanted to be somewhere else. I knew it was silly, because he was a nice guy who didn't seem to have any illusions about himself or to be trying to impress me, but I recalled some past experiences – Claude, Michel, Luc in particular who has a little mini-career on TV now, but who talks about himself as if he were the Québécois James Dean – and I wanted to get the hell out.

As he talked, Mathieu's tone became more and more confidential. As if he were opening up to a friend. I should have been touched, but I was scared.

"Since I left the children's theatre company I haven't been doing much ... Little things now and then. Bit parts, the odd commercial. If you've only worked for kids and you haven't gone to theatre school it doesn't help your reputation much. But I'm patient. You never know when the right person's going to turn up."

He stopped talking for a moment.

"Are you listening?"

I nearly jumped.

"Yes, sure, I'm listening ... You're right, I'm sure it can't be easy."

He finished his lemon pie in silence as I watched the passing scene. I wished I'd been more tactful but if I hadn't stopped myself I'd have got up and left without a word, leaving him there with his crumb-strewn plate and his half-drunk glass of milk.

"Do you like being a French teacher?"

Once again, as when he'd asked my age, the words came out before I had a chance to think about them.

"No, I don't."

"You don't look like a French teacher to me. Anyway, you don't talk like the ones I had in CEGEP. You know the type, they sound like defrocked priests or Outremont matrons from the fifties ... "

I felt like telling him that Outremont had changed a lot and its matrons aren't what they used to be, but that would have led us straight into where-do-you-live, do-you-live-alone and all the rest, and I didn't feel like going in that direction.

When he realized that I wasn't going to return his attempts at confidences, he started to talk about himself again and that brought the conversation to an end.

"I take singing lessons too. I don't know if I could ever become a singer: probably not, but I love it ... "

The next thing I knew I was standing beside the table with

some dollar bills in my hand. Mathieu was staring as if he'd been slapped. I've never felt like such a boor but I couldn't stop myself. I put the money on the table without really looking at him.

"Listen ... I have to go. Sorry. I've got a bad headache and if I don't go to bed right away I know I'll be up all night ... See you some time ... "

I know what I'd have done in his place: delivered a few choice words to the son-of-a-bitch who'd dared to behave like that. But I think he just sat there, stunned, staring at his empty plate. It must have taken him a couple of minutes to realize what was happening.

At the corner of St-Laurent I shuddered with relief and jumped in a cab.

I was furious when I went to bed that night. Furious with myself for the way I'd behaved, but at the same time feeling as if I'd escaped from a possible danger. The years with Luc had marked me, I know that, his frustrations exasperated me, his bitterness sometimes made me cynical with him, but I'd never realized just how hostile I felt towards actors. Especially those who haven't made it yet. Why not give Mathieu the benefit of the doubt? He was only twenty-four, with his whole future ahead of him. I think I preferred to let him hold on to his illusions and simply disappear before I told him something I might regret. All night I relived some painful scenes with Luc, his crises, his doubts, his certainties that were often so pathetic. No, never again. Really.

The Mother of Us All doesn't laugh, she barks. A cute little yap, like a puppy that's happy and doesn't mind showing it. Her eyes crease, she reveals teeth that are perfectly white in spite of a heavy cigarette habit, and she throws back her head like a child abandoning herself to pleasure. I love to hear her laugh and she adores laughing, so together we're like a pair of idiotic clowns, a little suspect in the eyes of other people who don't always understand what we find so funny. I also have to admit that nothing's sacred when the two of us get together: absolutely nothing and no one finds favour in our eyes. Beginning with ourselves. When something's bothering her she comes to me and laughs about it and I do the same when I feel an attack of the glooms. It's a form of therapy with the great advantage of being absolutely free. It can happen that the real laugh, the one that delivers you and brings tears to your eyes, keeps you waiting until you despair of its ever coming at all – which happens more often to me than to her because I'm more high-strung – but it always arrives in the end, nudging our sense of the absurd and soothing heavy hearts.

Her name is Marie-Hélène but we call her Mélène, the nickname her family gave her when she was little, or "the Mother of Us All," an expression we made up one night when we were partying and she'd taken it upon herself to solve *everybody*'s problems. Everybody – and I'll have more to say about that later – is the group of women I've been hanging around with for years now, my only true friends, my sisters; we're a family we've put together ourselves from scratch, one in which each member has a particular role to play though none of it's taken too seriously, an oasis of peace in the midst of our turbulent lives, a refuge that over the years has become essential to us all because it's based on specific needs. For some, it replaces a family life they've never had, for me it takes over from an perfectly ordinary childhood. You can laugh if you want, but it's wonderful to be able to relive part of your childhood in your late thirties.

So I was the only man in a group of lesbians.

I've always had a lot of trouble fraternizing with men. Gay or straight. The gay sense of humour is often too ghetto-bound for me, while it's rare for straights to have any sense of humour at all; gay men make me feel as if I'm always competing for sex, and straight men do too, but in a different way, and with a latent misogyny I find hard to take. With my group of women, though, I feel not only safe but confident. That's it: I never trust men. No matter what kind. Why lesbians then? Because of Mélène, actually, who introduced me to her group in the early seventies: I liked them right away and they adopted me at once. Because of the rights they demand, of course, which resemble mine, but mainly because of the way in which they conduct their struggle: my friends, my family. They're never heavy and instead of being hostile to men, they laugh at them. Laughter again.

My colleagues, both male and female, who'll always consider me a misfit, often tell me that laughing will either kill me or turn me into a total fool. I hope they're right.

Mélène set down a brush soaked in white paint, then wiped her eyes on a corner of the old chef's apron that she wears for painting.

"I can just see you, running down Prince-Arthur like a gazelle ... You must have looked like a lunatic! And the poor guy who thought he was set for the night, sitting there staring at an empty glass of milk ... How humiliating! I'd hate to hear what he'll say if you ever run into him again."

We were in the lane behind the house we'd bought together the year before, she, her lover Jeanne, another couple of women and myself. We were painting that day and

19

I'd been cursing since morning. Don't worry, I'm not about to hold forth on the joys of co-ownership; I'll just say that some days I'd gladly take an ax to the contract we all signed, which requires me to do a lot of things that make my flesh crawl. Such as, for instance, repainting our old fence on a Saturday morning when I'd rather get back in bed with my *Devoir*. But no, the phone had rung at half-past eight and Mélène had warbled with obvious bad faith verging on the sadistic: "Morning, honey, rise and shine! Traipse your lovely buns around the bars till all hours if you want, but don't forget your obligations! I hope you remembered our fabulous plans for the day: it's our turn to paint the gorgeous fence that keeps us safe and sound . . . "

The gorgeous fence in question is so old I was afraid it wouldn't stand up to the weight of the paint. We'd taken a vote some weeks before: no money for a new fence because of the new double windows, therefore purchase of white paint to do what we could to conceal the hideous structure that was the disgrace of our lane. Another vote had designated Mélène and me to start the painting because Jeanne works weekends. If we hadn't finished by Saturday night the two other occupants of the house would take over on Sunday morning. Just talking about it made me queasy. How had a solitary type like me got himself into such a boy-scout situation?

Yes, that's exactly it: for Mélène it was a wonderful way to bring us closer, to strengthen the ties between us, to form a true family core. She and Jeanne lived on the third floor, I had the second and the two others had the ground-floor flat. We didn't spend much time with the two others, who'd been chosen not from within the family, which would have been normal, but solely because they were the only women we knew with a little money. We all got together now and then for plenty of idiotic reasons, but we didn't socialize with

20

them. So the family core is far from complete, and we often find ourselves in situations that are absurd and infuriating.

I've never been any good with my hands. The paint I was applying to the dry grey wood was running in long sticky rivulets that kept disappearing into the brand new grass which was so hard to keep green. My right hand looked as if I was wearing a white glove and there were so many splotches on my jeans I lost all hope of salvaging them.

I was well aware that Mélène had been watching me out of the corner of her eye for a few minutes, that she was fed up with my clumsiness, she who could work miracles with a hammer and a couple of nails. Yet I can't say I wasn't applying myself; I really was trying, doing the best I could to cover the goddamn fence with white paint, but the brush kept slipping or the paint would drip or I'd bump my head against the freshly painted wood . . .

"Watch where you put your brush, Jean-Marc, you're dripping paint all over!"

That was probably what I'd been waiting for. I rammed my brush into the can of paint and got to my feet.

"Fuck off, sweetheart! If you're so goddamn good at it, do it yourself!"

I climbed up to my place, up the creaky staircase that's bound to collapse any day now since we can't afford to replace it either. I slammed my door hard, after smearing plenty of paint on the knob, then realized when I was in the kitchen that I didn't have anything to clean myself off with. I went out on the gallery, a pitiful sight. Mélène was standing in the middle of the lane, grinning.

"Coming down to clean up, or shall I bring the stuff up?"

"Come on up, we'll have a coffee."

The kitchen's the only room in my apartment that I'm really proud of. Raised in a house with a minuscule kitchen and accustomed to hearing my mother complain about the lack of space, I've always chosen apartments with huge kitchens, even before I cooked. I have two brothers and two sisters and, like most North Americans, I was brought up in the kitchen. It's the only place where we all gathered regularly, the site of our most spectacular scenes and our teariest reconciliations. We ate all our meals there, the dining room being reserved for possible visitors who hardly ever came. It was where my father, so often drunk, broke countless plates: my mother spent almost as much time crying there as cooking; I got some slaps on the wrist myself, because of marks that were less than satisfactory. During family parties, at Christmas time, I always ended up there with the women while the men, the real ones, not delicate little flowers like me, sat and chewed the fat in the living room, around a bunch of bottles of Bols gin. Sports, gin and sex in the living room; food, beer and sex in the kitchen. My adult preferences were already there: cooking over sports; beer over hard liquor; and as for the last, it's everybody's favourite topic – especially other people's sex lives.

My kitchen, then, which was huge, with a southeast exposure which makes for the loveliest morning light, and above all practical, played a decisive role in the choice of this house on Bloomfield just above Bernard. For me, in any case, because Jeanne and Mélène, perhaps in reaction to their own mothers' lives, spend as little time as possible in their own.

"You haven't cracked a smile all morning, Jean-Marc. Lose your sense of humour last night?"

She barked then, just a little, enough to put me in a really foul mood, while she put too much sugar in her coffee as usual.

In fact I was having trouble laughing at what had happened the night before. I didn't know why exactly, although I've made a fool of myself often enough not to get too upset about the misadventures that can occur in my life as a practising and rather reckless homosexual.

"I don't feel right and I don't know why. It's normal to feel ashamed about what I did, but I should be able to get over it . . . I didn't sleep all night, if you can imagine, me who snores like a lumberjack crew at the sight of a pillow. There's got to be something about that guy making me feel bad about how I behaved . . . But what? Sure I liked him, or I wouldn't have left La Cachette with him . . . But not enough to stay awake all night because I left him high and dry! Anyway I'm sure he just went back to the bar and looked for somebody else . . . "

To my horror Mélène stirred a little more sugar into her coffee, then said in a mock-lugubrious tone:

"Remorse may take many forms when it comes to prick the conscience of wrongdoers . . . "

"Mélène, for God's sake, I'm trying to be serious!"

"What'm I supposed to say, Jean-Marc! That you missed the chance of a lifetime? You'll probably never know! That you behaved like a son-of-a-bitch? That, you know. If you feel so guilty, try and find the guy, tell him you're sorry and let's get on with it! I'm sure as hell not going to let it spoil *my* weekend!"

I sighed and poured myself another coffee.

"That's exactly what I'd do if I could. But I haven't got his number. I don't know how to get in touch with him and that's why I'm in such a state."

"Go back to the bar tonight."

"I want to do something *now*!"

"Do you just want to apologize or do you want to see him again?"

"I don't know. Both, probably. If he hadn't told me he wanted to be an actor, likely I wouldn't have run away . . . "

"The Luc syndrome again . . . "

23

"What else? Every time I meet an actor, and God knows they aren't rationed in my wonderful world, I run like a scared rabbit. Which doesn't mean I'm going to see a shrink about my actorphobia! Listen, let's talk about something else, okay? Let's finish painting that rotten fence and I promise I'll be winsome and droll . . . "

Droll I wasn't. The very opposite, in fact. I was grouchy all day and I did a lousy job on the fence. Mélène got impatient once or twice, which led to our first real battle since we bought the house. The day ended as badly as it had begun: the family supper we'd been planning all week took place without me. All the others were there, I heard them enjoying themselves through the ceiling while I sat home and pouted, not knowing why.

I watched two terrible horror movies on pay TV, just to guarantee my evening would be a total write-off, then I went to bed too early, before I was sleepy. I tossed and turned for hours, unable to clear my mind of Ravel's *Bolero* which had been overused in one of the films I'd just seen and kept going through my head, insistent, hypnotic and exhausting.

The next day it was raining buckets, as they used to say when I was a child. A heavy August rain, not really refreshing. Diagonal nails of water flattened on hitting the sidewalk, tracing on the windows sweepings of liquid dust that would dry and leave a powdery residue made up of every form of pollution that infects Montreal.

In the past, a summer rain was usually welcome. When I was a teenager I'd often go for walks in a downpour, without an umbrella, just to feel the water pour over my face. I would drink it in, open-mouthed, as I headed for Parc Lafontaine or Parc Laurier. I could walk like that for hours without getting tired. When I came home, soaked to the skin, my mother would yell at me to dry myself properly or I'd catch my death, if not pleurisy or double pneumonia, depending on her mood. Nowadays the rain scares me. You just have to

24

look at the burnt, pitted, sticky leaves on the trees in Outremont and you'll lose any urge for a bucolic stroll to clear your head. At Mélène and Jeanne's place, where there's no roof over the gallery, the acid rain leaves a sticky deposit that's especially revolting.

So, I didn't stick my nose outside all day except to run over to the Librairie d'Outremont for my fat Sunday *New York Times*, which I flipped through while drinking countless cups of coffee. Around three p.m. I was totally wired, wandering from room to room, running actually, unable to concentrate on a book or even on the godawful Sunday afternoon TV. At five I couldn't take any more, so I called a cab and went to the Paradise for happy hour. It obviously wasn't the ideal way for me to relax, since happy hour, especially on Sunday, is one of the most depressing institutions invented by man, but I had to do something or I'd really get depressed. Was I hoping to run into Mathieu? No, I'd never seen him there and as I said before, the crowd at the Paradise was mostly regulars. An attack of fleeting self-destructiveness? A sudden onset of masochism? Probably. Five minutes after I arrived I was ready to climb the walls, howling in despair. They'd done their cruising the night before, a few, not many, had spent the night with someone, and now they were calmly cruising again, a glass of beer glued to their hands, eyes more often scrutinizing baskets than faces. At midnight they'd still be there, their gazes a little foggier, desire extinguished by alcohol in some cases, exacerbated in others, and all of them frustrated. I left in the middle of a conversation with Bernard Thibeault, I guy I quite like, but who turns sentimental with alcohol. Going to bed with somebody once, for want of anything better to do, doesn't create an inextricable tie. Bernard's been looking for the love of his life for thirty years now and he still doesn't understand that he's such a lousy lay, nobody's going to be interested in him for longer than one night.

It was still raining and la rue Ste-Catherine was deserted. Even the tourists, though there were plenty of them at this time of year, were staying in their hotels rather than braving such a miserable day.

I had a flash while I was eating a Mister Steer next door to the Cinéma Parisien: there might be a way to get in touch with Mathieu after all, without having to wait for La Cachette to open. I made a mad dash for the pay phone and called 411 for the number of the P'tit Café.

"Hello? Is François working today?"

"François who? There's two."

And I thought I was simplifying my life.

"Don't know. He was working on the terrace Friday night."

"Oh, François Simard ... Yeah, he's here. But the staff isn't supposed to take personal calls ... "

"This is urgent ... it won't take long ... "

The sound of a receiver being plunked down, then:

"François! Another proposal!"

I waited a good two minutes, I even figured François had forgotten me. The P'tit Café must have been mobbed; I could hear snatches of conversation, food and drink orders, laughter. The straights' Happy Hour seemed livelier than ours.

"Hello?"

I jumped; I hadn't heard him coming.

"Hello. Umm ... you don't know me ... You probably don't remember, I was with Mathieu on the terrace Friday night ... "

I'd expected silence and I got it. Finally he said:

"Yeah ... I remember. What do you want?"

"To apologize to Mathieu, but I haven't got his number ... "

26

Mathieu

Sprawled on the living room carpet with the Festival des Films du Monde programme unfolded in front of him, Mathieu was using a yellow hi-liter to mark the films he wanted to see. This initial selection was perhaps the most interesting one, because it would allow him to dream of seeing everything, from the blockbusters that would bring out le tout Montréal to the obscure little offerings that wouldn't attract a soul and would disappear forever as soon as the Festival was over. His leaflet had yellow splotches on both sides; black Xs, check marks and circles would be added later, to indicate his first, second and third choices, steps that got harder and harder as concessions and sacrifices became a drag.

For two years now Mathieu had taken his holidays at the end of August so he could disappear into the Cinéma Parisien from morning till night, eat bland-burgers on the run, stuff himself with chips and Coke, run from theatre to theatre without even taking time for a pee, happy, excited, often exhausted, constantly alert. He was one of the first to arrive every morning, his I.D. card pinned to his shirt, and he often stayed on at night to discuss the day's offerings with acquaintances or total strangers. He would emerge from the festival pale and burned-out, his brain on fire. Then he'd go to Ogunquit or Provincetown to recuperate after Labour Day, at the blessed moment when the raucous tourists had left New England and the resort towns reverted to simple fishing villages.

When he came back to work in mid-September his colleagues said, "Here's our film freak! He'll tell us about every movie that's on in Montreal so we won't have to see one till Christmas!"

Which he did: he'd describe the Bulgarian films, the American tourists, the international celebrities, the local stars (not nearly as discreet and sometimes downright loud), the screenings that brought reverent crowds, others that were booed ... At Eaton's he was known as "the Festival freak" and he didn't mind at all. He'd even converted to "serious" films a few of the people he worked with, who now patronized the Dauphin and the Elysée almost as often as the mainstream theatres – a fairly stunning victory and one he was glad to claim.

He laid down the felt pen, took off his glasses and rubbed his eyes, stretching. His mother, who'd been vigorously punching the remote-control for a good half hour because there was nothing decent on TV, heaved an exasperated sigh.

"You'll ruin your eyes with that schedule, the print's so small! Anyway why don't you just wait and see those movies when they come out? You're going to waste your holidays again, shut up in the dark for ten days! You haven't got a brain in your head!"

He rolled onto his back, hands behind his head.

"The ceiling needs painting."

Rose rolled her eyes and shrugged.

"Don't change the subject, Mathieu."

"Ma, we've had this conversation a hundred times! Not all those films are released commercially ... There's some you never get another chance to see ... And if I enjoy seeing four or five films a day ... "

"I don't understand you ... "

"How many films do you watch on TV? How many hours

28

do you spend in front of the box, punching your remote like a fanatic as if you wanted to smash it because there's never anything good?"

"I don't punch like a fanatic ... "

The phone rang, interrupting a conversation they'd had all too often; it was a relief to both of them. Mathieu grabbed it on the first ring.

"Hello?"

"May I speak to Mathieu, please?"

He had trouble hearing the person at the other end, because the background noise, conversations, laughter, dishes, seemed to be in the foreground, masking the voice.

"Speaking ... But can you talk louder please, I'm having trouble hearing you ... "

"It's Jean-Marc ... I'm not sure if you remember me ... We met Friday night, at La Cachette ... "

His mother watched him turn pale, take the receiver from his ear, and stare at it as if he'd never seen one before.

"Oh ... yes ... I remember ... Hold on, I'll be right back."

Mathieu held out the phone to his mother.

"I'm going to take it in my room ... Don't hang up till I start talking."

Rose put her hand over the receiver.

"Maybe I watch two or three on Sunday, but weekdays I work, I don't go waste my time at festivals!"

When he recognized Jean-Marc's voice, Mathieu had been tempted to hang up. He'd been deeply humiliated by the events of Friday night: he'd spent Saturday wondering what it was he'd said or done to make Jean-Marc take off like that; he even found himself wondering if it was the glass of milk and the lemon pie that had turned him off ... He'd suffered his share of rejections, but never one like that, so

29

incomprehensible and so sudden – and after such a good start.

He'd gone back to La Cachette on Saturday night, in the hope of seeing Jean-Marc and asking for an explanation. There'd been only the customary crowd, maybe a little more vapid than usual. He'd come home early, disappointed and even more intrigued.

At the other end of the phone, Jean-Marc was obviously choosing his words carefully.

"I really behaved like a jerk the other night ... You must've thought you'd never hear from me again ... But I want to apologize. It had nothing to do with you ... Listen, it's kind of hard to go into all this on the phone ... We talked a lot about films at the restaurant, and I noticed in the TV Guide Radio-Québec's showing that old French one, *L'assassinat du Père Noël*, about killing Santa Claus. It terrified me when I was a kid."

Mathieu said nothing, just waited for what would come next. He merely grunted after each of Jean-Marc's sentences, like someone who's not really listening.

"If you feel like coming over and watching it I could try and explain about Friday."

"Maybe I don't want any explanations."

A brief silence. Mathieu could hear a woman laughing very loud in the background.

"Listen, Mathieu, what I'm trying to say is, I want to see you again, you must realize that ... It's hard enough as it is ... If you really don't want to see me, just say so and that'll be that. We don't even have to say hello if we run into each other, if you want ... "

Mathieu smiled. Curiosity would win out as usual, he knew it. The situation was so ridiculous, Jean-Marc's pretext was so crystal-clear, he was tempted to go through with it just to see where it would lead. It wasn't because of any particular liking for risk, he'd realized at once that Jean-

Marc was perfectly harmless, no, it was plain old-fashioned curiosity, which more than once had dragged him down paths that were not hazardous but, let's say, unaccustomed. And he had to admit it, he'd liked Jean-Marc. A lot.

"Where do you live?"

Jean-Marc

The jitters hit me a few minutes before Mathieu arrived. Would he have eaten? All I had was some cold cuts drying out in the fridge and a bottle of grocery-store wine. Was he a drinker? Long ago, back in the days when I used to drink too much, I'd decided to keep the bare minimum in the house; therefore I had exactly three cans of beer. I went up to Mélène and Jeanne's; they weren't home. I went out again in the rain. Besides beer I bought fifty-six kinds of garbage – chips, peanuts, even one of those gadgets for making popcorn I've always thought were useless.

I don't know why, but food was suddenly assuming a vital importance: instead of thinking what I'd say or do that evening, I was obsessed with what would happen if we got hungry. It wasn't until I remembered the ever obliging Laurier Bar-B-Q that my anxiety lifted a little. With that aspect of the evening taken care of, I had the other, more important one to deal with: I'd been determined to get in touch with Mathieu and now I'd done it, but I wasn't too sure about my intentions. It was like when you've been dreaming for months about buying something and then after you have it, you realize that desire was a lot more exciting than possession. Now that Mathieu was on his way I didn't know if I even wanted to see him.

And when he rang the bell I almost didn't answer it. It wasn't the jitters now, it was a full-blown panic attack: I was chilled, my chest felt too small for my heart, my hands were shaking ... If only Mélène had been there, her little bark would have comforted me. In fact it was the thought of her that made me decide to open the door: we'd laugh about it tomorrow morning over a good cup of coffee; I'd give her every detail, even add a few to spice it up. Another chapter in the madcap adventures of a wild, foolhardy, gay Montrealer. In New York I'd have run the risk of torture, even decapitation; in Montreal the worst that could happen would be an evening of boredom. But I was just as scared!

The first thing I did after I opened the door was tell him to dry his hair, the way my mother nagged me when I was little. There was rain running down his neck and he could catch his death. And the first thing he said to me was: "I don't know what I'm doing out on a night like this!"

He didn't just dry his hair, he took a shower. Luckily there was a clean bath towel and for once my bathroom didn't look too disgusting. I'm very careful about how I look but I have a tendency to splash ...

After his shower, Mathieu sat in the living room, on his best behaviour. In a bathrobe. His shirt and jeans were spinning in the dryer. And that was when I sensed that the evening wouldn't be a write-off: I felt as if I was the visitor, with no responsibilities to entertain. And probably because of that I was the perfect host. My apologies weren't embarrassing but actually quite amusing; I told him with disconcerting ease why young actors scared me; I even confessed that I'd called him out of stubbornness, to help shed my guilt.

He listened, smiling, as he sat on the sofa with his legs squeezed together, his head in his right hand. He looked even younger than he had the other night, more like an intelligent teenager who lets the grownups talk and keeps his impressions to himself. And conceals his own reactions behind an impenetrable smile.

No, I wasn't going to panic again!

"You could've told me all that on the phone. Why did you

33

make me come halfway across town in the rain just to hear your apologies?"

I confess, it caught me off guard.

"Did you think I was going to make a pass at you the minute you were in the door?"

His smile broadened, his eyes creased; he seemed to be enjoying himself.

"What I think is, I don't know why I came any more than you know why you asked me. Let's talk about something else or we'll just keep going in circles. Besides, I'm hungry. You got anything to eat?"

My dried-up cold cuts gave us a laugh. Mathieu insisted on eating them, even after I tried to tempt him with the Laurier Bar-B-Q.

"I eat barbecued chicken three times a week, but I don't often see horrors like those cold cuts every day of the week."

He didn't want either beer or wine and we knocked back a bottle of new-style Coke which provided a topic of conversation for another ten minutes. Complicity was established very quickly. Too quickly almost. After all, I wasn't looking for a pal, if I was looking for anything at all – and I wasn't sure I was, in fact – yet I felt safe with him, as if I'd known him for a long time. Once we'd polished off our meal Mathieu reminded me of the corny pretext I'd used on the phone to entice him into my lair and we watched *L'assassinat du Père Noël* on Radio-Québec. The whole thing. In silence. Like old friends.

Mathieu didn't put his clothes on until it was time to leave, around eleven o'clock.

We shook hands affectionately, if you can say that about a handshake. I asked if we could get together again that week, he said sure, then he ran to his taxi after giving me his phone number at Eaton's.

After he'd left I felt as if I'd learned something in the

34

course of the evening. But what? I felt hokey as hell – and absolutely wonderful.

I fell asleep the minute my head hit the pillow.

"We must have looked like a couple of kids. I felt like a fifteen-year-old about to sin for the first time!"

Everybody laughed. It felt good.

Jeanne set down her cup of coffee, slowly, as she does everything. She wiped her mouth meticulously, then folded her napkin almost the way it had been when she sat down. This signified that the meal was over. We all rose together and made our way to the living room where there awaited, we knew, a vast selection of liqueurs: from a simple Amaretto to a very rare Hierba, which comes from Ibiza and tastes like Thrill chewing gum if you ask me, along with a complete assortment of the most exquisite cognacs and the strongest vodkas. I slouched in an armchair and continued my account.

"We were sitting there like fence-posts, staring at the TV . . . We were still drinking Coke, the new kind, a bottle I found in the back of the fridge, and eating popcorn. Romantic, eh?"

After she'd given her little bark, Mélène touched my forearm.

"And you mean *nothing* happened?"

"Nothing, my dear, not even rubbing elbows!"

Johanne, one of our partners in the house, who smoked cigarillos that stank up the room, said in what was meant to be a light tone but in which I detected a hint of contempt:

"Did you sing 'Feu, feu, joli feu'?"

To which Marguerite, her lover, added contemptuously:

"What's wrong, Jean-Marc, have you lost your famous touch?"

That did it as far as I was concerned: the two of them were absolutely despicable. Previously, I hadn't liked them, but now what I felt was hatred pure and simple. I appreciate irony and even sarcasm – they're my own weapons, I use them freely and don't mind when they're used against me – but venomous persiflage disguised as friendly ribbing, especially from people who aren't even my friends, that makes me livid, it disgusts me, and I let them know by simply not reacting. My eyes didn't leave Mélène's face and I went on as if nothing had happened.

"The worst is, I'm seeing him tomorrow and who knows if the same thing won't just happen again."

Jeanne brought over the cognac and set the bottles down very carefully so as not to damage her fine Italian coffee table.

"I think it's a good sign."

Mélène gave her a swat on the rear, friendly and affectionate.

"Look who's talking ... You take yourself too seriously, kiddo."

"If I wasn't here to take certain things seriously the place would go to wrack and ruin ... "

Mélène smiled, her head resting against the back of her chair.

"There she goes again, playing indispensable!"

Jeanne offered her a snifter of cognac.

"I'm not playing indispensable, I know I am!"

Laughter and applause. Especially from Johanne and Marguerite who thought, wrongly, that they had ringside seats for a domestic squabble, whereas the other two were just teasing each other in their usual way, with no bitchiness.

The evening was drawing to a close. I was almost sorry I'd recounted my misadventure in the presence of people who weren't part of the family and might, who knows, enjoy spreading the word that I'd gone senile or that the first good-looking guy I'd met had made me impotent. So while I'd felt relieved during dinner, now the glooms that had been prey-ing on me all day were back in force.

Jeanne must have noticed because she said softly:

"Come on, Jean-Marc ... we think it's cute, what's hap-pening to you ... "

"Cute! That's exactly what's wrong! I'll tell you some-thing, at thirty-nine the last thing you want to be is 'cute'! You don't have all the details yet, right? I told you we've got a date tomorrow, but I didn't say where ... "

At once I regretted my words. Johanne and Marguerite, who were preparing to leave, casually settled a little deeper into their chairs to hear the end of my story.

Mélène was fidgeting with excitement.

"Jean-Marc, you're a joy to have around. I don't know what I'd do without you ... Where are you meeting him? Come on, quick, I can't take any more ... "

I took a deep breath, then plunged:

"On Saint-Denis."

Triumph! They laughed, they slapped their thighs, Mélène even shouted, writhing in her chair: "Oh wow, a macramé!"

"Come off it girls, don't lay it on so thick ... It's not that funny ... "

Assuming a contrite expression that oozed insincerity, Marguerite said:

"You're right, let's not pass judgment yet ... After all, we don't know if they're meeting above Sherbrooke or below ... "

I was almost expecting Johanne to nudge her like a schoolgirl who's just made a gaffe, but no, they both kept their serious expressions while the other two were still doubled up with laughter.

The Mother of Us All wasn't barking now, she was trumpeting.

"That's right, Jean-Marc, where are you going? A

trendoid terrace north of Sherbrooke or a subsidized hang-out for fake welfare bums down around Emery?"

I waited for the laughter to cool down before I replied.

"Don't lay the Saint-Denis trip on me, girls . . . You're always dumping on it, but I notice you don't stay away."

Johanne reacted as if she'd been stung by a horsefly.

"Not us! Ever since they've started developing Bernard we hardly ever leave Outremont . . . I don't know why we'd go to Saint-Denis when we have everything we need right at our doorstep!"

And we were off. We'd had this argument many times before and Mélène, Jeanne and I had sworn we'd never bring it up again. It had been a mistake for me to mention Saint-Denis and suddenly I felt very weary. I really wasn't up to an attack by Johanne and Marguerite after such a good dinner.

But Jeanne put an end to the evening as she'd put an end to the meal, with a single remark. Turning towards her guests she said with obvious bad faith:

"Correct me if I'm wrong, but I think the bars where you two go every weekend are on Saint-Denis, no?"

Marguerite stiffened, Johanne gulped down the sentence she had ready. They rose in perfect unison and made a single rush for the door, like geese raised in the same barnyard. Before she left, Marguerite turned towards Jeanne who was seeing them out.

"You have to take the bars where you find them."

"There's other bars, and a lot more chic. Don't try and justify yourselves. Do the Outremont ladies want to go slumming? Then let them accept the consequences!"

She almost slammed the door in their faces.

We didn't laugh too loud because the living-room windows were open and we were afraid they'd hear us on their way down the stairs. Mélène looked tired; between giggles she kept dabbing at her eyes with a Kleenex and struggling to get her breath back.

Jeanne poured her one last little glass of cognac.

"Here, drink this, it's good for what ails you. But don't gulp it when you're so tired, it'll knock you out ... "

I took one too, which I sipped in silence. Jeanne had gone to load the dishwasher and Mélène, like me, was sprawled out in an over-sized armchair. She yawned once or twice. I didn't take offense: it didn't mean she wanted to go to bed but that she felt comfortable. She stretched like a cat who's deciding whether to go eat between naps.

"Good thing they left when they did, I was ready to claw them! God, I wish they'd get fed up and sell us their third of the house!"

"What would we use for money? It's hard enough to pay what we owe already ... For me, anyway ... "

"We could find somebody else ... "

"We don't know anybody who's got the money ... And as for getting involved with strangers, you see where that gets you ... "

Jeanne came back carrying a Coke. She sat on the arm of Mélène's chair and planted a kiss on her shoulder. Such tenderness emanated from the two of them, such serenity, I felt a pinch in my heart. They've been together for more than ten years now and they're a cliché-sort of old couple that touches me as my parents did when I was a teenager, with their little habits and their ways of being thoughtful to each other, their childish rows, their exuberant reconciliations, their troubling silences. Why is it that I find old couples so moving while new ones always seem almost silly? Mélène claims it's because I'm afraid of getting involved in a relationship that might be a lasting one even though it's what I really want. That's simplistic, but it makes sense: with what had been happening to me over the past few days I was thinking she could be right. I was attracted by Mathieu but I was pushing him away, as if I were scared by how important he could become in my life if I let him. Maybe my suspicion of young actors was been just an excuse to protect my fragile independence.

All at once I felt transparent, too simple; I felt as if I lacked density, I understood myself too easily and I bored myself – something that happens a little too often for my liking. I got up to leave. They both kissed me very affectionately, as if to console me.

"We had a good laugh just now, Jean-Marc, but it really doesn't matter if you're meeting him on Saint-Denis . . . "

"I know that. Anyway, we're meeting at the corner of Sherbrooke. We'll see whether we go north or south."

Mélène took one last sip of cognac.

"If you go north I'll let you see him again; but if you go south, it's bye-bye Mathieu."

I took a walk through Outremont before turning in. I knew that if I went to bed in my present state I wouldn't fall asleep but would toss and turn, cursing and pounding my pillow.

Since it was fairly early, la rue Bernard, which in the past few years had undergone frantic, nearly hysterical development, was buzzing with activity. It was the hour when film-goers were emerging from the Cinéma Outremont. The terraces were packed. Some even overflowed onto the side-walk, blocking traffic. To avoid being jostled you had to walk around the scrawny trees that were languishing in their squares of earth and the more robust flowers proliferating in their green metal tubs, or walk right on the road. I wasn't in the mood to hear people sing the praises of Alain Tanner so I kept heading west, without stopping for the espresso I craved. After l'avenue Outremont, things suddenly became calmer, as if I'd crossed a frontier. A few couples were looking for their cars and the line outside Bilboquet, the trendy ice cream parlour, was quite impressive, but after that, nothing. Immutable Outremont, hated by some, secretly dreamed of by others, former fortress of wealthy French Canadians, cradle of most of the influential politi-cians of the sixties and seventies, both far right and moderate left, of both the federalist and the nationalist persuasion, favourite target of east-end workers, the tight-lipped snob who had long thought the French she spoke was interna-tional when in point of fact her accent would set your teeth on edge, Outremont, for so long had been not a place to live but a way of life, a social status, sleeping Outremont now offered me her luxuriant lawns, her flowerbeds, her pretty, always-empty balconies (you wonder why they were built,

42

since nobody ever sits on them) and most of all, her magnificent, tranquil parks.

I walked for a long time, craning my neck to peek inside subtly lit living rooms, stopping in front of my favourite houses, the ones I'd singled out when I first arrived in Outremont, the ones that make me wish I were rich, though I've never had that kind of ambition, rich and powerful and owner of a home on Kelvin or Pratt or Antonine-Maillet. Walking through the streets of Outremont at night makes you ambitious though; I should have acquired that quality when I was younger, then maybe I wouldn't be living on Bloomfield today, but farther west, on the flank of the mountain or opposite a park. In the end, these morose thoughts made me smile. I needed that. I saw myself emerging from my castle to turn on the automatic sprinklers or check to see if my domain was truly safe from intruders, and the absurdity of it cheered me up.

I know a few professors who, because they'd reached a certain social level, bled themselves white to buy what they thought they had to have, which turned out to be a bottomless pit in which they lost themselves: their money and their sanity. Killing yourself for a house seems to come from an irresistible passion among CEGEP teachers, and the situation's so widespread you hardly notice it any more: most conversations seem directed at people who aren't yet homeowners, pariahs who included me until barely a year ago, whom people point to and who don't know how lucky they are. When they found out I was buying a house in partnership with my woman friends, some of my colleagues snickered and told me I was a jerk, while lauding the merits of their little garden in Notre-Dame-de-Grâce or of the superimposed terraces in Outremont or even Westmount. It got me down for a couple of weeks, made me feel really useless because I hadn't set my sights high enough; but then the sudden bankruptcy of one of my colleagues put things back in perspective: I didn't know if I was really cut out to be a landlord, so why embark on an adventure that I already suspected was beyond me? I shrugged off the snickers. And on the night in question, right in the middle of la rue Dunlop, outside a house that was perfectly dazzling but, thank God, inaccessible, for the first time I was proud of what I'd done. No, not proud, relieved. I pictured myself going back inside my house after I'd turned on the sprinklers, climbing the broad staircase, heading for the bathroom, taking my heartburn tablets or my headache pills ... I saw again the downcast look of some of my colleagues on Monday morning, their red eyes, furrowed brows, the circles under their eyes, and I went home to la rue Bloomfield as happy as a clam.

Bernard was empty. Totally. It was hard to imagine that an hour earlier people had nearly come to blows over a seat on the terrace of La Moulerie or Le Café du Théâtre. Unlike la rue Laurier, which is still lively into the small hours, around one a.m. Bernard, because of some idiotic new law, seems to drop dead, as if struck by lightning, although until a few weeks ago the streets had been full of people till all hours and in total freedom.

When I turned in I realized I hadn't thought about Mathieu once during my walk.

Both the terrace and the restaurant of Le Train Bleu on Saint-Denis are very popular. It's a meeting place for artists of all sorts: actors, writers and film-makers come there, noisy and often too comfortable, to eat mussels or French sausages as they settle the fate of the world. To their liking. Rarely for the common good and often to their own advantage. Trendy restaurants like that exist everywhere, in every city with even a hint of cultural life, and they attract a second clientele, who come to gawk – and be scoffed at by – the first. And it includes me. I love to sit in a corner of the European-looking dining room and listen in on the conversations of those who make our culture. They often amuse but rarely surprise me. And I think that a lot of what they say is crap. They repeat themselves night after night, especially when they've been drinking. They're always on display, like homosexuals in the bars, but theirs is a verbal performance, which is much more dangerous. And revealing. You can change your clothes every day but speech, especially when it's tinged with bitterness or envy, evolves more slowly than fashion. By sniffing out rivalries I've even worked out the composition of the various clans; I've caught them in the act of hypocrisy or double-dealing, I've witnessed reunions that were a little too noisy to be genuine, I've watched some faces turn away, others flaunt themselves to be seen. But what I remember mostly is the truly awful things that are said after someone leaves. If I were ever invited to eat at a table of artists I'd make sure I didn't leave first.

In the days when I was seeing Luc, my circle of friends bored him and his scared me, so we didn't mix our two worlds much. That meant I wasn't known as the "lover of" which is what often happens in that sort of misalliance.

Over a well-chilled kir I told Mathieu everything. I described the past three days in the most intimate detail, sketching a none-too-flattering picture of myself, even exaggerating some of my characteristics. Not to discourage him: on the contrary, I felt very comfortable with him. It was so he wouldn't delude himself, so he'd know perfectly well who he was dealing with and what an ass I'd been since Friday night. I even confessed how relieved I was that we were eating on this terrace located *above* Sherbrooke ... What I said amused him. And, as he admitted himself, relieved him too.

"I've got something to tell you too, and it's hard for me, so I'm glad you went first."

Our table was the worst one on the terrace, under the outside staircase, but it was also the most private. The waiter had to bend over to avoid being knocked out when he served us and he didn't always remember.

Mathieu didn't tuck into his main course right away.

"If we're going to see each other again, and I hope we will, there's something you have to know."

"You aren't going to tell me you've got a lover ... "

"No. I'm married ... and I've got a four-year-old son."

This was so totally unexpected that I thought at first it was a joke. But from his serious, almost pained expression, I realized that it was true. It took me a minute to respond.

"I'm sorry ... I don't know what to say ... I was ready for anything but that."

"I'm not surprised ... "

"But you told me you were twenty-four! And you look nineteen!"

"What can I say? Life starts early for some people. I got married when I was eighteen, to my childhood sweetheart. We'd known each other forever and I suppose we were very fond of each other, but obviously we had no idea what we were doing ... Even our parents were against it! We had less sense than they did, if you can imagine! I really think we did it more for the presents and the wedding itself than to live together. We were children. We got caught in the trap like everybody else who gets married, we went into debt for ten years to buy incredibly expensive things for our apartment ... I'll still be paying them off five years from now."

"But that wasn't who answered when I phoned the other day ... "

"No, no, we've been separated nearly two years. I went back to live with my mother, because of all the debts."

Mathieu pushed away his plate of *crudités* as if it were making him sick.

"I left Louise very suddenly when ... when I realized ... I'm sorry, it's hard to say because I never talk about it to anybody."

"I understand ... You don't have to if you don't want ... We can pick it up another time."

"No, no, it'll be good for me."

He became more animated. I felt he must have been holding himself back for a long time, looking for someone to confide in. But why me?

"It hurt so much, Jean-Marc. Me as much as Louise. I realized I must have seemed like a real son-of-a-bitch when I told her, but I was too honest to try and hide it ... I thought if I explained my problems to her I'd be able to understand myself ... She's very smart, smarter than me anyway. I figured she'd catch on faster and maybe be able to explain to me what was going on ... "

He blew his nose in his napkin, then realized what he'd done and looked around to see if anyone had noticed.

"Did she keep the child?"

"Obviously."

"Are you on good terms?"

"Yes, better now ... It's been two years, so things have settled down. I see the boy as much as I want."

He moved his plate back, fiddled with his beets, then pushed it away again with a sigh.

"And I was so hungry ... "

"Yeah, come on, you should eat."

"I've got a lump in my throat ... "

"You've never talked to anybody about this?"

"Who? For sure not my mother, even if she suspects. And the guys you meet, you know as well as I do, you don't exactly want to trust them with the story of your life."

The waiter came for our plates. Mathieu handed him the napkin and asked for another. I watched regretfully as the *crudités* vanished into the kitchen. Nothing, absolutely nothing could stop me from eating: what Mathieu was telling me had no effect whatever on my appetite and I would have gladly helped myself from his plate, but under the circumstances I didn't think I should.

Mathieu lit a cigarette, after asking if it bothered me.

"Maybe I should cancel the rest of my dinner ... "

He was very upset; his eyes, his beautiful black eyes, shone in the orange light of the setting sun. I wanted to get up and take in my arms to console him for those two years of enforced silence.

"Excuse me for coming back to it, Mathieu, but didn't you know you were gay when you got married?"

He gave me a helpless little smile before replying.

"I've asked myself a hundred times, as you can imagine ... As far as I was concerned I was straight ... I swear, I was positive ... I'd never had any problems with girls ... It was very good with Louise ... That's ... my wife. I won't tell you how it happened, it's so banal ... But anyway it happened, and it turned my life inside out. I was so far from being ready for it, you can't imagine ... It was like changing my skin, my personality, my whole life ... Overnight every-

48

thing changed, absolutely everything, without my wanting it! Can you understand? I wasn't like some guys or girls who hesitate for years, it had never crossed my mind! My first experiences were . . . fantastic, Jean-Marc, and that made up my mind. But there was no way I was going to go on living my little domestic life alongside, as if nothing had changed, I can't . . . I can't cheat. That's something that has to be clear in my life and I couldn't live with . . . with that weight, that shadow . . . "

My veal kidneys and his lamb chops arrived. I hesitated before digging in. To my great surprise Mathieu had picked up his knife and fork as if they were weapons.

"Ah! No reason to stop eating . . . It's such a relief to talk, now my appetite's back."

We ate in silence for a few minutes. I didn't dare tell Mathieu it was impossible for it to have happened out of the blue, with no warning, that he must have given it some thought, had secret desires since childhood which he still refused to acknowledge. I've had so few problems coming to terms with what I am, it's hard for me to understand the development of those others, so many of them, for whom sexual choice was a Calvary, sometimes long and painful. And so often disastrous.

I've met lots of married men – the bushes on Mont Royal are full of them from May to November – but none, I think, with Mathieu's honesty. The duplicity of some so-called bisexuals makes me sick; too often it reeks of a conspiracy of misogyny on the part of those men, a fear of the truth, a sort of bitterness because of what they haven't been able to come to face. The openness of Mathieu, who didn't hesitate to turn his life upside down when the first signs of his new sexuality appeared, filled me with admiration. What courage it must have taken to confess everything, and to assume the consequences . . . And what a shock for his wife! I didn't dare mention her again during dinner. Better let things develop gradually. I was convinced now that I'd have the pleasure of seeing Mathieu again, and the prospect made me very happy.

I also tried not to think about the child too much.

Just before dessert, Mathieu asked me with a big grin:

"Are you going to run away now like you did the first time?"

"How about a nightcap?"

It was an unoriginal but always effective way to find out if someone wants the evening to go on . . .

"No thanks, I have to work tomorrow. Actually my vacation starts Friday but I won't be all around all that much . . . I bought a pass for the film festival, so I'll be in the dark for ten days – from morning till night."

This relationship was definitely getting off to a bizarre start: if I wasn't shying away then he was doing a disappearing act. Without thinking I replied, though it was an outright lie:

"Funny, I've been thinking of doing that too!"

Was I checking to see if he really wanted to see me again, or just playing games? I really don't know. But as it turned out, he was thrilled. Fortunately.

"Fantastic, we can do the Festival together. I've never done it with somebody. Usually I'm all by myself . . . But I warn you, I take it seriously . . . No breaks, no hanging around, nothing but films all day long . . . "

I swore I felt the same way, while asking myself if I really wanted to spend ten days staring at a movie screen. Another treat for Mélène and Jeanne.

I walked him to the Laurier Métro station. We hesitated before taking our leave. We walked around the station a couple of times, talking about this and that, about nothing actually, because our minds were elsewhere; mine was at any rate. I wanted to see him the next evening and I was searching for a reason. And hoping he felt the same way.

As he was about to enter the station I found it.

"Listen ... If you get off on romance, tomorrow night's the greatest show on earth, at the chalet on the mountain ... It's the August full moon. Or almost."

Sniffing a pretext, Mathieu smiled.

"A little fresh air before ten days' seclusion ... Call me at Eaton's tomorrow afternoon ... I'll let you know if I'm feeling romantic."

He came over and kissed me on the cheek.

"Meanwhile, thanks for tonight. You must know how good it's been for me ... "

Thirty-nine years old and I melt at a kiss on the cheek! *That*, I thought, is something I won't tell the girls.

Mathieu

The humidity was unbearable. There wasn't a breath of air in the apartment; Mathieu, dazed and dripping sweat, poured himself a glass of Contrex water and went to sit on the balcony. His mother was already out there, dozing in her chaise longue.

What he'd told Jean-Marc over dinner had awakened some old demons, reopened some old wounds that had been very hard to treat, that he'd thought were almost healed, more definitively scarred over. By putting up a wall between that period of his life which had been at once so terrifying and so exhilarating and his present life, more passive, almost vegetative, he'd been able to forget the intensity of the pain, the gravity of the dilemma in which he'd found himself, as well as his doubts, his certainties, all the questions, the outbursts of self-affirmation, the other, far more violent outbursts of rebellion as he came to terms with a revelation that he didn't understand and refused with all his might, while experiencing it with an intensity that stunned him.

Once again he lived through the amazement, the denial, the suffering in Louise's face; the rage during that brief period when her reaction had been violent; the horror he'd inspired in her, which she'd thrown back at him with desperate force; and then, acceptance, after battles of surprising brutality and arguments that went on forever. Acceptance, but not comprehension. He'd been unable to make his wife understand what was happening to him because he hadn't really understood it himself, or hadn't wanted to. Not right away, in any case.

For a while he'd thought it was a reaction to responsibilities too great for someone his age, to his refusal of the head-of-the-household straitjacket that had been thrust on him when the child – an accident – came too soon into his life; to the role in which he found himself frozen for the rest of his existence. But why men? Why not other women? And then old memories that had been buried, deliberately or not, resurfaced, clearer now, more obvious: troubles that had regularly cast him into melancholy during adolescence; hesitant reactions, incomprehensible at the time, to advances, whether timid or direct, that should have brought a more vigorous response; inexplicable crushes; images that had been rejected as soon as they occurred to him.

He also relived the pettiness of the incident that had started it all, the childish taste for revenge that he'd felt when he betrayed Louise, who had betrayed him first – and to make matters worse, with a guy he detested. Above all, the revelation in the face of what should always have been, and which was now happening too late. And was, fundamentally, so simple.

He'd even wondered if his true nature would ever have shown itself if Louise hadn't cheated on him, or if he hadn't found out. Then he had to acknowledge that it was just a pretext, his wounded pride serving as a catalyst for something that eventually, inevitably, would have been revealed. The timing couldn't have been worse, though, so soon after the birth of Sébastien, for whom Mathieu discovered an almost painful passion. He had lost at the same time the love and esteem of a woman he had deeply loved and his rights to a creature who was part of him, whom he'd created – somewhat unconsciously, granted – but who had quickly become his reason for living. His other reason for living, because his recent discovery had struck like lightning and he was giving himself over to it with the energy of despair. Mathieu remembered the period right after his separation as a kind of semi-hell in which he had revelled with an evil joy, a perverse masochism, an appetite for danger that astonished him.

Since then, things had changed considerably. He'd quickly had enough of the orgy at any price, of adolescent gropings in dark corners, of the furtive and pitiful encounters between anonymous skins scarcely touched, of sex quickly performed and soon forgotten; of the sadness, the hopelessness of it all. And especially of the tremendous futility of such ill-controlled gorging.

Now he found himself bruised, tired, disillusioned. Almost bitter at twenty-four, unhappy at his salesman's job and harbouring few illusions about his chances of becoming an actor.

Jean-Marc was turning up at this point in his life not as a saviour, then, or a last hope, but as a positive force at a particularly difficult time. He was grateful now that Jean-Marc hadn't tried anything the Friday before. He'd been upset at first, for he'd become accustomed to men succumbing to his charms, which were many and certain, without his having to lift a finger; he was always sure of his effect, of being able to pick and choose; but that was just his pride talking again, and Jean-Marc's tact now struck him as more precious than a quickie that would probably be already forgotten.

He'd have liked a sustained and straightforward relationship with Jean-Marc; for the first time in two years he even felt an urge to build something; not necessarily a love story: love was a word he'd more or less erased from his vocabulary for some time now, but perhaps a privileged friendship that would approach love, but without the consequences, which were so often disastrous. But none of that was very clear because Jean-Marc appealed to him physically and, inevitably, the time would come when that problem would assert its importance.

He was also anxious to know what Jean-Marc wanted from him. Their platonic association, so unusual in a sub-culture where sexuality is usually the cement and essence of a relationship, both surprised him and piqued his curiosity. There was something pleasant and exciting about this peacock dance they'd both been performing without daring to take the next step, something he'd never experienced before, but now was avid to explore. It entailed some danger, obviously, the danger of unrequited passion, but wasn't that a risk in any relationship?

After smoking a good half-package of cigarettes, he decided that he'd be as open and honest with Jean-Marc as possible, trying not to get so involved that he couldn't pull back if he realized that things were going badly. He wanted to be absolutely open with Jean-Marc, not to hurt him, but he didn't want to suffer either. He'd have to learn caution, something that was almost foreign to him.

He watched his mother for a long time as she slept. How would she react if she ever learned the truth? He'd often asked himself that question; he'd even come to the conclusion that she'd suspected something for ages now but kept postponing the explanations so she wouldn't have to come to grips with a situation that would change so many things in her own life.

It wasn't getting any cooler and he decided he should go to bed since he had to work the next day.

He slept amazingly well, woke up in a good mood and hummed on his way to work.

Jean-Marc

The moon was far from being full, but it was a glorious night with astonishing blues that slowly succeeded one another in the empty sky, from the nearly white post-sunset hue to the navy verging on red of the encroaching night; with its disturbing greys that slithered and crept into everything close to the ground, blurring human silhouettes while accentuating the shapes of trees, the contours of bushes; its ambers too, soaring above the city and veiled in a humid mist that made Montreal look like a huge Chinese lantern hanging in the void, unswayed by the slightest breath of wind. In the distance you could make out the St. Lawrence River, a black, irregular hole broken by the exaggerated straight line of the Seaway. The three bridges to the south shore, in contrast, were perfectly visible, their aerial structures like motionless ships.

I told Mathieu that when I'd started going up to the lookout at the Chalet on the mountain, when I was a child, the Sun Life Building was the highest in town. Montreal was just a small provincial city then, still absorbed by its Catholic complexes and its unhealthy fear of growth. Not that it's the world class super-metropolis of its dreams, but now at least it's a city that for the past twenty-five years has been trying to look like something, even if that meant getting shot down, which has happened more than once.

"We'd take the trolley up to Beaver Lake, along the Camilien-Houde Parkway which didn't have a name back then, I think, then we'd walk to here. Every Tuesday night in summer the symphony orchestra gave a concert. They'd put chairs out all around the Chalet and the orchestra played on the steps. The kids in my gang didn't have any money, so we'd bring blankets and lie around the lookout. We couldn't see or hear a thing but we were *there*. Sometimes we'd hug the stone wall that holds the place up, we'd stand just there, look, down below where we are now, we'd look down on the city while we tried to hear a few bars of the 'Danse macabre' or the 'Capriccio Italien.'"

Mathieu said nothing. He was smiling, probably amused at my sudden attack of nostalgia. He was leaning on his elbows and looking more at the sky than at the city.

The moon had put in its appearance later than expected. We must have waited a good hour and a half before we spotted it, somewhere to the right of Place Ville-Marie, a little yellow ball like half a lemon, nothing like the flashy, orgiastic full moon that I'd promised Mathieu. When he saw it he shook his head.

"Do you do this often – promise the moon and deliver a lemon?"

I simply told him that the end justified the means, then put my arm around his shoulders. He rested his head against mine. It was our first somewhat intimate contact; I sensed it was fragile, easily broken. One untoward remark, one awkward move could have spoiled it, we both knew that. So we just stood there, lost between our joy at this first furtive caress and our fear of seeing it vanish.

We walked very slowly down towards avenue du Parc. I didn't dare pop the big question and he didn't dare ask to spend the night. We were both guessing what the other wanted and we found it both funny and touching.

So we passed through the outside gayland of Montreal's nights, the famous bushes of Mont Royal, celebrated all over

North America and very popular, even since the appearance of AIDS which, it had been predicted, would put an end to such sexual manifestations that cause God-fearing souls to blush and bring policemen running through the shadows, from San Francisco to New York and from New Orleans to Quebec City.

What's always surprised me about that sort of open-air cruising, whether it's in the Tuileries or Central Park, on Mont Royal or the Plains of Abraham, is the total silence in which it takes place. You don't even dare to come out loud, whereas elsewhere, especially in the bars, sound is the natural element for the winking and groping, the propositions and assents. Here, along little paths where every tree risks being turned not into an Iroquois but into a sexual partner – who can be effective or not, but always discreet – silence is as much part of the game as the darkness. Something like the backrooms but without the stifling atmosphere, the suspect odours, the dirt you expect to find on the walls and especially on the sticky floors. The underbrush is strewn with Kleenex, granted, and empty cigarette boxes form paler spots on the more secluded paths, but it's still the open air, almost rural. In moments of irony, in the days when I still indulged in such practices, I'd named the bushes on Mont Royal my "outdoor backrooms" or my "dangerous resorts," because along with everything else, you never know what's going to turn up. Unpleasant surprises are numerous and varied, more so than pleasant ones, but then pleasant surprises are generally worth the trouble. That's why hundreds of men of all ages and all convictions climb the steep slopes of Mont Royal every night, in the hope of ending up either as part of the wildest group of the century or in the most discreet, romantic spot in town, in the arms of a partner they'll never see again, who'll fuck as if he was doing it for the last time in his life.

A lot of them fuck that way every night, as if it was indeed the last time, but they're already speculating about what their luck might be the next day. It's sexuality marked by despair at ever finding another one who's worth the trouble, and by the hope of being surprised again, one final time – the ultimate time.

A few silhouettes were moving around us, even on the main road where's it's bright enough to distinguish faces. I recognized a few, the same old companions in cruising I always thought I knew, they'd become so familiar, but I pretended I didn't see them, as if they'd never existed. Phantoms for whom I too am only a phantom, whom I've watched grow older, fatter, thinner, worse or better looking, never knowing who they were, but well aware of what they were looking for . . . and it wasn't me. At one point Mathieu moved closer and wrapped his arm around my waist.

"It's not what you'd call a romantic stroll but it's nice anyway."

We'd left the area of the burning bushes with a strong sense of relief. We got the giggles as we hurtled down the final slopes of the mountain, the ones that lead to the corner of Parc and Mont-Royal. In the distance, we'd spotted a patrol car beginning its rounds. Shorts and jeans would be pulled up in frantic haste, more than one coitus would be irrevocably interruptus, shadows bent double would speed through the trees, warning whistles shrilled amid the weighty silence of the night.

We'd gone back up Côte Sainte-Catherine, admiring the magnificent houses that line the street. Mathieu thought they were pretentious, while I told him my long-cherished dream which I now found so laughable. I didn't ask Mathieu back to the house and he didn't invite himself either. But at two a.m. he was in my bed.

It was a night filled with tenderness. I hadn't made love with a man for whom I'd felt something resembling affection for a very long time; I'd forgotten the pleasure of giving that's as important as receiving, the sense of sharing that occurs when love is made not only well but with generosity and feeling.

And, something that's very important for me, we laughed a lot. At our fears and our shyness and our hesitations. While finding it all very touching, of course. We got all emotional about the hokey, almost adolescent side of our relations, which we found it amusing to call our dates, and we swore we'd keep on that way because adult love is usually intolerable and always painful. We weren't missing a single cliché.

The next morning he got up to go to work. Since the Cinéma Parisien is near Eaton's I went along with him to buy a pass for the Festival des Films du Monde. Luckily there were still some left. I bought the programme and spent the rest of the morning looking through it. So I was going to spend the rest of my vacation in front of a movie screen – I, whose knowledge of world films is limited to what's shown in Montreal, i.e., practically nothing. But to be with Mathieu I'd have done a lot worse. I realized that and refused to succumb to my usual anxiety.

The Mother of Us All adores grains and granola. Especially in the morning. But sometimes she fixes herself a big bowl-ful at noon, with yoghurt, fruit and wheat-germ. And offers some to you. She claims it puts everything where it's sup-posed to be, that no other food has the nutritional value of that disgusting mash and that we should eat nothing else, since after all man is nothing but a seed-eater who was diverted from the right path by the disastrous discovery of meat, the cause of all his ills. I tried it once and felt as if my stomach would be blocked for at least three days: I felt heavy and listless and I had a doughy taste in my mouth that produced an annoying tickle in my throat. Health food makes me sick, I've always said so. My system's used to the garbage I'm always stuffing it with and it reacts just fine, thank you very much. So now when I go to Mélène's for lunch I bring my own junk food and I disgust her with my poison while she nauseates me with her panacea.

So there we sat talking, Mélène with her bowl of cereal the mere colour of which made me gag, and I over a plate of canned meatball stew that nobody else in the gang would be able to stomach.

Mélène seemed delighted at my account of the night before. She listened without interrupting me, in itself an event, an emotional little smile on her lips. I already knew what she'd tell me, but maybe that was precisely why I'd come. And in fact I didn't get away.

"It's been a while since you've gone out with someone for so long, Jean-Marc. Four times, wow! that's serious. Usually you get turned off right away, after one night. The next morning you give them a huge breakfast, then tactfully kick them out."

She'd assumed her Mother of Us All voice, high-pitched, ironic, almost condescending. A real mom making gentle fun of her naughty child.

"Just a year ago you were swearing up and down you'd never get caught again – no more lovers, only tricks."

I was wiping the last of the gravy from my plate with a slice of six-grain bread, my one concession to Mélène's regimen.

"Things were bad last year, you know that as well as I do. I wasn't ready for another love story that would tear the skin off my heart."

"Who says this one won't?"

"Who says it's a love story?"

"Well it sure didn't start as casual sex. I just hope you aren't deluding yourself, Jean-Marc; it sounds to me like one

61

of those fine little romances you swear you've given up for good!"

"When I said that last year the whole family laughed ... Now I see you were right. As usual. It bugs me sometimes how you girls know what's going on inside me better than I do myself ... "

"You don't see because you don't look hard enough."

"Mélène, please, no sermon."

She laid her spoon on her plate after deliberately licking it clean, perhaps to irritate me.

"That's exactly why you're here, Jean-Marc, for my sermons! So stop complaining."

Of course she was right. Like all the members of our little chosen family, I often came and consulted Mélène, to hear things I already knew but didn't want to admit, in a reproving tone that was a lot like the kind of Judeo-Christian sermons we'd all resisted during our adolescence, whose injustices and dangers we all condemned aloud. We'd delegated Mélène to play the role of mom that we'd refused our own mothers and now we had to accept the consequences. I won't let a contradiction get in my way.

"You're in deeper than I thought, Jean-Marc ... "

"I'm in deeper than I intended, if you want to know. You'll tell me what you think when you meet him, but there's something about this guy ... something *genuine*, to use an unfashionable word I always used to sneer at. It's touching, and it's very appealing. He comes across as a little kid, and it's true he can be very childish, but then suddenly he'll come out with something amazing ... When I think of what he's been through, at his age, I feel as if he's lived more than I have! And you get the sense that there's a wound, a scar somewhere that he wants to hide and I want to discover ... "

"You make him sound like the eighth wonder of the world ... Watch out, Jean-Marc ... "

"He may not be a wonder, but at least he's alive! You meet so many walking corpses in my circles, when you find a spark of life it's almost shocking!"

Mélène smiled, shaking her head. I'd made this speech dozens of times before, sometimes when I was on the brink of despair at ever finding anybody appropriate as my peregrinations became more and more rocky, more and more hysterical, sometimes marked by a bitterness she was quick to point out, because we'd long ago decreed that bitterness is one of the worst feelings you can experience.

"Anyway, let us know if we'll be celebrating for a change or consoling you as usual."

The first day of the Festival des Films du Monde was an endurance test. I enjoy movies but I've never been an immoderate consumer, just following what comes out of France, at least the ones that make it here – and less so, what's done in the States, because I find most American movies have too much noise and not enough sensitivity – and then, out of solidarity if I dare to use the word, what's been done here for the past twenty years or so.

I don't think I was even twenty when *Valérie* came out. My memory of it's confused, like a feeling of embarrassment because I'd thought the film was idiotic, though at the same time I was relieved to see our grotesque censorship being held up to ridicule, the same censorship that in 1960 had devastated and violated *Hiroshima mon amour* under the pretext of preserving public morality. So there I was, on the first day of the festival standing in line at a quarter to nine – a.m. – outside the Parisien with Mathieu, who was so keyed up he couldn't stand still.

"This year I'm aiming at an average of four films a day . . . It's easy at first, but towards the middle of the Festival, you'll see, you reach a kind of plateau . . . you can't take in any more, it's like a kind of indigestion ... but it gets sorted out and the final sprint's always exhilarating."

Since I was afraid I wouldn't even make it through the first day, I didn't reply.

It was Mathieu, of course, who'd drawn up our schedule. At breakfast he'd held out a leaflet covered with yellow and black splotches, totally unintelligible to me, and tried, in vain, to explain them. All that got through to me was that on day one, we were going to see a film from Poland, one from Britain, one from Japan and, if there was still time, one from Australia. So in just one day I was going to see what I usually take in over a month and I didn't even feel like going to the movies.

No, what I wanted to do was stay home with Mathieu, savouring one of those mornings that are unique to the beginning of a relationship, so sweet, so gentle, that nothing afterwards can replace them, that remain among the most beautiful. I'd have been attentive enough to risk being cloying, tender in a way you rarely admit you're capable of being. Willingly and with talent galore I'd have played the part of the star-struck lover who gets on everybody's nerves till they want to punch him. Instead, there I was surrounded by a mob of leaflet-waving film buffs who were already trumpeting in peremptory and superior tones their personal favourites: "I saw the latest Beineix at Cannes, it's total trash" or: "Skip the Blier, it's sillier than usual!" or again, and with the proper accent to show how plugged-in you are: "You *must* see the Schlöndorff! Really, the Schlöndorff is *the* film to see!" And I, poor ignoramus who'd never been able to pronounce the name without being laughed at, stood with my nose in my programme while Mathieu kissed the cheeks of overwrought girls and shook hands with incredible sixties leftovers, complete with beards and lugging those paper shopping bags that were known in my childhood as "les sacs à Tousignant."

In the distance I spotted two colleagues deep in conversation, and I turned my back for fear they'd notice me. Just the thought that in one week I'd have to rub shoulders with them every day made my legs turn to rubber. When the doors opened the excitement, already high, moved up a notch. For a minute I thought the crowd would shout "Hurray!" the way we used to on Saturday afternoons when I was a kid, when the doors of the parish hall opened and we took out our ten cents with a squeal.

Mathieu grabbed my arm.

"Exciting, eh?"

I said yes, sure, as I followed the crowd that was surging into the theater. A lady behind me gave me a push in the back, just hard enough to be unpleasant. I turned around. She didn't get it. I felt her schedule against my shoulder blade, the pressure of her hand grazing my shirt, and I wanted to scream.

A heavy, violent Polish film, with English subtitles, at nine a.m.: everybody should try it – once! The only films I've ever seen in the morning were those old fifties melodramas they showed us in high school to warn us about intimate physical contact or drugs, which were sometimes so terrifying they'd keep us awake at night. The violence in this Polish offering was a different kind, more psychological than physical, but it was still nine a.m. and I had a lot of trouble concentrating on the misfortunes of the woman who was being humiliated by her husband, even though the film was excellent. I felt a vague discomfort the way you do when you change your schedule at the last minute and find yourself somewhere at an unaccustomed time: the lighting in the room is the same but the light is different, because the sun isn't in the same place. You feel displaced, but required to go on functioning as usual, in a waking dream.

After the second film – from England this one, fascinating and admirably filmed but which I was already beginning to confuse with the preceding one – I was hungry. Obviously a quiet lunch at a good little restaurant was out of the question; it was over a Mister Steer, number six, that Mathieu and I discussed what we'd just seen . . .

My buttocks started to ache during the first film of the afternoon, a deadly bore about peasant life in rural Japan, almost impossible to sit through till the end. While I was watching it I thought that if a Québécois filmmaker dared to make a movie like that he'd be massacred and his film wouldn't have a chance of being shown outside the country; he'd be called a "misérabiliste", accused of fascination with the sordid side of life (the sordid aspects of Japanese life being automatically universal, I suppose, but not ours), worst of all a regionalist: we must keep our peasants to ourselves, they're shameful, but by all means let's share other people's, they're *culture*. But then I told myself I was being unfair: no great film about peasant life has ever been made here, I think. But would we manage to impose it on the Japanese if it existed, or must we always suffer the folklore of others?

The last screening of the day did me in: I haven't seen many of those Australian films people have been raving about in recent years and if this one was typical I was very glad I've been staying at home watching soaps; they don't cost anything and at least I can laugh.

I brought out all the tact I can muster at delicate moments to tell Mathieu, over supper, that I found it hard to imagine that the next ten days would be like the one just ending. Not only because of the films, which I doubted I'd be able to keep ingurgitating in such heavy doses over such a long time, but especially because our new intimacy was going to be disturbed in a way that struck me as abnormal. He understood very quickly, before I'd even finished my explanations, and I think he was hurt, not at having dragged me into this adventure for nothing, he'd done that in good faith, thinking I'd enjoy it, and he didn't know me well enough yet to be able to guess my tastes, but because he was being criticized so early in a relationship, for not being sufficiently present.

Already a dead end. Each of us understood the other's arguments, while maintaining his own position: for Mathieu the film festival was one of the highlights of the year and he didn't want to sacrifice it, whereas all I wanted was to lock myself away with my new lover and not see another soul.

Still, I have to admit that he was the one who worked out the solution for this first conflict, but only after a really vicious exchange. (I was even afraid, towards the end of our meal, that he'd get up from the table and disappear, it was that bad.) But he found a compromise that would more or less satisfy us both: he'd sacrifice the first film of the morning if I'd follow him for the rest of the day. Negotiations were tight: I wanted the whole morning for the two of us and just two films a day. But I lost. Because I gave in: I suddenly realized I sounded like an ass, a late-blooming romantic making demands like a young virgin lover. After all, Mathieu was probably right: the festival would soon be over, but if we wanted, our intimacy would remain, brand-new and passionate, still undefined and waiting to be formed.

Mathieu

At Jean-Marc's first incoherent and tormented words Mathieu had clung to him, hoping that would silence him. Or wake him up. Jean-Marc had turned to him, hugged his chest with his right arm, and smiled vaguely, moaning. But then he kept talking. It sounded complicated and very strange; there was hostility mixed with helplessness, all expressed in quick, brief gasps like the cries of a small sick animal. Mathieu had taken Jean-Marc's head in his hands.

An overgrown child of thirty-nine. Who was dreaming just the way his four-year-old son did. Sébastien dreamed a lot, enough to worry his father who, encouraged by guilt, was sometimes sure that the boy was restless at night because he was unhappy. Did Sébastien – a child of divorce, separated from his father very young – re-live in his sleep the hideous hours of his early childhood when rage, violence, even brutality had exploded in their lives, ugly, irreparable and destructive? Sébastien slept on the living-room sofa with Mathieu when he came to visit his father and grandmother. Bedtime was always accompanied by the joy of kisses and tickling and stories told in hushed tones, by secrets that ended with great declarations of love. But often, just as Mathieu was stretching out beside his son to go to sleep, little whimpers would emerge from the mouth of Sébastien, who seemed to be protesting some terrible injustice. Rose maintained that it was because the child was used to sleeping alone and that his father's presence disturbed him, but Mathieu saw it as a reproach, almost an accusation. Or

68

worse, a rejection. When it happened he would gently awaken Sébastien, tell him he loved him, then put him back to sleep as tenderly as he could. Most of the time it worked and gave Mathieu a tremendous sense of deliverance.

He tried to awaken Jean-Marc, who merely muttered and turned his back. Then Mathieu reached out his arm and pressed his hand against Jean-Marc's neck, where an artery was beating softly.

This fight, their first, had upset him a lot. He'd promised himself for years, since he and Louise had separated in fact, that he wouldn't put up with any more of those pitiful, searing domestic squabbles that always leave a scar, even when you think the problems are solved, those endless, exhausting analyses the mere memory of which was enough to keep him from making a commitment to someone when he wanted to, or even felt he was in danger of doing so. He'd had plenty of affairs, sometimes exalting, sometimes depressing, too often run-of-the-mill, but until now he'd always managed to pull back in time, even at the risk of seeming like a bastard if the break was too abrupt, or shallow if there was no logical reason for it. He never caused gratuitous pain to anyone. But when a relationship seemed not to be just dragging on – if he enjoyed seeing the same guy for a long time – but becoming official, something in him resisted, he'd feel out of his depth, and he'd start seeking a way out. And take it, despite whatever tenderness or consideration he'd been feeling for the other man, whom he generally left feeling stunned and wounded, not knowing what had hit him, or how, or, above all, why.

With Jean-Marc, though, something new was happening and he couldn't account for it. Jean-Marc wasn't better looking or sharper or more intelligent than some of the men he'd gone out with since discovering his homosexuality; in many ways he was even less mature, like some belated adolescent who would venture into the adult world but never actually manage to become part of it. But it was precisely the way he expressed his immaturity, his self-restraint, too, which he'd given proof of during those first few days when they'd been seeing each other without sex, usually so inevitable in their circles, getting in the way, his very special way of treating Mathieu not as spoils of war to be consumed as fast as possible in case he disappeared on some whim, but as a privileged partner to be treated carefully, that touched Mathieu, even though he'd seen it all before. But all this attentiveness, though it was considerable and Mathieu appreciated it tremendously, didn't explain his desire to be with Jean-Marc, despite the tiresome tirade over dinner that normally would have sent him running.

Jean-Marc was talking again, but his voice was softer now. Mathieu allowed himself the pleasure of thinking that it was because of his hand on the sleeping man's neck. Which made him suddenly aware that for the first time in his life, perhaps, he felt not superior to, but stronger than his partner, that he could, if he wanted, have the power to transform a life, shake up an existence, "protect" someone as he so often wanted to "protect" his child: in a word to love someone who truly needed him. Until now he had left men because he wouldn't allow himself to be loved; this time he wanted to stay, so that he could love. He sat up in bed and lit a cigarette, very cautiously to avoid waking Jean-Marc. Was this love or condescension? Was he being patronizing? Was he going to play daddy with Jean-Marc as he did with Sébastien one weekend in four? Or was he simply afraid to acknowledge that he was on the point of throwing himself into something tremendous, something incomprehensible, that he wasn't yet ready to face? Were his superiority and strength an act he was putting on to conceal from himself the state of dependency and weakness into which he felt he was sinking? For a very brief moment he was tempted to get up and run after freedom as he usually did, not looking back,

70

not allowing himself any regret, his arms stretched out towards other episodes, other meetings that he'd make sure would lead nowhere, would be free of pain, bland and totally innocuous.

But then he pictured Jean-Marc's dazed look after seeing four films in one day, his indignation at Mathieu's refusal to spend their mornings together, the shared joy of their love-making and the laughter they exchanged afterwards. He put out his cigarette and moulded his body against Jean-Marc's. And immediately fell asleep.

Jean-Marc

Everything was fine that weekend. We got up fairly late, had breakfast in bed (a big meal that I prepared with pleasure if not talent, while Mathieu read with imperturbable seriousness the reviews of the Festival in *Le Devoir* and *La Presse*, which fortunately I subscribe to), then, calmly, without rushing around as we'd had to on the first day to be on time for the nine a.m. screening, we headed downtown to the Cinéma Parisien. The number 80 bus was less crowded than at eight-thirty, and faster too. With our passes we were able to go directly to the theatre we wanted, without having to stand in line.

We'd seen nine films in three days at that point, and to my amazement, with no pain on my part. On the contrary, I felt festival fever growing on me: I'd be more and more excited when we arrived at the Parisien, I'd listen to what people were saying about the first show, I'd underline the films they were raving about and strike out those we'd intended to see that were being panned, I'd get worked up over a Mexican film everybody else was ignoring, I had even caught myself snickering at the mention of one of the French blockbusters whose director I couldn't stand; in short, I was becoming a full-fledged festival-freak, to the great pleasure of Mathieu who kept saying: "I told you, didn't I, the tension builds and you can't resist the excitement . . . "

On the Sunday night, around half-past seven, we were coming out of a very fine Danish film that had disturbed us both deeply and we were lingering in the lobby, animated, overwrought even, trying to decide where to eat, when I heard a familiar voice:

"Jean-Marc! Jean-Marc! We thought you were dead!"

The whole family was there, emerging from another theatre. There were six of them, forming a compact, homogeneous group, all with the same style, the same ease, the same humour in the depths of their eyes, a vaguely tomboyish look that was just enough to remove any doubt but not enough to draw attention to itself; they were noisy of course, but not loud like some men. Kisses, embraces, brief introductions. They literally devoured Mathieu with their eyes, weighed him and judged him. He sensed it at once and shut himself off completely. Observations crossed and tangled, laughter welled up, nervous when a remark had been too obvious, conspiratorial when it was too obscure. Mélène gestured her approval while Jeanne gave Mathieu a look that was much too offhand. Mathieu leaned towards me in the midst of a widespread guffaw (subtle Mélène had just said to no one in particular: "I think I understand why you've been tied up around the clock: breaking in the new home entertainment centre?") and asked, furiously: "Was this a setup, this little chance meeting?" I swore that it wasn't. I couldn't help smiling, and that seemed to shock him even more than my friends' remarks. Zouzou, in her nasal voice that sometimes has an embarrassing way of carrying, laid her hand on Mathieu's shoulder: "No billing and cooing, lovebirds!" A few heads turned and there were some smiles when people realized who the two "lovebirds" were. I thought Mathieu would crash to the sidewalk. Mélène tapped Zouzou's arm, and she shrugged. "Mélène, quit behaving like my mother! And anyway I wasn't nearly as bad as you!"

Right away, of course there was talk of "going somewhere to grab a bite." I drew Mathieu aside.

"They're my best friends, Mathieu, my only friends as a

73

matter of fact ... and it's true I've been out of touch with them ... "

"They aren't exactly discreet ... "

"They're probably embarrassed."

"Embarrassed! It sure as hell doesn't show!"

"Well, nervous then ... I've talked about you to Mélène a lot and she probably repeated it all to the rest of them, and they're happy about us ... They're fantastic women, you'll see ... "

"But I'm embarrassed too, Jean-Marc! I mean, I'm out-numbered, seven to one! How am I supposed to please them, with my back against the wall? Seduce them? Show them my terrific sense of humour, my great cultivation, my enormous I.Q.? They're all older than me, Jean-Marc, I haven't got a chance!"

I'd never seen him like this; I was startled and a little frightened too.

"Mathieu, you don't have to do *anything*! This isn't an exam you have to pass, it's a chance meeting as you said, that's all ... We're going to get something to eat, we're going to try and enjoy ourselves ... "

"And you mean if they decide I'm 'inappropriate' or 'unfit for human consumption' you'll tell me to get lost so your friends won't be unhappy?"

So we'd reached that point already. Everything was happening too fast and there was no time for explanations, there at the door of the Parisien, standing between the impatient line of people waiting to go in and the noisy, unruly crowd that was coming out.

"There's nothing to be scared of ... They aren't ogresses, you know, I've told you a lot about them ... "

"I didn't want to meet them all at once like that, in a gang. It's terrifying ... I was hoping you'd introduce them one at a time ... But ... I don't care if you say it's not an exam, I still feel as if I'm being judged!"

74

He was absolutely right.

Mélène came over, as discreetly as possible. She had that preoccupied look I never see on her except at moments of great importance. She smiled at Mathieu, a gorgeous smile, irresistible because it's sincere, that she reserves for people she really cares for.

"If you don't want to eat with us, we understand ... We were just talking about it ... It can't be easy for you, Mathieu, meeting so many of us all at once ... We're not exactly shrinking violets ... "

Oddly enough, Mathieu's about-face didn't surprise me at all. He heaved a sigh that sounded like one of relief and made an effort to return Mélène's smile, hugging his chest as if he were cold.

"You're right, it's not easy ... But since I'm here now I might as well be brave and go through with it ... I need your help, though, my teeth are chattering! This is going to be one of the deepest dives I've ever taken!"

We all met at the check-out counter of Le Commensal, having our food weighed amid widespread giggling that seemed to puzzle Mathieu. I couldn't explain to him here and now the contradiction that for years had made us giggle at this neighbourhood restaurant with its wan granola-eating clientele and its excellent food, heavy but delicious, too stodgy perhaps but all-natural, it would have taken too long and might have sounded cruel. Zouzou or Arielle just had to jerk her chin in the direction of a long-haired girl in Roman sandals and a flowered skirt that trailed along the terrazzo floor, and groans of pleasure would rise up from the entire family, with heads dropping towards plates and shoulders shaking in uncontrollable spasms. Unlike Mélène who was pure granola but whom we forgave because we loved her, the genuine post-hippie article drove us to bitchiness that was unprovoked and, I have to say, generous – in the sense that it was neither held back nor openly malicious. This bitchiness was perfectly good-natured, open and almost affectionate, probably contemptuous and patronizing, the sort you might feel for a sick person who's dependent and complaining. We'd play busy nurse with these poor, peace-loving creatures, motionless and pale, who'd never done anything to us, as they calmly, like satisfied monks, devoured their tofu steaks and carrot cake.

Mélène, in her role as Mother of Us All, and Jeanne, the moderator of the group, took places on either side of Mathieu as soon as we'd picked our table; the others arranged themselves like obedient apostles, leaving me the seat across from him, between Zouzou and Arielle, who were exchanging knowing looks as usual. The complicity between those two girls is stupefying; you sometimes feel as if they're communicating through a sixth sense they don't share with anyone else for the simple reason that they don't realize they possess it: you're always catching them in the midst of a silent conversation, the eyes of one riveted on the other's and an almost tangible electric current passing between them, little signs of complicity being traced within their secret world, subtle and ethereal, understood by them alone and excluding any possibility of a third source of energy.

The conversation was mainly about films, of course. The girls had seen one from China, with French subtitles, and Michèle, the youngest, who was a bit lazy but very funny, with a cat-like slyness, complained about having had to spend two hours reading instead of concentrating on the images. It was an old quarrel that will never be resolved because all the arguments are worn-out by now. Michèle repeated once again: "I don't care what you say about subtitles, I still need a course in speed-reading ... All they did in that film was *talk*!" and Mélène replied: "But it's so much better than listening to the same damn Paris accents all the time! Sometimes I think if I had a rifle I'd go to France and shoot Nadine Alari point blank!" A few shrugs, some knowing smiles.

Mathieu leaned across the table towards me.

"Who's Nadine Alari?"

Triumphant applause. The girls envied him his youth, they extolled his good fortune at being unacquainted with Nadine Alari's nasal voice, they officially christened him "the kid." He blushed to the roots of his hair, nearly choked on his garlic spaghetti, then wiped both his brow and his mouth. I smiled my encouragement as best I could, but I could see that his discomfort was very deep, that he probably thought he was being laughed at, while the truth was that we were making fun of our own advancing years. It was Michèle, finally, who put an end to the incident by telling him: "I'll gladly pass you the sceptre of youth, Mathieu. But let me warn you: it's no picnic, being the scapegoat for these old fogeys who deal with their fear of aging by laughing at anything younger than them! Just remember, they aren't laughing at you. Ever! Or you'll be as paranoid as I used to be. Remember, it's not you, it's your age!"

Loud applause greeted her outburst. Mélène stood up, grasped Michèle's shoulders and kissed her, clasping her ostentatiously to her bosom.

"Welcome to the golden oldies, my child!"

The atmosphere for the rest of the meal was good-humoured. Mathieu gradually relaxed, even started to confide in Jeanne, who was gently and tactfully grilling him. I was glad to see that things were turning out so well; that my friends, whose opinion matters so much to me, seemed to like Mathieu a lot. Because I'd have known right away if they were rejecting him, I'd have sensed it from any excessive (and therefore false) interest, any ill-concealed irony in their glances, any overdone courtesy. They weren't polite with Mathieu; that meant a lot. Of course I'd been through plenty of those first meetings where everybody spies on the new recruit while pretending not to; I'd been one of those who sat in judgment myself when one of the women brought us her new flame, the poor girl livid and terrified.

Families like ours, born of each member's visceral need, that are almost too close, smooth and hard as rocks, with nothing officially holding them together, but sufficient unto themselves, are formidable to any foreign body that tries to penetrate them. I'd seen so many girls come up against a stubborn refusal, so many guys unceremoniously sent packing, that for some time now I'd been reluctant to introduce any casual friends to the rest of the family. I preferred to disappear for a few days, follow my adventure to the end, then reappear at an official supper, the prodigal child, the black sheep whose return is eagerly celebrated, his brief fling forgiven, but whose definitive flight would be taken very badly. I'd have been happy to wait a few weeks, then, before "producing" Mathieu, but circumstances had decided otherwise.

Over coffee, too strong but delicious, Jeanne, Mélène and Mathieu were deep in a conversation in which I already sensed a reassuring complicity. Mathieu was talking about the uncertainties of the actor's trade and the other two, although they'd cordially hated Luc, were listening with surprising attentiveness. Why had they found Luc so disagreeable and why did they find Mathieu so nice? Bad vibes or bad faith? I decided not to analyze, but take advantage of it, and so I listened in on what they were saying.

Jeanne was leaning against the back of Mathieu's chair, her head on her fist.

"You mean as soon as you get an acting job you'll have to quit Eaton's?"

"Well, it's not that simple . . . First of all, there aren't all that many acting jobs these days . . . "

"With looks like yours it shouldn't be too hard . . . "

"It doesn't always work that way . . . There's more than

looks involved ... and anyway Montreal has no shortage of good-looking actors ... "

Mélène, whose bluntness still surprises me, it's so brusque sometimes, asked him point blank:

"Have you got any talent?"

"Yes. I know I have. But nobody knows me because I didn't go to theatre school, so I have to fight harder than the others ... "

Mélène, visible pleased at his reply, lit a cigarette.

"Is that really necessary? I mean the theatre schools, the conservatory, whatever ... "

I didn't hear the rest of the conversation, I was literally assaulted by Arielle, whom I hadn't seen for several weeks, who'd moved her chair between Lucie's and mine. Lucie didn't object. She never protests and if you ask me she's much too tolerant. She's the silent member of our group, discreet and to some extent our Patira, as my mother, a fervent reader of Raoul de Navery, would have said. She's Michèle's lover, and Michèle takes tremendous advantage of her, too much in fact: she's demanding, temperamental, almost inquisitorial with her, and gets nothing in return but consent and submission. We call them the Babin sisters and we sometimes amuse ourselves too cruelly at Michèle's demands and Lucie's indulgence. Just now, Lucie had pushed her chair aside without even a sigh, while Arielle, tipsy after single glass of white wine, collared me with her unique brand of familiarity.

The cat-smell she's left in her wake for years caught in my throat right away and I recoiled slightly. She didn't even notice, sure as she was of my undeniable interest in the escapades she was about to recount. It was a long, raunchy, rambling, incomprehensible story. After what seemed like hours, I heard Jeanne give the signal to leave and I was grateful.

On the sidewalk it was all noisy kisses and affectionate

hugs. Arielle, Zouzou, Lucie and Michèle were going to a bar on Saint-Denis; Jeanne and Mélène, who have a car, offered us a lift.

When he found out that they lived in the apartment above mine Mathieu seemed first surprised, then very uneasy.

Well, I saw thirty-four films in eleven days, but I never reached the "plateau" Mathieu had talked about. Towards the middle of the second week, though, he began to flag; his concentration wavered a little, headaches made him grouchy – especially since I was still fresh as a daisy – he traded his contact lenses for a pair of glasses I hadn't seen him wear before, which I found very comical. They made him look like a pointy-headed intellectual and, fortunately, a little older too, so I didn't feel so much as if I was tagging along with my oldest child.

Because, obviously, in the course of the week I'd caught some unambiguous, even frankly mocking, stares: other gay men, especially ones my age, watched us go by appreciatively, because he was good-looking; they were probably envious of my good luck, but they were always ironic and not often friendly, as if our casual manner didn't shock but provoked them. In contrast, the guys of Mathieu's age seemed totally indifferent to me and openly cruised him as if he were alone. A few even gravitated around us for days, I'm not exaggerating, in the hope of some sign from Mathieu, thinking it was impossible that he wouldn't show duplicity at some point. As no such sign appeared, they must have thought Mathieu was just weird, turning down their proferred charms in favour of an old man, so they left us to our discussions and didn't push it.

At a few screenings of gay films, where we were of course the majority, the straight men – and this was both amusing and very revealing – would scowl a little in their seats, as if afraid of being taken for one of "them." Or they'd clutch at their dates as if they were lifebuoys, or irrefutable alibis. I thought it was funny but Mathieu, in whom I was beginning to sense a fairly lively intolerance, grew impatient. His bad faith was quite simplistic in fact: "Should I worry about passing for straight when I go to a film by Sautet?" But then he saw the difference and shrugged, laughing. "Anyway, they're the ones with hangups ... "

The days sped by at a dazzling rate; the summer holiday was ending in a final sprint that was new to me, I who always stretch out the last weeks of August by sleeping as much as possible, slowing down my activities, adopting an almost vegetative rhythm, because for too many years now the resumption of classes has become so loathsome.

We hadn't seen my women friends again during the Festival. I'd run into Mélène on the stairs a couple of times and she kept telling me how charming she thought Mathieu was; and he confessed that he'd fallen under the spell of my adopted family, but on both sides there was something missing – some conviction, some sign of sincerity – as if both were telling me what I wanted to hear, not what they really thought. In Mélène I sensed caution dictated by her affection for me, and in Mathieu, reluctance to admit to me – or to himself – that all of it, the family, the way we lived in one another's pockets, the ties so close he assumed they were inextricable – just weren't his style. He didn't want to scare me off with premature possessiveness or a totally legitimate concern that, from the very beginning, he'd have to share with a group of people who were themselves too involved, a still-fragile relationship which the slightest thing, especially indiscretion, might compromise.

During the last weekend of the Festival, Mathieu turned gloomy; he became almost taciturn, easily distracted, less passionate in our discussions, I even caught his attention wandering during a wonderful Argentinian film that was one of the high points of the ten days, one he'd been looking forward to with great excitement.

On the Sunday night, as we were heading to the Latini for

the last meal there, I asked him what was going on. At first he said it was the fatigue, the edginess of the past ten days, the overdose of films that were making him grumpy and irritable; then all at once he changed his mind, and confessed that he was leaving for Provincetown the next day, as he did every year after the Festival.

"See, I've got a week of holidays left, and I've had my reservations for two months ... I honestly don't want to go all that badly now, because of you, because of what's happening between us, but I have to tell you I'd have trouble going back to Eaton's without seeing the ocean ... I should've told you ages ago, I know, but I kept putting it off. I didn't want to spoil the Festival and I didn't want you to freak out because of Provincetown ... I even considered cancelling, but ... "

I reassured him, though I wasn't all that reassured myself. No matter how much you trust someone, Provincetown is still one of the most active hot-spots on the North American homosexual scene. Gay men rarely go there just to admire the reflection of the sunsets in the ocean; the world-famous dunes are the real reason, even more than the bars and the nightlife, for the invasion of that pretty New England village, so quiet in the winter, impersonal even, by a scented, noisy, flashy population, ready for anything, especially for heavy-duty emotions and sex, during their hyperactive holidays.

I watched us for a moment, Mathieu and myself, reflected in the restaurant window: in spite of everything that bound us together, the growing passion, the mutual discovery, the games of seduction, so gentle and all-absorbing, the fact remained that there was a fourteen-year age difference between us, and the image we projected was far more one of father and son than of star-struck lovers. And I knew that this image, if I let myself stand back and look on from a distance, was one I'd judge severely myself, probably out of fear. Fear of being ridiculous, of course. My sense of the ridiculous has often stopped me from making a fool of myself and I was terrified at the thought of discovering that I was lapsing into what I think is the most pitiful condition in the world: an old man – which I know I'm not – rejected by an unscrupulous young one – which of course Mathieu wasn't either.

I didn't mention any of that to Mathieu; I just reassured him, wished him bon voyage, even made a few wisecracks about the danger of spreading his mucus membranes too thin in this age of the killer AIDS. We laughed, but half-heartedly. Mathieu perhaps because of the warning, which was relevant after all, I because I thought I was being an asshole, unable to express my real fears.

He didn't spend that night at my place. He was taking the bus very early the next morning, he had to pack ... I was pissed off because he'd postponed telling me for so long and I told him so. He offered a humble apology and we took our leave of one another at the restaurant door like old acquaintances who see one another more out of habit than enthusiasm.

I walked back up to Outremont, depressed, furious, my morale as low as the sidewalk. I crossed Parc Jeanne-Mance without seeing much of the glorious late summer evening that spread its aromas onto Mont-Royal, its moisture gliding over the skin of strollers, making them nervous, oversensitive. Nervous and oversensitive: that described me too, but not because of the splendours of the evening.

School was about to resume. The thought made me sick to my stomach.

Mathieu

The wind and rain came in gusts so violent that the restaurant window vibrated with a muffled sound. From time to time Mathieu would press his palm against the glass to feel it shudder. The rain was battering down just a few millimetres from his hand, tracing watery lenses around his outspread fingers. He felt then as if he were holding back the storm with one hand: if he took it away, the window would shatter and everything inside the restaurant would be submerged, starting with him, with his nagging conscience and the first signs of a head cold.

A gigantic force was shaking Provincetown to its foundations; the sea was hurling itself against the beach, sudden gusts would lop the heads off waves and the spouts of water thus set free lashed against the first houses on the coast, smacking into them at full force. A premature hurricane whose effects would be felt much farther north than usual, according to the local radio announcer, in between the neo-macho slogans of Bruce Springsteen and the neo-bimbo growling of Madonna. "It's not normal for the season – but in Provincetown, what is?"

Mathieu put out his cigarette – how many had he smoked since he'd been standing there, holding back the hurricane? Fifteen? A whole package? – in the overflowing ashtray that no one came to empty now that the tourist season was over. The handsome young men who had signed on for the summer and had screwed off on a whim had gone South, to the Carolinas or Florida, to continue emptying ashtrays amid the heat and the vacationing gay men in search of a variety of strong, brief and clandestine emotions. By night they would serve as means of release for the men whose ashtrays they'd cleared away during the day, whom they wouldn't recognize the day after and who probably wouldn't recognize them either. In a year or two though, they'd end up at this same table, where they'd be served by a new arrival whom they'd debauch in turn, with the satisfied manner of initiates who know the routine, and so on and on . . .

It was not so much his foul humour and the storm that made Mathieu furious as his sense of impotence, which was basically pretty hilarious, he knew that, but he was in no mood to laugh at the unrelieved boredom and the *uselessness*, above all the futility of this week's holiday away from Jean-Marc. The hurricane was a sustained note, the coda to what had been a series of almost intolerable empty moments between barely containable outbursts of rage.

He had known when he boarded the bus that he really had no good reason for leaving, but he'd left anyway, telling himself that the sea, the iodine, the seafood, the seagulls, anything at all, in fact, would be good for him, that distance would give him the perspective he needed to see and properly understand what was happening to him, though he didn't want to see or understand anything whatever. At customs, he'd been tempted to get off the bus, ask for his overnight bag and wait for the next bus, or hitchhike back to Montreal, his heart swollen, but shameless, feeling like a jerk, but proud, deep down, to return on a whim, just like that, when he hadn't had the courage to stay. But his pride, his fear of being ridiculous, and the apathy that struck him every time he had a difficult choice to make had glued him to his seat, beaten him to a pulp emotionally, convinced that it was a mistake to stay, but left him unable to act. He'd called himself every name in the book but he let the bus carry him along, after meekly showing his passport and stating like a nerd and in an accent that would make your hair stand on end – his English was extremely rough – that he was taking a few days' holiday to recharge his batteries. A very good-looking guy had eyed him during the whole trip, and that too had got on his nerves.

The closer they got to Provincetown the more helpless he'd felt: the evidence of the uselessness of this journey had become so acute that he'd got panicky and jittery, thinking, to console himself, it's just five days, it'll go fast, it'll be fine, I'll fill my lungs with fresh air and sunshine ... and I'll be that much happier when I go home ... But what he wanted to do was wrench the window out of the bus, throw up, howl with rage. The last hour of the trip had been hideous. He felt pathetic and childish, but he couldn't control his feelings: he made ridiculous plans (imagining himself boarding a plane the minute he arrived in Provincetown or even getting back on the same bus, which would return him to Montreal the next morning), he invented sudden, violent illnesses, imagining Jean-Marc running for an ambulance or waiting for him at Dorval with flowers ... A child unjustly punished who wants to die in order to punish others, so he'll be missed. But the child was twenty-four years old and he'd inflicted his own punishment which was, as it happens, a punishment only because he'd decided that it was.

He was so sure his holidays would be a complete write-off, he'd been caught off guard at first by the gentle beauty of Provincetown. When he got off the bus the iodine smell that he loved so much brought tears to his eyes and all at once he felt calmer, as you do when you've wept after a great sorrow. The sea was omnipresent, in the salt in the atmosphere, in the blue of the sky, in the strong odours that saturated the air. Before he went back to the hotel he sat on a wharf and for ten long minutes, he was happy.

But that same evening clouds had gathered above the Bay, concealing what appeared to be a magnificent sunset and casting over Provincetown a harsh, heart-wrenching light. It had all broken with great solemnity around nine o'clock and it had been raining ever since.

He ordered one last coffee. The afternoon was dragging. Provincetown was deserted and there was nothing to do. With the wind and rain even walking was impossible, especially with the cold he'd felt coming on in the middle of the night. So he drank coffee, read, and, from meal to meal, watched the rain fall, not daring to leave the hotel except to run across the street to the Italian restaurant where they let him hang around and didn't make him feel as if he was in the way. And of course he kept going over everything that had happened to him in the past few weeks.

It was only inertia that kept him there drinking cup after cup of coffee, smoking cigarette after cigarette, turning over thoughts, each one more depressing than the one before, when it would have been so easy to hop on the first plane to Montreal. He didn't understand why he persisted in staying here, not enjoying himself, being bored; he had the impression that he was bolted to the restaurant chair, he felt as if he had to suffer every day, every hour of every day, to expiate some sin or other perhaps, or to prepare to commit one that would be irreparable. Because he knew now that he loved Jean-Marc, that he would tell him so when he got home, simply but unequivocally, trying not to push him too hard, while remaining firm in his intentions: it would be all or nothing, all being life together, built as much as possible on mutual respect and humour, and nothing . . .

The mere thought that Jean-Marc might turn him down made him sick, but he would prefer separation to that kind of dubious camaraderie that could develop if one of them didn't put his cards on the table. In that sort of uneasy friendship the emotional risks are as great as they are in love, precisely because of the ever-present danger that one of the partners might fall in love, and it was hard for Mathieu to imagine himself suffering in silence with Jean-Marc if neither of them decided to make his intentions clear. Until now he had always refused to live with another man because he'd never met one whom he trusted; all that had changed with Jean-Marc, but he didn't know if it was for the better. Sometimes he was even convinced that the opposite was true, that he believed he was heading for failure with no chance of remission. But why failure? Why not success?

He grimaced as he swallowed the last of his coffee.

The rain had stopped but not the wind.

"Maybe because failure's easier to deal with than success."

Jean-Marc

The new school year was greeted by general indifference. No enthusiasm on the part of the students, who barely said hello, not even the ones who liked me well enough, no excitement from my colleagues either, who seemed to be as blasé as I was. I remembered the first day of school when I was a child, the smell of new bookbags, the happy shouts when you spotted a friend you hadn't seen since June, the sound of footsteps on the marble steps, the voices of the teachers we liked and of the ones we hated, who scared us, the twinge when you got the home-room teacher you wanted, the disappointment when you inherited the notorious creep who'd keep you bored to death for ten long months . . .

I don't think I'm a notorious creep myself; no, I see myself as a non-traditional French teacher, appreciated by his students, relatively interesting, enough so at any rate that nobody sneers when I walk into a classroom, moderately demanding where assignments are concerned – the trick is to know how to ask without being peremptory or pleading – amusing enough so they don't laugh *at* me when I make a joke and, most important of all, with enough psychological smarts never, *never* to have a sexual involvement, not even a flirtation, with a student. They all know I'm homosexual, usually don't give a damn, sometimes make a try if they are, too – they're just learning about seduction so they'll try it out on the nice, friendly teacher, that's quite normal – rarely making a joke of it, though that sometimes happens and it hurts. In any case, relations between us haven't been the same for the past few years: the heroic era when students and teachers got together regularly to have a beer and remake the world in general and the educational system in particular, is ancient history now. The new race of CEGEP students doesn't give a sweet damn about us and I think we feel pretty much the same way about them.

One by one the students presented themselves, some of them shy to the point of giddiness, others too snooty to be really at ease, a few – whose names I'd ordinarily have remembered because they were the ones who would become the basis, the foundation of my courses, on whose account I'd remind myself I was working when I got discouraged at the others' lack of interest – these were more laid-back, they'd look me straight in the eye, sometimes even give me a smile to let me know my subject doesn't disgust them too much, even though it's required. I counted three of them, two girls and a boy, one more than last year. But last year was especially depressing: granted they didn't have to be talked into taking my courses, but they didn't work too hard either, French being for most CEGEP students a superfluous subject, a ridiculously complicated mechanism it was considered cool to mock and to ignore, and that class in particular had been totally impervious to the beauties of the perfect subjunctive and to the subtle differences between litotes and euphemism. That same class, though they did brilliantly in other subjects, had put up more resistance, so much that it finally became a point of honour for me to win them over, no matter what, and in fact this had drained a fair amount of my energy and time, and almost claimed my health too. By the end of the year I had them all in the palm of my hand, but I didn't have much time to take advantage of it. I knew I was going to lose them and I'd have to start all over, which got me down.

I delivered my usual little speech. Zero. I didn't even feel

91

the boredom that comes over me when a class is going badly because I'm not up for it, or when I sense that the students are irretrievably lost. I even felt a little tremor of disgust as I skimmed over what I was going to try to instil in them by Christmas. I hoped it didn't show, but I know that I glanced in panic towards the door once or twice. If they noticed they didn't let on, and must have waited until after the class to talk among themselves about how the French prof who seemed like such a nice guy was actually as big a turkey as the rest of them.

I let them out earlier than they expected and holed up in the staff lounge where I could get a look at a few faces that were as long as mine, some of them even longer, desperate cases who saw teaching as the source of all their woes. I haven't reached that point, luckily, I still love my work, but that morning I had a foretaste of what could very well happen to me if I became as blasé as they were, and I quaked at the thought.

When I'm very down, which I was as soon as I stepped outside the CEGEP, I go to see a porno film. I've never tried to analyze it; all I know is that those films, which are always bad and often totally ridiculous, drag me to the very depths of my depression, pin me there for a few hours as if I were mired in the bed of a muddy lake, allowing me to wallow in self-pity and at the same time laugh at myself, because there's something very adolescent about my reaction that finally amuses me. And the surroundings fascinate me. The sight of those gentlemen, not all of them old, contrary to popular belief, jerking off under their hats in front of some pretty repulsive bimbos, makes my depression shift; not that I feel superior to them, or more highly evolved, I'm not impervious to suggestive images, but there's something so desperate and at the same time hilarious about such a straightforward way of getting it off in public, it makes me forget my own troubles.

Which means that in the four corners of Montreal, in movie houses subdivided into four or in magnificent, abandoned old theatres, I've seen some ineffable productions with incredible titles, the prints so mishandled they were all scratched and faded and, every time, whether it was the one o'clock screening or the last one with a nearly full house, I was surrounded by the same weighty silence, even when the movie was funny, as if the viewers gathered there weren't listening to the soundtrack but were just waiting until the right moment in the action, or for the bimbo of their dreams, to lower their zippers and let their fantasies carry them far away from wives and everyday problems and the uniform grey of their lives. That muffled silence in movie houses darker than most, scarcely disturbed by a few abrupt, regular little movements and the occasional suppressed heavy breathing, always disconcerted me. I feel out of place because what's happening on the screen doesn't affect me very much, and calm because I usually go there in search of a release I don't understand but one that's always been effective.

I haven't seen any really heavy gay porn since my first visits to New York in the early seventies, when I was discovering the real big city, with its countless possibilities for all sorts of vice, when I ran through the streets of Manhattan like a horny rooster, wrung out after three days of too much walking, too much drinking, too much sex, not enough food and convinced I'd caught every kind of bug and disease in the book. Which was too often the case, and I'd come home to Montreal more tired and depressed than when I'd left, a well-deserved present blossoming between my legs. But a shot of penicillin and I was ready to resume my activities, needless to say, like any person who's been too careful all his life and is suddenly turned on to the thrill of danger.

I'd been hearing a lot in the past few months about the Cinéma du Village on rue Sainte-Catherine – it used to be the Théâtre National, a mecca of Québécois music hall in the forties and fifties, converted now into a porn house – where for some time apparently they'd been showing uncut films that every gay man in Montreal made it a point of honour to see at least once, probably to make them feel as if they were back in some dark corner of New York or San Francisco.

I was skeptical. I'd seen so many butchered sex scenes in Montreal, so many straight films that gave spectators an occasional glimpse of a woman's crotch but scrupulously banished the male genitalia, or gay films that had practically nothing left after the censor's scissors had had their frenzied way, that I figured there was no chance this theatre would show films intact. Especially the kind that leave me with a slightly bitter aftertaste, as if I were still awash in their aggressive breeziness and their raw familiarity.

Boy was I wrong! Once inside the pitch-black theatre I was greeted by a bouquet of furiously agitated dicks about to spout, nothing censored, by some poorly synchronized but very audible orgasmic grunts and groans, and by the same damn weighty silence I'd recognize anywhere. Since it really was pitch-black I waited behind the velvet curtain that screened the door until my eyes grew accustomed to the dark before I took a seat. I was afraid of bumping into a spectator in mid-fantasy or, who knows, if Montreal really is becoming a den of iniquity, into a couple in mid-action. I felt a little weird just standing there at the door, afraid to move, watching some spectacularly handsome musclemen horsing around in the cubicles of a public toilet from which the doors had been ripped off, perhaps in the course of the action, and with holes punched in the walls for the easy passage of a coveted cock. For the first time in ages I felt involved in a porno film and it was almost embarrassing. This kind of sexuality wasn't the sort that interested me now. It's been ages since I've gone in for those frantic orgies

94

where you don't know which way to turn and where the individual partners are less interesting than how many of them there are.

Someone opened the door on my right and bumped into me. We apologized simultaneously. He walked past me but stopped after a couple of steps because he couldn't see anything either. Two blind men surprised in an unfamiliar environment. We were planted there, both of us, eyes glued to the screen, not daring to move. After a minute the other man held out his arms, took a few timid steps, bumped into a seat and stopped short. I got the giggles but tried to hold it in. Two guys came running out, allowing me a better look. The theatre was almost empty. I slipped into the first empty seat, which was much closer than I'd thought, and transferred my attention to the screen.

Truckers in jeans and T-shirts, the leitmotif of all the American porno films, were cruising beautiful young men – another constant – on a powdery desert road. Every sequence was totally predictable, and proceeded exactly as anticipated: looking, touching, stripping and fucking followed in order with an infuriating lack of inventiveness. But you don't go to these movies for a feast of the imagination and good taste ... Every fantasy that's been part of American homosexuality and picked up years afterwards by the colonized French who live and breathe America was there: the leather you knew was aromatic, the longish mustache, proof of virility, the conspicuous basket to show we weren't kidding, the inevitable cock ring that seems about to separate the penis from the rest of the body, while giving it a semblance of life, the public toilets, the trucks, the beer and the poppers.

The movie lasted just over an hour; I was bored after five minutes, in fifteen minutes I got the giggles again, and the rest of the time I kept looking at my watch. I was neither titillated nor sickened: I didn't feel a thing. No, actually I was reminded of my New York debauches, my first tentative explorations of the back rooms and specialty cinemas that smelled of sperm and urine. Instead of casting me into the depths of depression as dirty movies usually do, this one made me nostalgic, and the last thing I needed was to pine over my youthful escapades, besides being fed up by the start of school and missing Mathieu. The movie ended without my really being aware of it: one final sex scene just like all the others, a quick dissolve, a few particularly scratchy images, and no transition before the word *End*; the lights came up suddenly and I found myself sitting there somewhat dazed with a dozen other guys as surprised as I was, who quickly got to their feet and rushed to the door, heads down. I followed them.

And came out just as depressed as I'd gone in, maybe a little more.

It was dinner time and Montreal's gay village was springing to life. Mustachioed clones, skimpily clad or dressed to kill, were on the prowl, their faces fierce as hunting dogs, hard on the heels of the first passing figure that tempted them. It was a warm blue evening, the night was young, all hopes were allowed. Leather, though it was early in the humid month of September, gleamed in the neon glow, strides were virile, there was serious cruising in the air, the sort that's pursued without a hint of humour and inevitably ends up in furtive, impersonal groping with no tomorrow. Open air restaurants – a novelty in Montreal, where genuine terraces are hard to set up because the sidewalks are so narrow, where they compensate for the lack of space with sliding doors that more or less create the illusion – were already crammed full of guys sprawled in their chairs, feigning coolness, looking vague and super-laid-back, fingers encircling the first glass of beer but perfectly aware of anything that moved and everything that could be hunted in the area.

I wolfed down a rubbery pizza, staring into my plate because I wasn't up to dealing with a come-on – I'd donned my own cruising duds and I looked quite pretty if I do say so myself – or to pretending I didn't notice one, then I headed west. I left the gay village, which was becoming more and more animated, for the realm of the hooker of every variety, between Saint-Denis and Saint-Laurent. Which didn't cheer me up either.

This really wasn't my day. I decided to go home, flop in front of the TV and channel-flip until death ensued.

The week ended the way it had begun. Mathieu's absence weighed on me more and more, I felt as I'd been deprived of a piece of my very existence, as if I were walking around amputated, disoriented, in a dream I couldn't analyze. Relations with my new students verged on indifference and, for once, it didn't come from them: I taught my classes like a zombie, unable to derive the slightest interest, the smallest satisfaction from them. I caught myself insisting that they respect the rules of grammar to the letter, I who've always enjoyed getting around them, manhandling them, sometimes even mocking, with my students, rules that are unworkable or frankly silly. I've always advocated a simplified French, a language appropriate to the situation of the person using it: correct and clear, of course, but not stilted or pompous and, most important, neither emasculated nor colourless. After all, my own French isn't exactly a hymn to orthodoxy ... But I watched myself over just a few days turn from a kind and accommodating French teacher into a chauvinistic torturer, a language cop, a breed I've always abhorred, and I couldn't do a thing about it. I saw myself slipping towards regions I'd always avoided, and I could find nothing to cling to; I'd even reached the conclusion that I was taking out my frustration on my students, though previously I'd always managed to keep my personal and professional lives separate.

That depressed me even more than Mathieu's absence. I saw myself grow old, turn sour, succumb to bitterness and cynicism, and I was ready to jump out the window.

And did I do anything to pull myself out of it? Not on your life. I sank to the very depths, discouraged to see myself so bereft of resources, but lacking even the will to pull myself out.

I reached the lower depths I'd been seeking in the porno film the previous Monday; I came dangerously close to depression – the real thing – during the first weekend of the new academic year. I prowled in circles like a caged lion (I know the image is trite, but it's how I felt); I couldn't concentrate, I was sick with boredom and frustration, constantly looking at my watch, bringing it to my ear and shaking it, I was foul-tempered – Mélène phoned twice and twice I told her to get lost – on the verge of tears for no reason – I blew up because an element in the toaster had burned out – now a slave to my unhappiness, which I saw as insurmountable, now furious with myself for getting into such a state over nothing, I was wound up and I couldn't reason with myself.

Needless to say, when the time came to meet Mathieu at the bus on Sunday night, all I wanted to do was get into bed and go to sleep.

Of course nothing worked out as I'd imagined. It was much more wonderful and much easier than I'd expected. And amazingly silent. I'd been expecting a stream of explanations, some delicate scenes wherein I'd justify my requirements and my needs; I'd prepared arguments that were persuasive if not definitive and I'd even left open the possibility of trying to appeal to his pity – that's how desperate I was. But it was all unnecessary.

The Voyageur bus station was crammed as it always is on Sunday night. Prostitutes and bums mingled with the travellers arriving from all over North America, and disembarking from buses exhausted and hollow-eyed, rarely in a good humour and certainly in no mood for sex with some slender adolescent in a depressing room nearby. I've always been amazed at the number of hookers who hang around the bus station, but somebody once explained that they come there not for the tourists, but for clients from east-end Montreal who know they can find there, at better rates, the same quality of merchandise as in the city's west-end parks.

Departing travellers, who were fewer now that summer holidays were over, silently took their places in quickly disinfected buses, a herd far more docile than the ones who travel by plane, younger too, and obviously less well-heeled.

There were knapsacks all over the place, crammed to bursting, clattering with dangling cooking implements, stained, faded by countless downpours, many of them ripped in strategic places from which emerged old sweaters and walking shoes in an advanced state of decrepitude. Their owners lumbered along in couples, the girls more heavily burdened than the guys and generally in charge of the cigarette-making apparatus. They pull it out while they sit on a bench or at a restaurant table or even while they're walking. They concentrate on their work, the package of tobacco on their knees when they're seated, or sticking out of their shirt pockets if they're moving, their hands expert, the tips of their tongues ready to moisten the edge of the Zig-Zag paper. Another thing I've never understood, the girls always walk behind the guys. Maybe it's to avoid collisions, because of the size of their backpacks. If the guys want to talk to their girls, they have to make a quarter-turn; but they rarely talk while they're walking. In fact I'm not sure I've ever seen a couple talking.

It was because of one of those couples, a beefy three-hundred-pounder and a near-dwarf with an impressive but untended mane of red hair, that I didn't see Mathieu get off his bus. I was busy watching them load themselves down like pack-mules, the girl standing on a wooden bench to help the guy fasten the straps on his knapsack, the guy dripping sweat and swearing in an accent I've never heard outside an American movie, when I heard my name.

100

I must have looked pretty odd when I jumped, because Mathieu laughed.

There was no need for words. I could see at once in his eyes what kind of week he'd spent, and he knew as soon as he saw me all about my questions, hesitations, uncertainties and depression of the past few days.

My image of Mathieu had grown disproportionately as the rest of the world dissolved. One thing struck me before I put my arms around him, a little flash of awareness that irritated me and could have spoiled my pleasure: Mathieu looked even younger than I remembered him!

"When I was a kid, around twelve or thirteen, I'd run away at night in the summer and go to Parc Lafontaine to watch the sun rise ... I'd sit there across from the Hôpital Notre-Dame and wait for the sky to turn pale ... Believe me, in the late fifties, that took guts!"

Outremont Park is one of the most beautiful places in Montreal, especially at night when the amber glow of the streetlights gilds the trees, and the lapping of the fountain is undisturbed by any automobile noise, not even from la rue Bloomfield. The little paths that wind just enough, the perfect grass, the benches which are few in number but judiciously arranged, all make it a treat for the eye, a peaceful oasis barely disturbed in the summertime by the local preppy teenagers who say hello instead of insulting you. I have my own favourite bench, near the pool; I come and sit there fairly often, in the daytime to read, or to daydream at night if I have trouble sleeping.

It was six a.m. and as a matter of fact, the sky in the east was turning pale. We were almost lying on the bench, legs stretched out onto the path, elbows resting on the back. My mother always used to scold me for lazing around like that, on my tailbone; she'd warn me about all the terrible back problems that would turn me into a hunchback, but it's the only position that relaxes me when I'm tense. This time, though, I wasn't tense at all. We had made love in silence, with a tenderness that was, it seemed, becoming our way of proving our feelings to one another – we'd said nothing about the past week, there was no need to – Mathieu had smoked while the sweat dried on our bodies, I think we even slept a little. Then at five-thirty I felt like going for a walk.

102

With our arms around each other's waists, we'd gone for a stroll around Parc Outremont.

One of my great frustrations when I'm in love has always been my inability to walk around freely with my lover, holding his hand or with my arm around his neck, without seeming to defy society. I did it when I was younger and right away we became a focal point – black sheep or fatuous exhibitionists going out of their way to be noticed – for people's mockery and gossip. (Guys do it nowadays, in the gay village, but it's still self-conscious and it still bothers me: it's as if the atavism of thousands of years of clandestine behaviour were interfering with our spontaneity. We've attained a certain casualness, true, but it's still not natural, though I hate to admit it.)

So sitting there in the middle of the night, with Mathieu's head on my shoulder, I admit I wasn't thinking of any problems, but feeling totally at ease.

Mathieu straightened up on the bench and rubbed his back, grimacing.

"You ever been arrested?"

There had been a long silence before his question and I couldn't remember exactly what I'd been talking about.

"Well, once in Parc Lafontaine . . . I nearly . . . A cop car drove by . . . They asked me all kinds of questions . . . See, in those days Parc Lafontaine wasn't the fast food fun fair it is now . . . There was cruising, but not so open, it was more, I don't know, discreet, I guess . . . Anyway, I told them the truth, that I was waiting for the sunrise . . . and they believed me!"

"You were lucky . . . "

"No, convincing. But they gave me an earful and sent me home to my parents."

And that was when I asked the wrong question. I realized it as I was speaking, but it was too late.

"What about you? What were you doing at that age?"

Mathieu was wearing a cruel sort of smile, the first time I'd seen it, one that completely transformed his face.

"Smoking my first joints, dropping my first sunshines, lying around the corridors at school ... taking my first cafeteria courses, actually ... You should know, you were already a prof ... "

The ground was slippery, but inevitable.

"That's true ... I keep forgetting you're part of the sacrificial generation."

Mathieu almost jumped.

"You say that as if it has nothing to do with you ... "

"It's not that, Mathieu, but I sure as hell can't be blamed for all your generation's problems ... "

He got up abruptly, walked over to the pool, touched the surface of the water with the tip of his toe.

"I must really love you if I don't tell you to fuck off for saying that ... I was thinking about all that in Provincetown, the age difference, your job ... I'd sworn I'd never have anything to do with a guy of your generation! Especially not a prof! I'm pissed off enough at the whole bunch of you for making me an ignoramus!"

"Okay, first of all you aren't an ignoramus ... "

"I am! If you only knew how hard I'm working now to give myself something that resembles an education! Can you imagine what it's like, trying to catch up after ten years of bullshit? I got married right out of school, Jean-Marc, and I hardly knew how to read and I couldn't write worth shit! I know, I know, it's as much my fault as yours, but you guys didn't even bother giving us a kick in the ass and make us interested in anything whatever! Now don't take this personally, for all I know you're a model prof, but big fucking deal ... You're guilty collectively even if you aren't personally! If my teachers had bothered to let me know there's such a thing as culture, maybe I'd've wanted to find out something about it! We had absolutely no curiosity and no sense of wonder because our teachers were lazy jerks who'd rather argue than teach, and cared more about being *accepted* by us for Christ's sake than in passing on any knowledge! I spent ten years of my life in a windowless bunker, Jean-Marc, so how can you expect me to care about any of it?"

He stopped short, then turned to me. He looked truly sorry.

"I picked a good time for that little number, didn't I? But you'll be going off to teach in a couple of hours and I don't know why, but that really pisses me off! I wish you'd been anything, anything at all except a French teacher! You can't imagine how lousy I was in French!"

A police car drove along Bloomfield; we crept over towards avenue Outremont, a little like thieves. Always that backward glance.

Mathieu looked at me, trying to smile, but it wasn't very successful.

"There's so much stuff I wish I knew, Jean-Marc!"

Curiously enough I didn't even try to find something to say. We went home a little sadly, neither of us could get to sleep and we both decided not to go to work.

Mathieu moved in with me little by little. I began to find his underwear in the laundry, then a pair of jeans, then shirts, socks, T-shirts. I washed them all, folded them, put them away on the same shelf in the pine armoire where I'd always put Yves's things, and Luc's, and the others who'd been only passing through or who'd been part of my life for a little while or longer. At one point, in fact, that shelf had become a sort of treasure trove; you could find everything, in every size and every colour, for every taste. I dipped into it myself occasionally – I remember in particular a fabulous black leather belt with a silver buckle that I wore for a long time, until its owner, whom I hadn't seen for years, confiscated it one night at Bud's – or made presents of some of the finest items to guys they suited particularly well.

By early October, Mathieu started doing his own laundry, then mine. On the Saturday mornings when he didn't have to work he'd get up before me and stuff all the dirty clothes in the machine while he fixed breakfast. I'd be awakened by the wonderful aroma of coffee and the hideous sound of the old Inglis I've had for ten years. Of course I didn't tell him that I couldn't stand so much noise first thing in the morning; he was so proud of himself when I came into the kitchen, yawning and dishevelled, I couldn't scold him.

One Saturday morning when, as a matter of fact, the old Inglis was making the kitchen walls shake while I was spreading a quarter of the contents of a jar of Nutella on a slice of toast, the phone rang. It was the Mother of Us All complaining that she never saw me any more and inviting the two of us to a family dinner it night. I figured it would give me a chance to make my relationship with Mathieu official in the eyes of my friends – the rest of the family

106

hadn't seen him again since the film festival, and they were probably thinking he'd gone up in smoke some time ago, like his many predecessors. So I accepted.

Mathieu seemed cool, but he said nothing, only stuck his nose back into *Le Devoir*. I was going to ask if he'd rather spend the evening alone, or go out to a play or a movie, but then I thought selfishly that I felt like seeing my friends, so I poured myself another coffee and made no comment either.

When she came down to let us in I saw right away that Mélène was in a foul mood. Usually so excited at the prospect of our family suppers, that evening she had one of those ox-like expressions that makes her look so ugly whenever she and Jeanne have a fight or when something particularly unpleasant is on her mind. A little peck that just grazed the cheek, no hint of a smile, a frown as if she had a sinus headache: no, she was definitely not herself. I held out the two bottles of Brouilly that Mathieu and I had bought that afternoon and as gently as I could asked what was wrong.

"I've got some news for you . . . The terrible twosome decided to butt in and they got here first in case they might miss something . . . "

Yes, there they were: Johanne, her cigarillo stuck in the middle of her mouth, and Marguerite, all smiles but all eyes too, alert to the slightest tension, no matter how insignificant, even ready to invent some if necessary, were waiting in the living room, scotch in hand, the first in a long series because the two of them drink like fish. They were sitting in the same place I'd seen them last time and they had the same snotty look on their callow faces; they were a blot on my friends' living room and I resented their presence.

I made the introductions, hoping Mathieu wouldn't take a dislike to them too quickly.

Johanne waved her cigarillo above the ashtray she held on her lap and didn't even shake hands. Marguerite gave him a limp hand though, and a smile filled with such condescension I nearly screamed.

"So this is the young man who's always going in and out of your place ... You should have let us know about your new friend, Jean-Marc. Once when you were out I heard footsteps and nearly called the police ... You understand, there are so many thieves in those circles ... "

There was a brief silence that the women must have found juicy, but I was so taken aback I couldn't think of a thing to say. Mélène cleared her throat behind her fist, a sign between us that something has to be done, while Mathieu, standing and facing them, stiffened before our eyes.

Johanne threw her head back before expelling a long stream of nauseating smoke towards the ceiling.

"I guess you must have met him on Saint-Denis below Sherbrooke."

I know I was an asshole. I pretended this was a good joke; I laughed as I took Mathieu's shoulder to lead him to the big sofa, then asked for a beer just before Mélène disappeared with unaccustomed haste.

So there we sat, the four of us – Jeanne must have had her belly to the stove since morning, as she likes to tell us when she finally shows up with her hors-d'oeuvres, which are so complicated to prepare and which disappear much too fast for her liking – and I had no desire to start a conversation, so the silence went on and on. Mathieu lit a cigarette, resolutely refusing to look at them; he behaved as if they weren't there. Johanne and Marguerite exchanged a knowing look as if to say: just as we thought, he looks no better close up than at a distance; another one that won't be around too long, another name we'll forget in a couple of weeks ...

After a few drags on his cigarette Mathieu turned to me and asked in a perfectly offhand way, as if we'd been alone in the room:

"Who are those two twats?"

They literally went green. They froze in mid-thought-process, and didn't completely stifle a gag; in fact Johanne nearly retched (that would have been too sweet)!

Without thinking of the possible consequences, I decided to play along and replied in the same tone:

"They're nothing, never mind them. Outremont's turned them into such snobs they think anything from east of Park Avenue's dangerous. But don't worry, one's from la rue Valois and the other's from the ultra-chic town of Sorel."

I'd never displayed my antipathy so openly before (I'm a peaceful guy and I hate fights, which means I often put up for too long with situations I don't like) and it felt wonderful. Mathieu smiled, not to encourage me, but to thank me for taking a stand.

As far as we were concerned, the incident was closed; we hadn't come there to start a fight and I was anxious for the rest of the group to get there and inject a little life into an evening that had started so badly. Johanne, though, didn't want it to end like this. She hadn't completely extinguished her cigarillo and it was smoking in the ashtray; for the first time, she looked in our direction.

"We've been wanting to tell you this for a long time, Jean-Marc . . . We own part of this house too, you know, and it's easier to break into our flat than yours, because we're on the ground floor. We really wish you'd stop bringing people home . . . When we bought a house we didn't think we'd have to be worried sick about the people our neighbours hang around with!"

Mathieu was on his feet before I realized it. He went and planted himself in front of them – they'd shrunk back into their chair as if they were afraid he'd hit them – and told them, enunciating each word very clearly:

"Even if I was the poorest thief in the world I wouldn't stoop to burglarizing snobs like you! If your apartment's anything like you, I hope I never set foot inside it. I'd be too afraid of catching your disease!"

As he was leaving the room he ran into Mélène who was just arriving with our beers. He slammed the door; we could hear him tearing down the stairs four at a time. Mélène stood in the doorway, mouth agape. I apologized as I walked past her and went down to join Mathieu without even glancing at Johanne and Marguerite, who must have been simultaneously cursing and rejoicing.

"I don't want anything to do with people like that, Jean-Marc! And I don't want them as neighbours!"

"But you can't leave me because of my neighbours!"

"I didn't say I want to leave you! I'm happier with you than I've ever been in my life ... But think for a minute ... You aren't risking anything ... Your life's going on exactly like it was before, except you've got somebody new in your house ... But did you ever stop and think how my whole *life* is changing? I'm the one who's moving, Jean-Marc, I'm the one who's moving in little by little, I'm meeting new people that aren't necessarily dying to meet me, I see less and less of my own friends – and I end up being insulted by yours ... "

I was holding him very close, afraid he'd take flight. He was talking into my shoulder, a mixture of fury and pain, his voice halting like someone who's been crying, but he hadn't cried yet. His mouth was wetting my shirt at my right collarbone.

"I've told you a dozen times, Mathieu, those girls aren't

my friends. I know for a fact they weren't even invited ...
We hardly ever see them ... "

He moved away and stood at the window, shaking his head in vexation. It was already dark. The blues that invariably overcome me when the days start getting shorter suddenly gripped my heart. All this sounded too much like an end-of-the-romance explanation; I was frightened. My affair with Mathieu had got under way a little too slowly and now what seemed to be a dénouement was taking place with absurd haste. I felt we were close to a break-up and instead of wanting to fight, to preserve what had been the first happiness I'd allowed myself in years, I only wanted to give up. Was it the night that had fallen too quickly, catching me unawares, was it the sense of fatality I'd inherited from my mother, which colours everything that happens to me in melancholy tones? All I wanted to do was give in to the numbness that lay in wait for me, perhaps because of Mathieu's silhouette at the living-room window, a sad composition in grey and black, slightly out of focus actually, because my eyes were wet, a picture that was so disturbing in all its quiet sadness. Everything was still, inside as well as outside, and I felt helpless.

I switched on a lamp to chase away the lethargy that was preventing me from keeping Mathieu there with precise, definitive arguments. We'd been talking for a long time and I don't think I'd said one intelligent word. This banal incident – two uninvited guests showing up at the wrong time – wasn't going to screw up my life! I couldn't come up with anything better than a pitiful: "I don't stop you from seeing your friends!" which I knew was unforgivably idiotic even as I said it.

Mathieu snickered.

"You don't even know if I've *got* friends. You've never asked! Sometimes I think as far as you're concerned I came into the world when I stepped into your field of vision! I had a life before I met you, you know, and I seem to be giving it up so I can fit into yours! I'm not saying I don't want to, but you should know it isn't easy! It's hard to be called a parasite by people you're meeting for the first time, even without any witnesses!"

He sighed, came back to the armchair, and lit a cigarette.

"We're going around in circles and I'm talking bullshit. I've said all this a thousand times and we both know it by heart ... "

I slipped my hand onto his neck, where he loves to be stroked.

"You're talking bullshit and I can't think of anything to say. It's not what you'd call a constructive dialectic ... "

He smiled and I glimpsed a ray of hope. This wasn't the cynical smile with which he'd received every one of my arguments since the quarrel began; it was a genuine smile of amusement, a moment of respite I must take advantage of before it vanished. But what could I say?

"Mathieu, it's not that I don't care about your friends, I'm just afraid they'd find me boring! That's the truth! I'd rather not meet them than risk disappointing you ... "

"And meanwhile I'm supposed to change my life!"

The truce was over. The all too familiar vicious circle was creaking to a start again. I jumped in without thinking.

"Mathieu, those women are my only friends, the only human beings aside from you who really matter to me ... You can't ask me to choose."

I could see the end coming at breakneck speed; I could see Mathieu get up and tell me to go to hell, leaving me without a backward glance, without a wave, without regret; I could see a wall.

Then the doorbell sliced this vision in two.

I didn't move. I watched the profile of Mathieu who had started to tremble while I was contemplating the apocalypse.

It had been so long since I'd seen someone cry because of me, at first I thought he was laughing.

The bell rang again.

Mathieu put his hand to his forehead.

"Answer it, it's likely one of them wanting to know what's going on ... "

It was Jeanne holding two plates of roast veal.

"This may be tacky, but I thought you'd be hungry ... "

We had switched off the lamps and settled ourselves on the living-room floor with all the cushions and pillows in the house. The dirty dishes were by the radiator; breadcrumbs pricked at our necks and bellies. I saw to it that our wine-glasses were always half-full; I was getting a pleasant buzz and Mathieu would shut his eyes for long seconds before picking up the conversation, vaguer now than it had been early in the evening, because our thoughts were less clear – less aggressive too, because of the cozy atmosphere we'd managed to create. It was a time of confidences murmured in voices so soft that we both had the feeling the other didn't altogether want to be heard, that he was talking to himself; it was a precious moment, a magical one, and I savoured it, pricking up my ear to grasp everything Mathieu said while trying to be as articulate as I could when it was my turn to talk.

Mathieu drained his glass and covered it with his hand to let me know he didn't want any more.

"I don't think it's wise to move in with someone for good just like that, after such a short time ... You saw the fuss we made tonight, over nothing? I don't want to live my life that way ... Sure, it was sweet of her to bring us supper after everything, but you have to admit it wasn't very cool ... Those women are part of your daily life, Jean-Marc, so I'll have to get used to them! You practically live in a commune!

But it freaks me a little, Jean-Marc, having to deal with that every day!"

I was on my way to being seriously drunk. I'd rested my cheek on a pillow that felt surprisingly cool. I'd have gladly fallen asleep there, under Mathieu's nose, and slept straight through. Then I felt a hand in my hair; I smiled. When I opened my eyes Mathieu's face was very close to mine.

"Shall I put the icing on the cake right now, Jean-Marc? Have you given any thought to my son?"

I hadn't, but I pretended I had and I bluffed, even though the mere thought of a child in the house gave me the shakes:

"Bring him over! Introduce us! We'll see what happens then!"

Mathieu

"You still use too much salt . . . "

Mathieu looked up from his plate, ready to answer back. Louise was smiling, that little smile he used to love so much, even when he wasn't sure if it indicated amusement or mockery, though it always transformed her face suddenly and surprisingly, like a blush.

He scraped his plate with his spoon because he knew it got on Louise's nerves and returned her smile.

"Yes I am, and nobody nags me about it any more."

"Another of Jean-Marc's wonderful qualities . . . He lets you eat your brine without a word?"

They laughed, something they hadn't done since . . . Mathieu tried to recall the last time he'd laughed with his former wife. What came back to him were pillow fights and giggling under the blankets, but that had been in the earliest days of their marriage; he remembered one snowy Sunday afternoon when they'd started tickling each other until things nearly got out of hand, because Mathieu didn't know when to stop and Louise didn't want it to go any further, but that wasn't it either; then a tiny detail came back to him and a wave of emotion rose to his head: he saw himself, with Louise, leaning over Sébastien's cradle; he saw how rapturously they had gazed at their son's beauty as he slept so confidently, despite the little spasms that shook him from time to time, his body still too small for his head, his little bottom which he kept trying with great thrusts of his legs to lift as he lay on his stomach . . . then his first fart, loud, clear, unequivocal, emitted by a human being still unspoiled by society's hypocrisy, able to let himself go right under his parents' nose with a touching lack of constraint. Their eyes had filled with tears from laughing so hard, they'd taken off the child's diaper and religiously kissed his buttocks, which awakened him and made him howl with fury.

Louise had seen the emotion on Mathieu's face and she let him muse without interrupting him, as she'd had to learn to do when they first met. He was staring into space, holding his soup spoon midway between plate and mouth. She wanted to kiss him. They had never made an official declaration of peace; perhaps this was the time, now that he seemed to be doing all right. At last.

But Mathieu's dream was over. He went on eating his soup as if nothing had happened.

"Want anything else? There's some leftover veal in the fridge."

"No thanks. That was good."

Silence fell between them as it did every time they had something delicate to say to one another. Louise, amused, let him drift for a few moments, especially since Mathieu was the one with something to tell – she'd sensed it the minute he came inside – then she leaned over towards him, the eternal adolescent, so handsome and touching, whom she'd loved so much it had almost driven her mad, and hated so much it had almost made her sick.

"I haven't seen you in such a good mood for ages ... You were so miserable for so long! I can't wait to meet the great man who's actually been able to make you smile!"

"Oh you'll meet him – both of you ... How's Gaston doing, by the way?"

Louise picked up his empty soup plate, set it in the sink, and without turning around said:

"Gaston makes me smile too."

Mathieu remembered this same kitchen, painted

differently but with the same furniture in the same places, the same scalloped curtains and the same rather noisy refrigerator; but he also saw plates flying from one end of the room to the other and shattering against the stove or a wall, Louise's jerky way of moving when she was on the verge of hysterics, their sorrow because they hated one another and couldn't do otherwise; he heard Sébastien's howls, his sole defense when presented with something he could sense but not understand being to cry and so draw attention to himself. It was all so remote now, but still fresh enough in his memory that he felt briefly as if he were in the middle of one of those painful scenes, and he recoiled.

They both knew they had to create a diversion, that this room contained so many happy and unhappy memories it would be hard for them to be here together for very long without trouble.

Louise offered Mathieu a coffee, which he accepted eagerly.

"What time does Sébastien get back?"

The conversation could become normal again; Mathieu sensed that the danger of nostalgia had passed, like a storm you can feel in the air, but that hasn't quite decided to come crashing down on you.

"He should be here any minute. He loves going shopping with Gaston on Saturday morning. What're you going to do with him today?"

"Take him to the movies, as usual . . . Then we'll go for a walk . . . and as usual end up at some wonderful McDonald's . . . Unless I take him to Eaton's, to show him off and prove my virility to my colleagues."

Louise laughed, her head thrown back. Mathieu took advantage of this relaxed moment to make his big announcement.

"Would you mind packing a few things for him? Just

pyjamas, some toys ... those blocks he likes so much ...
He'll be sleeping over at our place tonight."

Louise wasn't sure she'd heard right and decided to play
dumb.

"At your mother's?"

Mathieu knew Louise well enough to understand her
game so he decided to bring everything out in the open right
away.

"You know very well I'm living at Jean-Marc's now. And
I think it's high time they met ... "

She'd brought the coffee pot to the table. Very slowly, she
poured the thick liquid – she made some of the strongest
coffee in Montreal and drank a good ten cups a day – and
Mathieu thought: I know her, she's gaining time, I caught
her off guard, she doesn't know what to say, either I'll get a
face full of coffee or she'll pretend to be enthusiastic about
my brilliant idea ... He felt himself on a tightrope once
again and wanted to shut his eyes and let things proceed
without him.

"What does he have to say about that?"

He admired her apparent calm, her brand-new self control, even the half-smile, so lovely, that had once turned him
inside out, that she was able to keep intact at this moment of
high emotion. She'd come a long way in two years.

"He's nervous, but he thinks it's right. He says he's scared
silly because he's never met a four-year-old before ... I
know he's doing it for me, because I don't think he cares that
much about kids, but what do you want, I mean he can't
ignore Sébastien, after all he's part of my life ... But what
about you ... how do you feel?"

"Well, surprised mostly, because you never introduced
Sébastien to any of your boyfriends ... Which means this is
more serious than I realized ... And also I don't know what
Gaston will think ... "

Mathieu was the first to lose his cool. He shoved away his

118

cup and it almost spilled on the refectory table gleaming with beeswax.

"It's none of Gaston's goddamn business, he's not the father!"

Louise replied in the same tone. All her fine false calm had vanished in a second and her voice had gone up an octave, disintegrating into an unpleasant shrillness that she had trouble controlling.

"Maybe not, but *we're* bringing him up!"

The danger was back. Not the danger of nostalgia this time, but the one still so fresh in their memories, of hurting one another, deeply, with that evil joy akin to bad faith. They saw it at the same time, at precisely the same moment; each could read it in the other's eyes, with frightening clarity. They dropped their gazes to their coffee cups. A brief, electric silence that a single misinterpreted word or gesture could turn to catastrophe.

After two or three deep breaths, Louise spoke without looking up. Her voice was almost normal again.

"I'm really happy for you, Mathieu, but you have to realize I've found somebody that matters to me too ... Gaston isn't just an onlooker who turns up now and then when you come for Sébastien every fourth Saturday ... I share my life with him, *everything* in my life, and that includes Sébastien, whether you like it or not ... You see Sébastien once a month because you work three Saturdays out of four, but Gaston sees him every day, he's like a father to him and he loves him as if he were his own child. In a way, Mathieu, Sébastien's as much his child as he is yours; that's hard for you, but you'd better get used to it ... If we decide Sébastien's going to spend the weekend with you and Jean-Marc, Gaston has to be involved and that's that."

Mathieu had been hit so hard, he could think of nothing to say. He felt as if he'd been knocked out and would need several hours to come back to his senses. He'd never thought of Gaston as a rival; he even felt a little contemptuous of him – a jock who was nuts about sports, whose macho manners had been somewhat softened by his enforced but ill-digested reading of a few feminist magazines. It's true he tended to think that Gaston stopped existing when he was out of his field of vision, that he was a negligible quantity, an on-looker as Louise had said, but now suddenly he'd become a full-fledged human being – who had rights over his own child on top of it! He was so caught off guard, he decided just to change the subject. He'd think it over later; for the moment, he was just too horrified.

"What about you, Louise, you haven't told me what *you* think ... "

"I don't know. I haven't had time to think about it, you just sprang it on me out of the blue ... You could have told me yesterday on the phone, you know ... It's probably okay if everybody thinks so ... But don't forget we have to ask Sébastien what he wants, it's his business too after all ... "

Mathieu felt drained. He had an urge to run away again, run away forever, without even kissing Sébastien, to go and lie down, to hide rather, and not get up again. Ever. They sat there for some time, not speaking, Louise drinking her coffee, Mathieu playing with his spoon.

"It's tough, all this ... "

He'd spoken almost without realizing it, as people do when they're alone but longing to be overheard.

"It's hard on everybody, Mathieu. Even Sébastien."

He laid his hand over Louise's.

"I don't know if we'll ever be able to talk without all the old problems coming up ... "

"I don't think we will. We've been too good for each other, and too bad, and I can't imagine us being just friendly and polite ... "

"But at least we can talk to each other without screaming."

Louise struggled to smile; it wasn't a complete success, but it was very touching.

"You mean *you* can talk to me without screaming!"

The key in the lock, Sébastien's voice – "Do you think Daddy's here?" – Gaston's – "Yup, I'm sure he is!"

Louise and Mathieu exchanged a look that was so intense it overwhelmed them.

Jean-Marc

While Mélène was struggling to cram a limp cushion into an undersized pillowcase, I was trying to fit an oversized sheet onto the mattress of the hide-a-bed in my office.

"That'll never look like a child's bed ... "

"What's important, Jean-Marc, is that he'll have a place to sleep. He's only four years old – I don't think his esthetic sense is all that well developed yet!"

"Maybe not, but putting the kid into a former pipe-smoking French prof's office that still reeks of tobacco, even the books and furniture, after I don't know how many housecleanings and a move ... The kid will be asphyxiated."

Mathieu and I had scrupulously checked out all the possibilities in the apartment the night before, considering the various places to put his son where he'd be relatively comfortable: the living room couch doesn't open up; the one in the dining room, an old stick I hang on to because it's the first piece of furniture I ever bought – fifteen bucks in an antique store – and which now sits in the bay window, is too lumpy to sleep on; our bedroom's too small to take a folding bed ... I even suggested that Mathieu sleep with Sébastien in our bed, but he refused. He said he wanted Sébastien to get used to seeing us sleep together right away; he didn't want to hide anything from him and it was essential for the child to realize from the outset that I was very important in his father's life.

Mélène and I had folded up the hide-a-bed, cursing

because the mechanism doesn't work very well (I still have an ugly scar from the time I caught my right thumb in it).

"At four he's too little for such a big bed . . . Just toss a sheet and a blanket on top, it'll be fine and he won't feel so lost . . . "

"No, I think he should have a real bed . . . And I'm going to buy a few things for the walls, for his next visit . . . This room's too severe for a child . . . "

"Jean-Marc, that child's going to spend one night here every now and then! You don't have to turn your office into a nursery school! Or fill your apartment with Mickey Mouse!"

"Poor Mélène, you're really behind the times! Mickey Mouse has been passé for ages. Nowadays it's Goldorak or Transformers or He-Man . . . The department stores sell stuff you can hang on the walls – you know, pictures, posters . . . "

"You mean you're going to redecorate your office every time he comes to visit? Hang up the He-Man, take down the He-Man, plug in the bunny rabbit night-light . . . Oh, you'll do it at first, but after a few weeks you'll get fed up and Sébastien's room will be just like it is now . . . "

She was sitting at my desk, in front of the papers I'd started marking that morning. Incredibly bad compositions churned out on Sunday night or Monday morning, wherein the poverty of the style rivalled the banality of the ideas and from which any hint of inventiveness had been banished, as if writing a few pages on a given subject automatically killed off any possibility of, or desire for, creativity. After nearly two months I still hadn't been able to motivate my students and the situation was profoundly depressing.

"Where will you mark your papers? Especially since you usually do it in the morning . . . "

I don't exactly know why I reacted badly to this, but suddenly I wanted Mélène out of the apartment. I thought she was nagging like an old maid and, even more, acting in bad faith.

"Listen, Mélène, get off my case! I didn't have an office in my old apartment and I still got my papers marked! I'll sit in the dining room, on my lumpy old sofa, it'll remind me of the early days when I still believed that teaching could be useful . . . "

Mélène got up, the way a person does who has abruptly decided that it's time to leave.

"Okay, I have to start supper . . . I was going to invite you, but under the circumstances . . . "

As she walked past me I took her hand.

"Listen, I'm afraid of that kid! What do you say to a four-year-old? What do you *do* with a four-year-old? I've never been around a four-year-old child in my life – because I've never wanted to!"

Mélène smiled. I told myself, okay, here it comes, she'll help, all is not lost . . . But her reply, amused though it was, flung me back into the abyss of uncertainty where I'd been foundering since the night before.

"Don't ask me, I've never talked to a four-year-old either! I can't even remember being one myself! Try kid's TV shows. Talk about 'Passe-Partout'!"

Indian Summer was late but violent. It had been very cold these past few weeks and everybody was sure that autumn had arrived for good, with no transition, when suddenly, overnight an amazing heat swooped down on Montreal, uncomfortably humid, reminiscent of August, even though now that it was late October we'd given up hope of it.

But you had the feeling it could change at any moment. A threat hovered over these last fine days: the wind could come up when you least expected it and in a few hours strip the trees. An endless downpour of red, yellow and orange leaves

124

swirling before they land on the sidewalk, one huge cloud, one icy rain, and it would all be over until April. The leaves would turn brown on the ground overnight and in the morning children would be wading through them, kicking them along the road to school. The creaking sound would delight them for five minutes, then they'd realize the implications and shuffle into their schoolrooms, cursing winter.

There are years like that, when the leaves don't even have time to dry on the branches. In the late afternoon Montreal is aflame in a frenzy of blazing colours, then the next morning everything's brown, dead and dry, like a fire that's been allowed to go out. You're overwhelmed by sorrow when you get out of bed and say for the thousandth time what a shitty country, this doesn't make sense, what the hell am I doing here, buried for six months of the year in dirty snow, slush, salt, cold, overheated houses, head colds, bronchitis, dammit to hell! I calculated recently that there are leaves on our trees only five months of the year and the absurdity of it appalled me. No wonder we're a defeatist nation!

All that to explain why I was taking advantage of one of those fine afternoons to sit out on the balcony and wait for Mathieu and Sébastien. I'd brought my papers with me but it was impossible to concentrate. The mild temperature, the beauty of the sun as it played in the leaves of the maple outside my house, along with my incredible nervousness about the appearance of this little creature in my life, made me feel at once exalted and depressed, if that's possible. A large part of me was enjoying the breathtaking spectacle of nature in its final convulsions, while the other was awaiting with terror the fast-approaching moment when I'd have to bend over the face of a child I hadn't chosen to know, who risked disturbing all my confirmed bachelor's little ways.

I saw them coming, hand-in-hand, Mathieu with his neck craned to see if I was on the balcony, Sébastien, good Lord, so small, trotting along at his side. In his free hand Mathieu was carrying a tiny blue suitcase. I don't know why – or rather, I do know, I was probably too uncomfortable to really look at Sébastien – I focussed my attention on that suitcase. I imagined the flannelette pyjamas, the teddy bear, maybe a couple of puzzles, twelve pieces depicting happy animals, some other favourite toy, a change of clothes. I wanted to cry. In panic.

I watched them come up the outside staircase. I was hoping my smile wouldn't look too forced. Sébastien, a breathtakingly beautiful child, gave me a "bonjour" devoid of embarrassment, then added, his eyes wide with greed:

"Am I really going to have my own room here too?"

He seemed to think "his" room was just fine and immediately lunged at the huge stuffed animal that had the place of honour on the chair by my desk.

"Wow! Is that ever neat! What's his name?"

It was a goofy-looking dog that you could make talk by slipping your hand inside its head. I'd found it at Toutalamain on la rue Laurier. It had cost a fortune but I'd told myself it would probably be just as well if there was something in the room that would make an impression on Sébastien when he arrived and would help make him accept the rest. My knowledge of child psychology was very rudimentary then, and I'm afraid it still is.

"He hasn't got one yet. You'll have to find one for him."

Mathieu leaned towards me, frowning.

"This is a new toy ... "

"I just bought it."

Sébastien was already holding the dog.

"I'm going to call him .... I'll call him ... "

His father bent over him and picked them both up.

126

"You don't have to give him a name right away, you know."

Sébastien appeared surprised.

"I don't? Why not?"

"A name's important. After you find one it'll be his name all the time ... So think it over carefully."

I took my courage in both hands and came over to them. Sébastien had that good smell of baby soap. He held out the doggy with amazing straightforwardness.

"How does it work?"

I'd slipped my hand inside the dog's head and assumed a voice I hoped was comical.

"Hello, Sébastien, how are you? So you want to give me a name, eh? Let's try and think of one together. I'd like to do that, pick my own name ... "

Sébastien was absolutely thrilled.

"He can talk! He can talk!"

My throat was already sore.

I was wrong. His puzzle had twenty-four pieces. It was his first one of that size and he was proud of it. Before, he'd explained with imperturbable seriousness, he'd just had baby puzzles that were too easy; and so the week before he'd asked his mother to buy him one that was really hard.

"At first I couldn't do it but now I'm pretty good ... Want to try it with me? You have to find the pieces that go together."

I hadn't put together a puzzle for at least thirty years. I remembered the 1000-piece Big Ben we'd had when I was little – the only one my parents ever owned, which they assembled every autumn when the bad weather started – it depicted an autumnal scene that my mother found particularly difficult: a black and white dog holding a partridge in its mouth in a wildly coloured forest. How I'd hated those bits of cardboard that lay on the dining-room table all week long, which we had to push out of the way at every meal so they wouldn't end up in our plates ... I could see my father and mother bending over the table, cursing the pieces that looked too much alike and the same colours that appeared all through the picture. What a nightmare for a child who's not allowed to join the adults, though he's sure he could help them.

Sébastien stopped in mid-puzzle.

"How come you aren't playing? Don't you know how?"

His father shouted from my office, where he was putting away the boy's things:

"Sébastien, leave Jean-Marc alone! He doesn't have to play with you, he's not a child!"

I protested because it seemed like the thing to do, but I confess I didn't have the slightest desire to go on playing.

The first hour had been delightful. Thanks to the doggy which Sébastien had responded to without being urged, we'd become acquainted. Then we showed Sébastien around the apartment, Mathieu and I being careful to show him the dangerous things he mustn't touch and those he could use whenever he wanted. He wanted to tell me all about nursery school – "Eric Boucher throws dirt at me!" as if I knew the little monster intimately – he mimed a couple of songs I thought were adorable and then described in intimate detail the games he played with his little friends on the street. I knew his likes and dislikes, the diseases he'd had and the colour of his new winter parka. I was exhausted. He'd filled the past three hours so completely, I felt as if he'd been there for three days. I needed a shower because my fear that he'd become bored had made me nervous.

I got up (needless to say we were lying on the dining room floor), telling him I'd be back after my shower. He seemed very surprised.

"Didn't you take one this morning?"

I said no because I didn't know what else to say and escaped to the bathroom. The hot water felt good but I kept thinking there were still two long hours before "Passe-Partout" came on and what were we going to do with him, he'd be bored stiff with two adults for company, we had to keep him busy – a walk? Are the parks still open? Hide-and-seek? The house is too small ... The movies? It's too late ... I think I'd have stayed in the shower till nightfall if Mathieu hadn't come and knocked on the bathroom door.

He sat on the toilet seat while I finished making myself beautiful. He told me things I already knew: that I wasn't obliged to look after Sébastien as I'd been doing since he arrived, that it was his role, and in any case a child has to learn to amuse himself when he comes to a new place, if you do everything for him it'll spoil him, and so forth.

I replied that was all fine in theory but impossible to put into practice: it wasn't just Sébastien's comfort I was seeking by keeping him busy, but my own peace of mind as well. I was so concerned about his happiness, I was ready to do anything to keep him from being bored.

"The child's come here for a day and a half, Mathieu, we aren't going to sit him in a corner, buried under a pile of toys!"

"Always extremes, eh, Jean-Marc? There has to be some compromise between sitting him in the corner and keeping him so busy you'll wear him out!"

Three knocks and a little face in the half-open doorway.

"You done yet, Jean-Mak?"

Mathieu – and I could sense that it was going to be like this for two days – frowned and bent over his son.

"Sébastien, leave Jean-Marc alone, he's busy."

"I want him to come and play . . . I finished the puzzle and the doggy won't talk to me."

I played with the doggy for another few minutes, until I finally lost my voice, so then we got out the poster paints and brushes and threw ourselves into a tremendous mural depicting Sébastien, Daddy, Jean-Marc and the doggy. Mathieu joined us and we were able to finish it before the start of the popular kids' show, "Passe-Partout."

As father and son sang along with the theme song – "Passe-Montagne aime les papillons, les souliers neufs et les beaux vestons . . ." I slipped into the kitchen to fix supper.

For the past few years, since I've been living alone in fact, I've made a specialty of wok-cooking. Because it's fast, simple and light. The trouble is, I'm the only one in my crowd who likes this Chinese-inspired cuisine. No, that's wrong, let's say I'm the only one who likes *my* version of it, for my friends think my cooking is incredibly bland and at times repulsive to look at. I admit that it's rarely a treat for the eye: either I'm too free with the cornstarch or I let loose with the soya sauce – in other words, I often end up with mush, one that tastes good to me because I know what's gone into it, though the sight of it makes my guests gag. Mathieu is more discreet. Or cautious. Usually, he'll eat my cooking without a word. Sometimes he'll even say that it's good, or at any rate healthy, and ask for seconds. He hates to cook so I suspect he'll do anything to avoid a stint at the stove.

Still, I followed to the letter the supposedly foolproof instructions in a highly recommended cookbook that had cost me a fortune. The results were grotesque. Apparently I just haven't got the knack . . .

So there I was with my vegetables ready to be chopped and my shrimps all set to shell. Why shrimps for a four-year-old? Not to impress him! I'd wondered, actually, when I was hesitating at Lemercier's between the crustaceans and some hamburger for a shepherd's pie, then I thought, if I'm in the mood for shrimp, why not ... But doubt returned as I was stripping the limp intestinal vein from the miserable creatures. "Maybe Sébastien's the kind of child who'll only eat his mother's cooking ... I should've asked Mathieu to find out from Louise if he likes shrimp ... A shepherd's pie would've been so simple ... " As my dish progressed I was convinced that Sébastien would turn up his nose at it, categorically refusing even to touch it. As far as that's concerned, did he use a fork or a spoon? Would I insult him if I gave him a spoon when he was allowed to use a fork like the grownups?

As my nervousness grew I decided I was just being silly. Honestly! All this fuss over a four year old who just eats because he's hungry ...

Right after "Passe-Partout," at six-thirty, Sébastien came to the kitchen.

"I'm hungry and I can't smell any supper!"

For the first time I showed some impatience, then immediately regretted it. I took him by the shoulders, turned him around and sent him back to his father, raising my voice to say something along the lines of I'm in charge in the kitchen, I don't like to be bothered when I'm cooking, go see Daddy, he'll tell you a story ...

Obviously I was trying to do things too fast because the child was hungry and I ended up with the most hideous dish I've produced yet: it was a pinkish-white that would make you shiver in disgust and it looked as if the shrimp and vegetables had been doused with glue that had thickened too fast.

I added some soya sauce to give it colour, but that only made it turn beige.

I marched into the dining room feeling far from triumphant but trying to put a good face on things: "Wait till you

131

see what I've made for supper!" Sébastien and Mathieu were already waiting, impatiently; Sébastien was clutching a soup spoon and pounding his plate to the tune of the endless theme from "Passe-Partout," the words distorted by his childish vocabulary, while his father mildly told him Now, now, big boys don't bang their plates with their spoons, big boys don't sing at the table, you aren't a baby, Sébastien ...

As soon as he saw me come into the room Sébastien dropped the spoon and waved his knife:

"I don't need this, I'm too little. *You* have to cut up my meat!"

I set the dish on the table; Sébastien stuck his nose in it.

"What's that?"

Mathieu sniffed, really overdoing his appreciation (years of children's theatre had given him some strange ways of behaving with his son).

"Mmm ... Doesn't that look good? And doesn't it smell yummy!"

"What is it?"

"All sorts of good things."

I hoped I was doing the right thing when I gave him a fairly small serving. It was steaming and Sébastien recoiled. His father blew on his empty plate like a clown – I hate clowns – miming a child who is blowing on his plate.

"Do this, sweetheart, it'll cool off faster."

After the blowing-on-the-food ceremony Sébastien finally stuck his spoon into the beige-coloured lumps that were smeared across his plate. And I asked the fateful question:

"Do you like it?"

Sébastien said nothing. His expression had become vacant as he chewed, a little like a cat who's doing his business as if the fate of the world depended on it. I looked at Mathieu, the word "panic" probably printed on my forehead.

"What do we do if he doesn't like it?"

Mathieu gestured impatiently.

"Let him taste it first!"

He went back to his son, still with his look of a reassuring clown.

"Chew it properly, that's a good baby . . . "

Sébastien dropped his spoon in the middle of his plate; sauce spattered the salt-shaker.

"I'm not a baby! Quit calling me that!"

He'd crossed his arms and gritted his teeth, which gave him a very nasty little prognathous look.

"I'm not hungry any more!"

There was no way to make him eat. His father tried everything – wheedling, threats, the sad clown number, the happy clown, the pouting clown: nothing worked. It was obvious that Sébastien was taking advantage of his hurt feelings at the insulting term "baby" to get out of eating something he disliked. I was sorry, especially because the shrimps were actually quite delicious (as I've mentioned before, nothing interferes with my appetite and I'd wolfed down two huge portions even as I watched the scene which was turning like mayonnaise in a thunderstorm, culminating as I was finishing my meal in a shrill and highly dramatic crying jag).

It went on for a long half-hour, during which I'd have given anything to be somewhere else. It was an all-out battle, briskly waged, a microcosm of the most violent plagues that strike without warning, then disappear the way they began: after three reconciliations, they fought again over some silly detail, exchanged countless kisses, came to blows only once – a slap on Sébastien's hand released a torrent of strident howls that made the hair on my neck stand on end – and, of course, they ended up in each other's arms, vowing eternal love, cloudless blue skies and other oaths they'd violate at once if either of them was foolish enough to utter a single nasty word.

Two minutes later, the fuss was over and it was as if it had never taken place. The happy clown was back and so was the happy child. As for me, I was wiped out. I'd lived through the drama in all its intensity, convinced at the worst moments that they truly hated one another, I'd been moved by their soggy reconciliations, then thrown for an emotional loop when the fight resumed. I was dripping sweat when Mathieu went to make a ham sandwich for his son, who blandly launched into the theme from "Passe-Partout" as if nothing had happened. Sébastien happily munched his sandwich while I heated up some shrimps for his father.

Dessert – an Italian cake I'd bought at Italissimo, across the street, along with a tartuffo – fortunately was received unanimously and the meal ended in harmony. Sébastien said a polite Thank you, that was good, then went and flopped in front of the TV set while Mathieu and I did the dishes in silence.

A very weighty silence, as a matter of fact, which neither of us dared to break.

Surprisingly, Sébastien went to bed without having to be coaxed. He let his father undress him, pretending to be a baby who can't do it himself – I heard his father's amused voice: "Stop going limp, I can't get your pants off!" – and came to kiss me goodnight, triumphant in an old sweater of his father's, a pair of socks that came up to his knees and a jacket of mine, the Prussian green one I haven't worn for ages, as a bathrobe. He looked very funny and he knew it. After some antics around my chair he disappeared into my office, calling for a bedtime story.

I heard Mathieu's voice reading a story about teddy bears and honey and bees and bee stings that cover you with bumps. Sébastien laughed a lot, shouting over and over, "Bees are mean!" and "Run, teddy, run!" – and probably fell asleep in the middle of the final punch line because he didn't say a thing when the teddy bear promised he'd never steal honey from the bees again ...

Mathieu came out of my office all nervous and tense.

Through the ceiling we could hear the laughter of our friends upstairs, who had just sat down to dinner. A clamour, the sound of chairs being shifted, an exclamation – Michèle, probably, who always goes into ecstasies over the arrangement of the table, even when nothing special has been done. I couldn't refrain from glancing towards the ceiling. Mathieu put his hand on my knee.

"Go on up if you want. I'll look after Sébastien."

"No, no, I'm fine ... "

"I don't want you to stop anything because of him, Jean-Marc ... I wanted you to meet him, but I don't want to impose him on you ... "

"Listen, I'm fine ... Let's spend a quiet evening watching TV ... We can even watch the French channel if you want a giggle ... "

Which we did. We sat there convulsed and appalled by the vulgar comedians; we sneered at the two-week-old news reports read by an announcer in thick pancake makeup that made him look embalmed; we shrieked at the first frames of yet *another* film describing the daily lives of peasants in minute detail (one sequence, nine minutes long by the clock, showed them peeling potatoes while exchanging inane remarks in a hilarious accent) the plot of which – another super-highway that was going to devastate the lovely landscape – was terminally boring.

It was Mathieu who had introduced me to this particular vice and I was starting to find it addictive. The French TV station that broadcasts in Quebec, marriage of a glaring lack of need and a shameful auto-colonialism, lost in the midst of the girly shows, shootouts, American quiz shows, sob stories, flops, false starts and acts of contrition of our own television, came across as a dotty granny who warms herself by the fire and makes other people happy by setting herself up as a laughing-stock. Naughty or nice. That night it was naughty, and we had a good laugh.

Before I met Mathieu I used to waste my time with the community TV channels, an endless source of cheap thrills with their televised macramé or crochet lessons given by well-meaning but hilarious ladies. Now, though, my boyfriend had gradually been introducing me to the pernicious pleasure of game shows like the "Jeux de vingt heures" whose lack of rhythm was equalled only by the total vapidity of the questions, or "Des chiffres et des lettres," which managed to make fifteen minutes seem like two hours of punishment.

Then, around midnight, came the inevitable Saturday night horror film. We huddled together, putting our intelligence, our sensitivity and all our critical faculties on hold, and were appropriately terrified when the girl went down to the cellar in search of the ancient trunk left to her by her old aunt, and when the guy opened the trap to the furnace that was the hiding place for the wicked little monsters who went running all over the house at night, killing off its inhabitants one by one, and at the end when the little monsters took over the sleeping city the next morning, after devouring the whole household. A great moment in cinema.

We didn't talk about Sébastien again. As far as I was concerned I didn't even want to think about the fact that he'd still be there the next morning, so cute but so present, and above all so demanding. I was used to cozy Sunday mornings; I had the feeling this one would be very different.

Before he came to bed Mathieu went into my office to kiss his son. I almost followed him, but a kind of prudishness, or call it self-censorship, held me back. I would have liked to go and kiss the child too, but I had the unpleasant feeling that I didn't deserve to.

I was in a half-sleep, the daylight had started to tickle my eyelids and an almost painful urge to piss had me bent double in bed when I became aware of a presence: noisy breathing (probably sinuses blocked during the night and a nose improperly blown on awakening) very close to my face and a movement, which wasn't the light but a person fidgeting. Mathieu never moved that way in bed in the morning, so it couldn't be he ... I admit I'd forgotten all about Sébastien, and I jumped when I opened my eyes. Two brown eyes, a turned-up nose and a big grin were floating a few centimetres from my face. It wasn't Mathieu but it bore a strange resemblance to him, as if Mathieu's face had become that of a child again.

"Hello!"

"Morning, Sébastien ... "

I shut my eyes again. The last thing I wanted was to be wakened by a child. Especially at 6:22 a.m.. I told myself, if I don't move, if I pretend I'm asleep he'll go away, he'll go back to bed or at worst, he'll wake up his father ...

A forefinger tapping my shoulder. Once, twice, three times ...

"Come and play!"

Hollow-eyed – I'd looked in the bathroom mirror and it was scary – and certainly dazed, I found myself at six-thirty a.m. on the living-room floor, assembling a twenty-four-piece jigsaw puzzle that depicted rabbits, squirrels and something that looked vaguely like a groundhog, all dancing in a circle around a campfire. The absurdity of the image hadn't struck me the night before but now, down on the floor, my head heavy with sleep, I looked at these animals whose behaviour was all too human and found them both hideous and just a little scary. The rabbits looked almost evil, the squirrels resembled curly-tailed rats, and the thing that may have been a groundhog, I swear, had perversion written across its face. And this was the image of animals that was being imposed on children . . .

I picked up the piece of the puzzle that showed the face of the perverted groundhog-thing and asked Sébastien:

"Do you like this puzzle?"

The response came promptly.

"Yes! It's my very favourite!"

"Why's that?"

"'Cause it's the biggest!"

Sébastien had insisted on spreading his toast with a slice of cheese that glistened like plastic in the wan morning light. I'd made some coffee, not too strong because I intended to go back to bed, and while Sébastien ingested his toast-and-poison I tried to think of some subterfuge that would both let me go back to bed with Mathieu and keep a four-year-old occupied . . .

I ended up with both Sébastien and the goddamn doggy in the bed.

In vain, I insisted that the doggy had lost his voice, that he was exhausted from his performance last night and desperately wanted to sleep, there was no way out of it: Sébastien was full of beans and he wanted, no *demanded* to play; no question of "let's pretend baby's asleep" or "let's be a good little boy who can play by himself like a *big* boy while Daddy and Jean-Marc sleep in on Sunday . . . " His agenda contained fun and that was that: *nothing* was going to change his mind.

Just as I was about to spring for his throat Mathieu woke up, gave his son hell for bothering me so early in the morning and got up, carrying Sébastien, screaming his lungs out and thrashing around like a devil in holy water, into the kitchen.

I didn't get back to sleep, Sébastien sulked for the rest of the morning and Mathieu looked miserable. The poor thing. He kept going back and forth between my office where his son had hunkered down and the bedroom where I was rereading some Maupassant to calm myself, one of those stories about some petit bourgeois Parisians who rent boats on the shores of the Marne, on a warm Sunday afternoon . . .

"Your first meeting's a flop. I knew it. It was too soon. We should've waited."

"Mathieu, quit pacing around the bed, you're making me dizzy."

"What will we do? I mean, I'm not going to *hide* him! I'll see him somewhere else . . . I'll take him to my mother's . . . that's it, I'll spend the weekends with Sébastien at my mother's . . . it'll bring them closer . . . "

I got up and took Mathieu in my arms.

"Give us time, Mathieu . . . All three of us . . . Sébastien will learn that he mustn't wake me up at 6:22 a.m., I'll learn that I don't have to make an ass of myself to keep him busy and you'll learn not to get in a state over nothing . . . "

I didn't believe a word. I'd come to exactly the same conclusion as Mathieu but didn't want to horrify him with it: our first meeting was a full-fledged disaster. But not because of Sébastien: because of me. I was a bachelor almost forty years old, firmly set in my ways, and I didn't want my weekends to be . . . embellished, shall we say, by the presence of a third person, a turbulent, irresponsible, dependent person who would insinuate himself between Mathieu and me, who would become the centre of interest and, above all, for whom we'd be responsible. In other words, I was jealous of a four-year-old, and knowing it made me furious.

The rest of the day, or rather the remaining few hours of Sébastien's visit, was a very bizarre time. I felt as if Mathieu was hiding Sébastien from me, trying to keep us apart, though the house wasn't all that big: I'd go into the kitchen where Sébastien was wolfing down a ham sandwich (it was barely eleven a.m, but it had been a long time since his six-thirty toast) and whoops, everything disappeared in seconds, child, dishes, father, leaving me standing there all by myself; same thing in the living room when I came back from Dumont's with the fat Sunday *Times* under my arm: colouring books, crayons, brushes, poster paints, everything had vanished and all that remained was the smell of water and paints in the air. In the end I felt as if I had the plague. All I needed was a bell around my neck to let people know where I was so they could run whenever I came near ...

In the end, of course, Sébastien asked for his doggy. Mathieu became a devoted, even a demented father, he went to tremendous lengths to bring to life the big floppy mutt that had given his son so much pleasure the night before, but it wasn't the same voice and Sébastien kept yelling for mine. Mathieu told him for the tenth time that I was busy – I was engrossed in the sports section, which I usually don't favour with a glance – and he had to leave me alone. Another ascent towards the peaks of an outburst was being mounted and I was in no mood to pass once more through the three great unchanging phases: exposition, development and conclusion – are the rules of discourse modelled on those of combat? – when I got up, crossed the house and leaned against the doorframe.

Mathieu looked absolutely miserable.

"We'll be leaving soon, Jean-Marc. It's a nice day, we'll go for a little walk before we take the bus ... "

I bent over Sébastien and assumed the doggy's voice.

"Well, I decided what my name is. It's Goofus. What do you think about that?"

Holding his little suitcase, serious as a pope, Sébastien was saying his farewells. He'd cried a little because he wanted to take Goofus, but we'd finally persuaded him that the doggy lived with us, that he'd be there waiting for him and especially – the ultimate argument – that his voice couldn't go with him. After endless cuddles and kisses, Sébastien finally sat Goofus in my office chair, telling him to work well. Mathieu and I were flabbergasted by that, but Sébastien gave me a look that was very eloquent. He had understood not only where the voice came from, but also that the room was my office, that I worked there and that, therefore, part of Goofus worked there too!

"Will you come back and visit again?"

I wasn't absolutely sure I was sincere, but what else can you say to a four-year-old?

"Sure."

For him it was the most natural thing on earth and I was surprised that he didn't look at all as if he'd had a bad time.

I embraced Mathieu, who looked pathetic, and kissed him.

"See you later . . . Don't worry now . . . "

Sébastien stood on tiptoe.

"Me too, give me a kiss too . . . "

The good weather was holding on, but it was stiller than the previous day. There had been a lot of wind during the night, the maple tree had thrashed about in a concert of creaking branches and rustling leaves, and I thought, that's it, tomorrow morning there won't be a trace of summer: depression time. But the leaves had held and our street was still shimmering with reds and golds when I went back to my chair on the balcony after Sébastien and Mathieu had gone.

I had only a few hours left to mark my papers but I

couldn't concentrate. I wanted to postpone everything until the next morning, like a lazy student. If I got up earlier, maybe I'd have enough time ... or if I went to bed earlier, my head burrowed under the pillow ... At the slightest movement in the street – a passing car, a neighbour coming down his stairs, a family returning from brunch on la rue Bernard – I looked up, grasping at the smallest diversion, inspecting people's dress, their walk, their behaviour which varied depending on whether they were alone or in a troop, and the way they reacted when they saw that I was observing them. In a word, I was doing everything possible to avoid thinking about the twenty-four hours that had just passed. Strangely enough, I wasn't able to concentrate on my work: snatches of conversation, raised voices, all the little events of the weekend kept going through my mind, taking me far from the theme imposed for French composition and the rules of grammar, while a stray dog or cat concentrating on a frolicking squirrel could send me into a sort of coma where I developed an amazing power to concentrate on utterly meaningless details I'd otherwise never have noticed.

My emotions were still a little unhinged, as if my train of thought had deliberately followed a track that ran parallel to my real concerns, to prevent me from suffering, but no matter, I quite enjoyed the sensation, which was somewhere between queasiness and a kind of bland well-being. I knew perfectly well that a huge problem was settling into my life and my mind was fixing things to derail my thought processes. Probably to gain time. Morose ideas like that generally amuse me, but now I was actually revelling in them. And that worried me.

What I needed was Mélène, her laughter, her warmth. And above all her wholesome sense of the ridiculous. But it was Luc who turned up. And Luc is anything but wholesome.

He's probably the best-looking guy I've ever been involved with, a "bête" as they say in our circles to designate someone who oozes sexuality. But unfortunately it's all he oozes and we'd soon exhausted that subject. No, that's unfair; he has plenty of good qualities but I wasn't in the mood for Luc and when I spotted him between the balcony uprights, sexy, self-assured, arrogantly handsome, I wanted to go in and hide, because those good qualities were so hard to reach.

With the tight leather pants, the carefully faded jean jacket, the shirt open to reveal the virile tuft of curly hair, he looked like a self-caricature, but I knew he was serious – "deadly serious" as they say in English – down to the slightest detail of his get-up, even the running shoes without socks because you never know, it might be a turn-on for some stranger at the back of a bus, provided that the foot is held at the proper angle, the leg folded comme il faut. Luc is a hunter and he's lost count of his prey. When he gets off a bus or the Métro hearts beat faster, erections are concealed, more or less, wet spots dry discreetly. It's true. He knows it and takes shameful advantage of it. In public he behaves like the last of the old time floozies and gets off on it far too much. Taking the bus or walking on the street with Luc is a singular experience: he cruises every gay man he meets and every one, even the most faithful of the closest couples, falls into the trap and is driven absolutely wild by him for ten long seconds. But I realize I'm describing him as a monster, when despite it all he's really a sweet guy. Provided you can be alone with him for more than fifteen minutes. And there's no homosexual within two miles . . .

And I was with him for seven years.

He threw back his head, shaking his curly locks, and I wanted to shout, Come off it, nobody's looking at you but me and your charms haven't done it for me for years now, come on, loosen up ... But his laughter was forced and I took a closer look. My God, Luc had wrinkles around his eyes! And a pallor on his face, usually tanned and bursting with health, an ill-concealed fatigue that was translated into sagging features, a softening of the profile, all told me he was worried about something. He hadn't come to see me, as he claimed, to talk about what they were saying about me in the wonderful gay world of the Paradise, he was here for some other reason, one that concerned him and that he postponed talking about, because it scared him. For the moment, he kept up his catty remarks about my "marriage."

"It's a neat trade-off: his youth for your money ... "

"Too bad you're aging into such a bitch, Luc ... "

I knew the word "aging" would provoke a response. Very abruptly he turned his head in my direction; all falseness, all affectation had disappeared from his face. For a moment he looked like an unhappy Sébastien.

"Too bad age is making you so naive, Jean-Marc!"

It was a very small barb for someone who'd always been ready with the devastating retort. No, definitely, he was not in top form.

"Luc, it's my life and I'll live it my own way if you don't mind, okay? You have no right to say he's after my money. He makes a pretty good living – unlike you when we were together ... "

"You mean he pays rent? The phone bills? Anything? If I was diplomatic I'd find some convoluted way to say that, but you know me, I spit out whatever I've got to say to whoever I'm saying it to ... I had an aunt who was a grandmother at your age, Jean-Marc. Do you want to look like a thirty-nine-year-old grandfather?"

I put my hand over my heart like an actor in a corny melodrama.

"Touché. That hurt. Bravo."

"People are talking, Jean-Marc ... "

144

And there we were, back again.

"People! What people? The tactful guys in the bars? The sensitive crowd at happy-hour? Or your actor friends who sneered when we were together because they never forgave you choosing me? Though come to think of it, they've probably forgotten I even exist ... "

"Mathieu looks like a kid beside you, Jean-Marc, you can't expect people not to talk. You really do look as if you're going around with your oldest son, you know."

"You really picked the wrong day for that ... Or maybe it's exactly the right one ... All right, go ahead, laugh behind my back, it'll keep you busy between acts and I don't give a shit ... "

"That's a lie and you know it ... "

"Okay, so it bothers me! That's exactly my problem these days! You should've seen me yesterday, with my oldest son's little boy ... *The Art of Being a Grandfather* in all its splendor! I played woof-woof with him, I watched 'Passe-Partout,' I built a fire station out of minibrix, I put together a twenty-four piece jigsaw puzzle twenty-four times, I blew a runny nose, and so what? Does that upset you? Does it change your life? Or your lifestyle?"

I was almost out of my chair. Luc, so unaccustomed to seeing me angry, was staring at me wide-eyed. I'd drained my beer in one gulp, I was coughing, almost choking, red with rage and humiliation.

Luc laid his hand on my arm, gently, which calmed me a little.

"I can't make you change your mind, eh?"

"No way ... I'm not going to drop the first good thing that's happened to me in years just because they're talking about me backstage at the Théâtre de Quat'Sous and in the back rooms of the gay bars in the Village!"

Luc scratched his balls, ostentatiously, his knees well apart. I immediately looked away towards the sidewalk. A very good-looking guy was going past the house, his eyes on my ex's crotch. I heaved an exasperated sigh.

"If that's what you came to talk about, Luc, you should know you aren't the first and anyway, I'm old enough to solve my problems by myself, thank you very much ... "

I watched the guy continue along Bloomfield. He turned around three times, almost walking into a tree. And then I attacked.

"If you're not after that guy already, sniffing his ass, you must have a serious problem ... Go ahead, I'm listening ... "

So then Luc let it all out. It was long, rambling and unrestrained, at times it approached verbal delirium then dropped to a murmur that was hard to follow but still crystal-clear, because a single theme kept recurring, like a litany: Luc, who'd never been afraid of anything, was terrified. You could see the panic in every uncontrolled gesture, in the new wrinkles that had made such an impression on me, in his voice which broke at certain words, in his way, which was also new, of sinking into his chair between sentences so he could catch his breath.

He was certain he had AIDS, no less, and if I hadn't known him to be such a showoff, such a braggart, such a loudmouth for all those years, I'd have laughed at the flimsiness of his evidence. But he was so terrified that I listened to him open-mouthed, without interrupting, not even his most extravagant suppositions. From what I could tell he had no symptom of AIDS, no fatigue, no lesions, he didn't feel the least bit sick, but he was positive he had it because of the life he'd led! I kept waiting for him to tell me he was being punished where he had sinned, or that the Lord Himself had decided to mortify him: the good old notion of well-deserved chastisement coloured everything he was saying, though he'd always been one to spit on fate, saying to whoever would listen: "I've got just one life and I intend to live it below the belt!"

Statistics from newspapers or gay magazines were thrown in along with the number of guys he'd been through per year for the past two decades, from the bushes on Mont Royal to the washrooms at The Bay, not to mention the meat-racks of the seventies, the darkened porno houses and the back lanes of Tupper Street; the appearances of partners who definitely "had it" came back to him after weeks or even months, a few "encounters" who he'd been told might be victims, the mere thought of whom gave him the shakes; one or two friends he'd slept with a long time ago, really ages, but who knows . . . and who had "passed away" recently . . .

"I can't *not* have it . . . It just isn't possible . . . Out of all the guys I've been with since I was a teenager it's impossible that there hasn't been a single one who hasn't been in contact with somebody who had it . . . "

"Have you had a blood test?"

"Yes. They didn't find anything, but big deal. Sometimes the symptoms don't show up for years . . . "

I began to feel that he wanted to be sick, that he'd be relieved if he learned that he was carrying the virus. But strangely enough, instead of calming his sexual appetite, which was what had happened to most gay men in North America, who were said to be changing their lifestyles for fear of contagion, his fear was exacerbating his desires, and he confessed, pitifully, that he'd never fucked as much as he had since the hideous idea had been running through his head. He was currently experiencing a sexual frenzy that worried him as much as the disease he thought he had, because now maybe he was actually spreading it himself!

"It's hard to explain . . . I should be afraid of infecting others . . . and I am, but at the same time I've got a monstrous, I think that's the word . . . a monstrous need to fuck while I still can ... before the symptoms ... the real ones, the ones you can't deny ... Five minutes before I go out cruising I convince myself I haven't got it, then as soon as I'm finished I tell myself that if I didn't have it before then I've caught it now, and if I did have it I've just passed it on! And then I start all over again! I can't take it, Jean-Marc. I know some guys who are too scared to fuck, so their problem's solved: they're condemned to frustration for a while, but me ... Some nights I go to bed exhausted but still unsatisfied, and I know it doesn't make any sense! I *know* I haven't got it, it's as plain as the nose on your face: if I did I'd've got sick ages ago, I'd be in some hospital or other, or 'dying with dignity' in my own bed, surrounded by my dearest friends, at any rate the ones who weren't too disgusted by the sight of me, so why worry? And then do you know what I do? I get up, Jean-Marc, I get up and go out and risk catching it one more time!"

Luc's account of his sexual escapades has always made my head spin. Ever since we split up it's as if he's chosen me as his confessor, his confidant at any rate, so he can hold on to at least some of my attention, stay in my life to some degree, as if he were refusing to let me completely disappear. We don't go out together at all any more but I regularly see him turning up with the latest gossip and, in particular, his latest exploits, all aflutter to tell me who in the artistic circles is sleeping with whom and serious as a pope as he describes his own latest conquests. I hear it all: the roundness of their asses, their experience, their kicks. Sometimes I find myself blushing when I watch TV, I know so much about the sexual proclivities of some of the young actors on the soaps.

Most of the time, though, he just gets me down, because he reminds me of a miserable period in my life – I was the most naive cuckold in Montreal for so many years I'm still humiliated by it – but that afternoon, in the unseasonably sweltering October heat, I pitied him, and that got to me.

Pity is a terrible sentiment, I know, but Luc was truly pitiful, with his contradictory convictions and his fears that were both hideous and legitimate. I could understand his fear of AIDS because he's been screwing all over the map since the beginning, and his frequent trips to New York are still the hottest – as my own used to be – but I was in no mood to console him because he was still reacting to a problem like a stubborn adolescent.

I watched him age before my eyes as he told his story: his face lost its attractive tan and became gray, his back hunched and frequently his hands would start to shake; I didn't forgive him for that either.

I did nothing for him. I left him in his slough of despair. But I wasn't sure he'd actually come for help in any case: maybe he just wanted to wave his unhappiness under my nose as he's so often done with his good luck. I know him well enough to realize you should never take what he says literally. He really was scared, that was clear, but I thought I also detected some morbid pleasure under the first layer of fear and that made me want to hit him. Perhaps he was still playing with fate. And the worst of it is, he has every chance of winning, because he's the luckiest man I know!

But I couldn't really be sure his cynicism went that far, so I didn't know what tack to take. In fact that's often the problem with Luc: he throws you so completely that in the end you don't know what to make of him.

I was about to let him go without doing anything for him – I'd dropped a few encouraging words, useless though they were, and a few bitchy remarks to try and cheer him up, but nothing serious because I didn't know what he really wanted from me – when I saw Mathieu heading up our street. Need I say that I had no desire for them to meet! I sat back in my chair. I felt like throwing my papers in the air like confetti, shouting *que sera sera*.

Luc is very civilized and would never have attacked

Mathieu head-on, but I had no intention of watching him try to seduce my boyfriend before my eyes while inwardly laughing at him. But there was another surprise in store for me – this was really a red-letter weekend.

They knew each other.

I didn't have to introduce them, they both started as they recognized each other and Mathieu went bright red, while Luc put on that little smile I've seen so often, which never augurs well.

"I should've realized it was you when I heard your name. There aren't that many Mathieus your age in Montreal . . . "

Mathieu held out his hand. Not very warmly. He was leaning against the balcony railing.

"I should've known who it was when Jean-Marc said you were in one of the soaps. Will your character, the one that stutters, be back this year?"

A hint of contempt had slipped into Mathieu's remark and it hit Luc right in the heart. His stammering character had been a joke all over Quebec for two years now and it had made him tremendously popular, but the show itself was a piece of shit and he knew it.

He cleared his throat, half-rose from his chair as if to say I'd better be going, but Mathieu kept him there.

"I've had something of yours for months, but I didn't know your phone number . . . "

He went inside the house.

I heard myself uttering one of the most fatuous remarks of all time:

"So you've met before . . . "

Luc sat down again, smiling.

"Yes . . . "

"Did you . . . "

"Of course. But just once. Lousy lay . . . "

For someone who was scared to death he knew where to hit.

"You used to say that about me, Luc, when you were pissed off with me, and I happen to know it's not true . . . "

He actually laughed. So that was what it took to restore his good humour, a situation that was somewhat equivocal. I leaned towards him.

"When did it happen, your little fling-ette?"

"Oof, early summer, May probably . . . "

"Which means that if you've really got AIDS . . . "

He slapped his thigh.

"If you see any spots on the soles of your feet you'll know who to thank . . . "

And there it was, his scorn had been cranked up, the real Luc was back. He'd been rejuvenated in two minutes, he'd lost his pallor, only the wrinkles remained and they were there for good.

Mathieu returned with the sweatshirt he'd been wearing the night we met.

Luc got up from his chair.

"So you're the one . . . "

"Right . . . It brought me luck. I was wearing it when I met Jean-Marc . . . I hope you didn't spend too much time looking for it . . . "

"At first, yes, but I couldn't remember where I'd left it . . . "

"I remember, you were bragging that I was your third conquest that weekend so I took off pretty fast, before we went to bed . . . "

Luc went pale, but only slightly. I could have kissed Mathieu. There's nothing Luc hates so much as being caught in a lie.

And I confess I was a little relieved that he didn't really think Mathieu was a lousy lay.

Luc stayed for another half-hour, either to prolong the unease that had settled over the balcony since Mathieu's arrival (that was his style) or, worse, *not* to give Mathieu the impression that he was driving him away. So I took on the burden of the conversation. It wrung me out. I looked like a nerd sitting there between the two of them, talking to each one in turn, with each one answering in monosyllables, like pouting children. We sat there in a tidy row, with our feet on the railing, and my head turning towards first one, then the other, like a weather-vane.

Infantile.

Luc finally got up, scratching his crotch. The goodbyes were chilly; I don't think Luc and Mathieu even looked each other in the eye. Luc didn't leave with his signature "Let's have lunch," which used to give us such a laugh when we were living together and which we'd hung on to as a private code. He set off in search of other adventures without looking back, an exaggerated sway in his walk, sure of the effect he was making, insolent even from the back.

We ate our shrimp salad almost in silence. I don't think we were ready yet to talk about the weekend that was coming to an end.

And I confess that as far as I was concerned, the child and the talk of AIDS was a lot for one weekend!

But we made love with particular tenderness that night. It wasn't the ultimate ecstasy, all fanfares and a technicolour finale, but a minor ceremony marked by attentiveness and emotion and restraint. We admitted our feelings of helplessness through caresses that were almost timid, and kisses that were far from feverish. I felt like a teenager; I wished I could prolong that moment to the end of time, like the first times we'd made love; I wished the entire world could be a bed filled with tenderness, with cool sheets and with love-making that brought rest, not exhaustion.

Of course I didn't sleep at all that night, or hardly, and my students suffered the consequences. I think I was actually pretty rotten to them, for the first time ever: rather than admit that I hadn't got my work done that weekend, I delivered a tirade against thoughtless students who don't give a damn not only about what they're being taught, but also about their teachers, whom they insult by turning in garbage assignments. But maybe I was on target after all, because they didn't react.

I threw their papers in the air, telling them to do them over for tomorrow. *That* got reactions. And ended badly. Now I had three dozen students against me, and it was only October!

"What upsets me most is, I feel as if I've been wasting my time, and that *really* pisses me off!"

Mélène hadn't laughed. On the contrary, she'd heard me out with great seriousness, even holding back her fury when I described the visit from Luc, whom she loathed, and merely smiling at my misadventures with Sébastien. I told her everything: the jigsaw, the doggy, the dinner disaster, the anxiety I'd felt because of a four-year-old child who had to be kept busy for hours, the big innocent eyes in search of affection or approval and, most of all, the impression that I was wasting my time because I'd never wanted anything like that and because I'd never been interested in children.

She and Jeanne hadn't seen Sébastien because they'd spent the weekend with some radical lesbian friends in the Eastern Townships, whom they didn't get along with all that well, but saw now and then for old time's sake.

They'd come back late Sunday night, depressed as they always were after these trips they forced on themselves two or three times a year. At first, a few years earlier, they'd been amused at the total rejection of men which their friends advocated, the stones they threw at the mail carrier, the way they shouted at the police officers who dared to turn up during a particularly noisy drinking bout, the excessive attempts to feminize their speech which led to horrors like "hersterectomy" and "goddessdamn" and made Mélène threaten more than once to bring along a male friend, a phallus in motherland, their exclusion of tomcats, their attempt to chase away everything that was masculine out of pure, simple hatred of the male, but finally, once that fad had degenerated into something that resembled madness, my friends had been turned off completely and had grown more and more remote from the group of women who were cutting themselves off from the world, closing themselves inside a ghetto from which there was no escape, choosing a deliberate, distressing intellectual and physical poverty. Mélène had known some of these women when they were much younger, she'd been fond of them and tolerated seeing them "throw themselves away" as she put it, on unforgivably childish concerns instead of tackling real issues.

She hadn't had time to tell me about her weekend; I'd taken her by storm the minute I arrived at her place, at lunch time.

For once I ate what she served me without really noticing. My beloved junk food was the farthest thing from my mind and she took advantage of the situation to feed me "naturally."

She gave me a second helping of a thick soup which tasted a little too green and which scratched my throat.

"Why don't you talk to Mathieu about it instead of me?"

Idiot woman! The reason seemed obvious enough to me! I blew on my soup.

"It's too delicate . . . for now. He adores his son, which is normal . . . All I hope is that I'll be able to adore the kid too . . . But I doubt it. And I'm scared. Our relationship's too complicated, Mélène, it never seems simple except when the two of us are alone!"

154

At that moment she's the one who thought I was being silly. And with reason. I wished I could be like her women-friends in the Eastern Townships and shut myself away in a ghetto, but with Mathieu. No more CEGEP for me, no more child for him. Elementary – and unthinkable.

I pushed away the bowl of green soup.

"I'll try and talk to him. But it won't be easy because I'm not sure he wants to talk about it either."

"Want me to talk to him?"

That was exactly what I'd come for, I knew it now. Why didn't I realize it before?

Mathieu

The waiting room was filled with young men sporting the latest look, smelling strongly and expensively of whatever scent was currently in, elaborately laid-back, a little too well-dressed for the early morning hour and, above all, alert to everything that was going on around the desk of Francine Beaupré, the secretary, who controlled the situation like the caller at a bingo game. Actually the secretary of a casting agency is a very important person: people smile at her as they probably never would in real life, they pay court to her, even screaming queens, compliment her on her clothes, her hairdo, her nail polish, her lipstick, her makeup; they bring her little presents (very small, of course, they don't want to seem to be buying favours), they tremble when the intercom sounds on her ultramodern grey smoked glass desk, they give her a hopeful glance as they enter the studio and, depending on how it goes, a look of triumph or defeat when they emerge.

Francine Beaupré had no power whatever over the final selection of candidates for commercials or movies, but it was she who phoned them, it was she who had the fullest knowledge of the agency's catalogue of photos and CVs, who often "recommended" one name over another to her bosses, depending on her mood – and on whether the bearer of the name was "nice" or not . . . So she had to be handled with kid gloves, to be cultivated like some rare plant, but casually, so no one could say: so-and-so buys the agency secretaries. All this took place then amid a sort of false bonhomie, as if nothing that was going on in the office had any importance, although every candidate present was prepared to wipe out all the others for a part in a soap opera, or in a commercial for soft-drinks or – since they paid so well – beer.

And if you landed something of course you had to "thank" her. Which meant that Francine Beaupré went out a lot. She was often seen on the arm of some very handsome young man, always different, always deferential, at the premières of eagerly awaited plays or the opening nights of French singers who had come here to try and revive a career that was fading at home, she turned up at rock concerts and even at the Opéra de Montréal, which she hated, while adoring the sophisticated – and, even more, the rich and influential – audience. At these premières she did the same things she did at the office: flattering the right people in the right way, but so cool that it all seemed invisible.

Her favourites praised her to the skies, while those she ignored dragged her name through the mud.

As for Mathieu, he thought she was a total fool.

Actually he'd been amazed that she'd called: they had never hit it off and she'd never forgive him for the blasé look he always sported at the agency. Incapable of any sort of flattery, at auditions Mathieu adopted a behaviour that he considered simply businesslike, but which the secretaries at talent agencies, accustomed to something very different, interpreted as arrogance or indifference.

So he hadn't fallen into Francine's arms when he walked through the door, or pecked her cheeks or paid her a compliment, he didn't ask for the name of the product he'd be asked to promote, or how many guys had been called or what she thought his chances were. He just gave her a polite hello and his name, then went and sat at the other end of the waiting room, near a fellow he saw at all the auditions, who wasn't too unbearable.

That was when he learned that a well-known brewery was

157

looking for new faces to sing at the top of their lungs in a super-macho commercial set in a hunting lodge, an incredibly vapid slogan that would probably be a catch phrase for a few months: "Bag yourself a real one!"

He had looked around him, discouraged. All the other guys were hefty and athletic-looking; next to them he looked like a slender Prince Charming from a kindergarten fairy tale.

Had Francine Beaupré been mocking him when she'd called? Or had she just made a mistake? He'd almost got up, taken his raincoat and left, but then he'd changed his mind. He'd hang in till the bitter end. He had nothing to lose in any case. A contact's a contact. If the director didn't need him for the beer commercial, maybe he'd remember him for something else, some other day . . .

So he'd taken refuge in his thoughts, which had been rather morose these past few days, while he waited for his call.

Mathieu had been devastated by the weekend with Sébastien and Jean-Marc. He felt responsible for its failure and annoyed with himself because he hadn't been able to make them like each other. No, that wasn't quite right. Sébastien had liked Jean-Marc. He'd said he was "nice" and "funny," even said he wanted to see him again. But Jean-Marc?

What was he supposed to do? How could he drop into the arms of a bachelor who was pushing forty and used to his own little ways and his peace and quiet, a boisterous, demanding child who felt at home everywhere and wanted nothing from life but to have as much fun as possible, as often as possible? How was he going to link these two poles of his existence, his two reasons for living, without forcing them on one another? Keep Sébastien away from Jean-Marc? But for how much longer?

He'd considered going back to his mother's, calling it all

off, succumbing to the semi-depression he'd fallen into after he left Louise, when he'd chosen to touch bottom all alone while hoping he'd be strong enough to resurface before it was too late – but that was childish and he knew it. He had a tendency to dramatize things, to revel in problems that usually could be solved, but he knew that his depressions were generally short-lived and he'd have to wait for this one to pass before he acted. He wished he had the energy to fight, but he had only enough strength to submit. Meanwhile, he was miserable and the audition he was about to try wouldn't fix anything, he was sure of that.

He'd been given a lumberjack shirt, a rifle and a bottle of beer with a twist-off cap. No less.

Behind the camera, aside from the director and the script assistant, were four gentlemen in three-piece suits, the clients from Toronto, who had frowned when they saw him walk into the studio. He'd felt like saying, yeah, I know, I'm too much of a sissy for you people, but it's not my fault, *they* called me ... But the director had been quite pleasant, instead of just saying you're wasting my time – explaining that the brewery wanted a more youthful image and was looking for good-looking new young faces, and the script assistant had given him a warm smile, so he'd decided to take the plunge. You never know.

The shirt was too big and the rifle weighed a ton. For the third time Mathieu slammed the bottle of beer on the table as hard as he could – "like a man," the script assistant had told him on the first take, with a knowing wink – then picked up the rifle and shouted at the top of his lungs: "Bag yourself a real one!!"

One of the clients from Toronto rolled his eyes in dismay, muttering, "My God!"

Mathieu dropped the rifle on the table.

"I don't want to waste my time either. I know I've got a nice young face, but I also know it's the wrong one for you. Sorry ... "

The lumberjack shirt joined the beer and the rifle on the table.

"Shoot that, it's a nice still-life!"

Before he left he snapped at Francine Beaupré, who was fluttering her eyelashes at a new candidate, a wrestler-type with little pig eyes and bulging muscles under a skintight shirt that was too thin for late October.

"Call me back when you've got a milk commercial!"

Fall had arrived overnight. All at once. No more Indian summer, no more mildness in the air, no more colours on the trees. The wind had blown the leaves away, the sky had become overcast, and then the rain, an autumn storm already smelling of November and the first frosts, had come and drenched everything, drowned everything. Montreal was hanging its head.

As he walked back up Bloomfield, Mathieu was thinking about how beautiful Outremont had looked just the day before, and of the emotions he'd felt when he got off the bus on his way to Jean-Marc's, remembering the treeless neighbourhood where he'd grown up. Overnight everything had turned ugly, as if Outremont were in transition between the extravagance of summer's final bouquet and the wait for the first snowstorm.

Everything matched his mood and he took a malicious pleasure from it, as he had in Provincetown a few weeks earlier.

Mélène was coming towards him carrying a huge bag of groceries. He offered to help. She refused pleasantly, claiming it was her only exercise of the day. They climbed the stairs together.

"Aren't you working today?"

They had stopped on the landing that separated Jean-Marc's balcony from Mélène's front door.

"I had an audition so I finished early . . . "

"How was it? From the look on your face . . . "

"It was my fourth flop in a row . . . They just want big oxes, so what can I do . . . "

Mélène shifted her package to her other arm.

"Want to come in for a coffee? You can tell me all about it . . . "

"Actually, I've been wanting to see you . . . Jean-Marc must've told you about last weekend . . . I think he's really upset!"

Jean-Marc

The phone rings.

I'm in mid-béchamel, a sauce I really hate to make but Mathieu adores it – oh yes, after two months it's still the intimate little dinners with candlelight and music, and why not. Never mind, they'll call back. Four rings. Five. Six. Must be important . . .

"Hello?"

A tiny voice, distant and feeble.

"Hello Jean-Mak? It's me!"

I feel my forehead break out in a sweat. On top of everything I hate talking on the telephone . . .

"Hi, Sébastien, how are you?"

A breath, some gurgles, a laugh, a few incomprehensible words. Then silence.

"Say it again, Sébastien, but slow down, I can't understand you."

Repeat performance. I still don't get one word.

Panic.

"Sébastien . . . Daddy isn't home from work yet . . . You wait and call back later, okay? No, listen, I'll tell him to phone you, alright? Kiss kiss."

I hang up like a heartless brute and go back to my béchamel.

Ten seconds later the phone rings again.

Is his mother dialing for him or has she shown him how to do it himself?

Gutless, I decide not to answer.

I thought I'd reassured Mathieu after his conversation with Mélène. At least until his son's next visit, in three weeks' time. No, Sébastien hadn't got on my nerves, yes I'd get used to having him around, of course he could come again. We'd both avoided going any deeper, Mathieu for fear he'd discover some truth that he wasn't prepared to confront, I to protect myself from making a confession that might wound him.

It was true that I was willing to see Sébastien again. It was a sacrifice I'd decided to make, thinking that after all, two days a month wasn't the end of the world. But I admit I was appalled at the approaching weekend which would probably find me once again on my hands and knees in the living-room, once again putting together that goddamn twenty-four-piece jigsaw puzzle.

Meanwhile, life went on, with improvements, even: Mélène, Jeanne and Mathieu were becoming good friends, which pleased me; the bitches downstairs were leaving us in peace; at the Saturday night family suppers our enjoyment verged on delirium; I wasn't nearly such a pain in the ass to my students.

All that in spite of a particularly vicious autumn.

I came home to Mathieu every evening with a joy that sometimes amazed me. There were times, totally insignificant moments, when I loved him so much that I wanted to grab him then and there, to thank him! Just for existing. And above all for being there. It's hard to admit things like that, you're afraid they sound tacky, but it's exalting to experience them.

Except for the prospect of seeing Sébastien in three weeks, two weeks, one week, my joy would have been complete. It had become almost a sickness. God in Heaven, the child wasn't a monster! But the thought of him gave me the shakes. I'd even started making plans to be away during his next visit!

He kept calling us regularly. I still couldn't understand a word and I'd finally stopped answering the phone between five-thirty and seven p.m. Mathieu knew, and thought it was funny. Whenever the phone rang at supper time he pretended not to hear it and I finally got impatient.

"Mathieu, you know very well it's Sébastien and you know it drives me round the bend to talk to him on the phone!"

"Come on! He always asks for you and I have to lie ... Do what I do ... I can't understand him either, but I just say 'yes' or 'no' and he's perfectly happy! Talk about nursery school and don't pay any attention to what he says, just give him a big hug and say it's his bedtime, say whatever comes into your head, he just wants to hear your voice ... "

Which was exactly what Mathieu did, sometimes for a good fifteen minutes; he'd sit on the kitchen counter, the receiver wedged between his ear and shoulder, and while he was doing something else – filing his nails or leafing through the paper – he'd let out a few grunts, laugh, feign surprise as he heard about some adventure he couldn't make head or tail of, or anger if Louise had told him about some misbehaviour, or interest when he was barely listening, then it would end with noisy kisses that were absolutely sincere: there was a big fuss about who gave the last kiss that could go on for ages. Each claimed not to want to hang up first, and they both seemed to enjoy it.

I tried a couple of times, to please Mathieu. Disaster. After two minutes I panicked, sweating, spluttering, more incoherent than the four year old at the other end of the line who at least was trying to make himself understood. A dialogue of dyslexics.

But it was true that Sébastien liked talking to me and in the end I found it touching. Even if I was cutting our "conversations" shorter and shorter.

The week after his second visit, despite some very serious efforts, I became irritable again.

November had been disgorging its heavy rainfalls for more than two weeks. Montreal had been sullied – it had been a long time since you could say "washed" – by the rain, polished, worn down, exhausted. The leaves had been swept away, leaving the pitiful sight of denuded trees, the streets were empty, waiting for the first sprinkling of snow that would shed a little gaiety over this sinister setting, at least for a few hours, before it turned to a sticky mud that would bring out Montreal's curses. Everything was waiting wetly for something to happen.

The days were becoming dangerously short. I was anxiously awaiting the day when it would already be dark when I left school. I think there's nothing more depressing than to come out at the end of classes into the hideous early evening of late November or early December, just before the snow, if by chance there is any, falls and turns everything blue. You feel as if you've lost a whole day because when you went inside that morning, it wasn't really light yet. You emerge from the wan CEGEP lighting into the dirty light of the streets and wonder what you're doing there. I don't know why, but I hate having to turn on the lights in my apartment when I come home from work. It seems like midnight and I feel like going to bed . . .

All this to say that November is the month I hate the most. And that November was particularly hard. On everybody.

On the eve of Sébastien's second visit, I was in a filthy mood. Despite the good will of my students, who, sensing it, had been amazingly attentive. I came home in a fury, phoned the Laurier Bar-B-Q because I didn't feel like cooking, and settled down in the living room with my *Journal de Montréal*, looking for a laugh, but even that didn't cheer me up. And Mathieu didn't get off work until nine!

I was feverish, I felt like chewing my nails, which I hadn't done for years and, more seriously, I'd have quite willingly got drunk, though I hardly drink any more. Oh yes, I'd have quite gladly got bombed ... A good weekend of adolescent boozing, complete with vomiting, dirty jokes, smutty songs, the works. Another form of escape, needless to say.

What would we do with Sébastien for two days?

Nightmare!

I'd wolfed my chicken, greasy french fries, sauce, bread, mocha, and Pepsi too fast, without thinking ... and of course I got indigestion. We were off and running. I could see the weekend coming in pretty well the same colours: queasiness followed by heartburn, nausea, and full-fledged panic.

Mathieu came in around nine forty-five, all smiles.

"I've solved your problems. This time, anyway. I'll take Sébastien to my mother's place tomorrow. They haven't seen each other for months. And we'll sleep over!"

Mathieu

Sébastien was asleep on the living-room sofa. Rose was holding his left foot, which protruded from the quilt, her thumb scarcely touching the sole so she wouldn't tickle him, the rest of her hand wrapping his foot like a blanket: Sébastien's toes emerged from his grandmother's hand the way his head did from the quilt.

Mathieu had a very clear recollection of his mother's mania for warming feet. She'd done it to him so often when he was a child, on this same sofa, while they watched *Les Beaux Dimanches* on Sunday night or those TV serials that "started too late." He would lie beside her, under the same sort of quilt, maybe this very one, which had come to them from her mother, a great Gaspesian artist who had salvaged every rag in the county in order to produce the star-patterned pieces that had made her reputation, under which you felt so secure; he would pretend to fall asleep during *Septième Nord* or *De neuf à cinq* and arrange himself so he could extend his foot towards her . . .

That thumb on the soles of his feet, that gentleness, all the tenderness concentrated on such a tiny surface . . . The soles of his feet tingled. He wished that he could become again the child who had once been so easily consoled, that he could lie down next to Sébastien and sleep, knowing that a light, beneficent hand would imprint upon one of the most sensitive spots on his body – he was very ticklish – a magical, soothing sign of her complicity.

He had wounded his mother deeply and he knew it, but he was the one who wanted consolation!

Rose let go of Sébastien's little foot and blew her nose.

Mathieu didn't feel like pursuing the conversation, but it had to be brought to an end: you don't leave such an important scene unresolved, you have to see it all the way through or not provoke it at all. (He'd already put it off for so many years!)

"Don't tell me you didn't suspect something, Mamma ... "

Silence. She seemed to be in the grip of emotions so powerful she couldn't speak.

"Mamma ... you knew ... and you've known for ages!"

Rose looked at him directly for the first time in half an hour. Throughout his confession she had watched Sébastien sleep, or nervously twisted the hem of her skirt, while she examined the flowers in the carpet.

"You were married ... you had a child ... "

"I explained all that ... I don't want to go over it again ... "

"I know, I know, I'm not stupid! You don't have to tell me again, it was painful enough the first time!"

She took Sébastien's foot again, but a little too roughly; the child stirred and moaned in his sleep.

"What's he going to say when he's old enough to understand?"

"We're talking about *you* now, not him. I'll take care of Sébastien. I'm going to bring him up so things like that aren't important ... What I want to know is how *you* feel!"

"But Mathieu, I don't *know*! Give me time! Half an hour ago we were splitting our sides over your adventures at the ad agencies, then you drop your bomb and want my reaction right away! I don't even know if I believe you!"

"Of course you do ... You've known for ages."

"Will you stop saying that, it's aggravating!"

Her good old temper was surfacing again; Rose was becoming the woman she was at her finest hour, who always came out of disasters on her feet, who would take the bull by the horns with a vigour you wouldn't have imagined she possessed a moment earlier, fighting to the bitter end and never giving way. How he wished he were like her . . .

"Okay, I had my suspicions . . . When you'd come home late Saturday night, early Sunday morning I should say, after you left Louise, you never smelled of woman's perfume, okay? . . . But *I didn't want to see it*, can you get that through your head? When you were just a kid your father used to worry so much that you weren't enough of a 'man,' and I didn't particularly want to admit he was right! I decided long ago, Mathieu, that your father was wrong about everything, *everything*, and I don't want him to be right about anything now!"

She heaved an exasperated sigh, then took a sip of cold coffee.

"I'm sorry, my trouble with your father has nothing to do with what you just told me . . . But it's true that's one of the reasons I didn't see it before: I didn't want him to know something before I did . . . "

"That's not all, I know you . . . "

"Well sure . . . I mean I've got my pride too . . . Can you see me going and telling all this to Georgette? It's been years now since her son told her he's that way, and all that time I was feeling sorry for her, bragging about you, your success with girls, your big healthy son . . . "

Mathieu realized he was out of cigarettes. Another reason to panic.

"Mamma, stop just thinking about yourself, think about me for a change! The reason I told you is because for the first time in my life I'm happy and I want to share it with you . . . "

Abruptly, she leaned towards him, as if to touch him, but stopped in mid-gesture. She spoke more softly.

"You weren't happy before?"

"Not really. But now I am, even though Sébastien could become a problem ... "

"You mean he doesn't want to see Sébastien?"

"Mamma, don't keep changing the subject! Listen ... I'm looking you in the eye and telling you, I love him ... I don't want you just to *understand* that, I want you to accept it ... "

Visibly moved, she got up and left the living room.

Mathieu thought it was all over now. Even here, he would find no response, no consolation. He knelt on the rug beside Sébastien and laid his forehead next to his son's head.

Rose came back almost immediately with a package of cigarettes, Mathieu's brand.

"You run out every time you come over ... I had these in the fridge so they wouldn't dry out."

She resumed her position, one hand on her grandson's foot, but her back was slightly bent.

"Go on. And this time tell me everything. You've never told me you loved somebody before, and I want to hear all about it. And afterwards ... afterwards I'll think about it. Right now I can't."

Mathieu was still sitting on the rug next to the sofa where Sébastien was sleeping. His second version had been much more detailed than the first. This time he hadn't merely skimmed over the subject, he had added details and emotion as he described something that, he realized as he told it, closely resembled happiness. This time his mother hadn't taken her eyes off him. He felt himself being scrutinized, judged, sized up; she frowned a little at delicate moments or when she didn't immediately grasp some

170

detail, but she gave him her full attention; he quickly realized that his description of how he'd met Jean-Marc was as important to her as the thing itself: she was judging him according to the sincerity of his account.

That was another of her specialties: she could sniff out a lie at once, he'd experienced it often enough when he was a child to remember very precisely. When she said: "Tell me that to my face so I can see!" you had to be careful, because the smallest sign of bad faith, the slightest hint of a lie or even a half-truth would be identified, denounced and stamped out. This wasn't the first time she'd asked him to repeat a confession, after merely listening to him with lowered gaze the first time. She wouldn't show her own feelings but ask him to start over, while she glared at him.

Because he was putting his entire soul into his account of the past few months, he realized that he'd won now, and he decided to spare his mother the problems with Sébastien, hoping she wouldn't realize that he was hiding something. Why upset her with a situation when he himself couldn't see all its implications and all its consequences?

He had smoked six or seven cigarettes and his throat was burning.

"I wouldn't mind something to drink but it's too late for coffee and I guess you wouldn't have beer ... "

"What do you mean, I wouldn't have beer! Go look in the fridge ... "

When he came back with a nice cold Heineken she was the one who looked nervous.

"Now I've got something to tell *you* ... "

"And on top of everything else he's married! Mamma, is this really you?"

"You're the last person to be preaching, young man!"

"I'm not preaching, I'm just surprised! Don't attack me before I even say anything!"

Rose had made her own confession, almost clinging to Sébastien's foot. She had kept a close watch on Mathieu's reactions as she spoke, interrupting herself when he started – this was the first time he'd ever heard a candid reference to his mother's sex life and he couldn't hide his amazement – stumbling over the words she found difficult, the ones with a loaded meaning that exploded between them like a small bomb, hesitating between letting doubt persist or telling him outright that it wasn't a platonic relationship . . . In the end she too told him everything, but she wasn't sure that she felt relieved.

Since the death of Mathieu's father fifteen years earlier, the question of other men had never come up. Rose had had several "pals" whom Mathieu had hated, persecuting them with well-aimed kicks and repeated hysterics until they went away, disgusted at the spoiled brat who wouldn't let anyone near his mother, but they'd never talked about them openly. Married very young, Mathieu had chosen to forget about his mother's escapades, though she was a healthy woman, still very beautiful and desirable, and men had always hovered around her, even when his father was still alive. And now he was picturing her in an enticing negligée on Saturday morning, waiting for the phone to ring, and then the doorbell . . .

"How long's this been going on?"

"Since before you left home . . . We met elsewhere . . . because of his wife . . . and you . . . Now, though, it's more . . . convenient."

She was as red as a tomato. She was breathing heavily, wiping her brow with a Kleenex and fanning herself with her hand.

"What a night! I won't forget this for a long time!"

Mathieu was both shocked and wounded. Shocked at his own selfishness, at not having realized earlier, because it had always been inconceivable, that his mother might have an active sex life, and wounded because of her lack of confidence and because she'd never breathed a word to him.

"Why didn't you tell me before? I could have made myself scarce on Saturday mornings, left you alone, I'm not a baby after all, I know about these things ... "

"And what about you, why didn't you breathe a word? Eh? It's the same thing, Mathieu! It's called being too damn discreet! If you hadn't told me what you did tonight, maybe I wouldn't have told you about Paul either ... Even though I've got one advantage over you ... "

"What's that?"

She leaned towards him and ran her hand through his hair, an abrupt little gesture that was almost a slap, as she used to do when he was little and she wanted to make a point during an argument.

"At least I had some suspicions about your secret ... "

At that he was frankly ashamed.

"Are you happy, even though he's married and you're stuck with being the other woman?"

"Yes. Absolutely. It suits me because he's not underfoot all the time like your father and ... well, you should know, sometimes it's exciting, sneaking around ... "

"Both of us are happy and we never said a word to each other ... "

"Some kinds of happiness are harder to take than others ... "

"Or to confess ... "

"Or to confess."

"So who is he anyway? You haven't even told me his full name! What does he do?"

"And what about yours?"

"How do you manage your Saturday mornings? Doesn't his wife suspect anything?"

"She isn't too bright . . . She thinks he goes to the gym to work out . . . He works out all right, but not the way she thinks . . . "

"Mamma, honestly!"

"Is he good to Sébastien at least?"

"He tries . . . but he's only seen him once."

It went on and on, passionate and impassioned, with plenty of tears and giggles; it was like a combined pyjama party and primal therapy session; it brought pain and relief, it was exalting but upsetting too, because it was so fragile: one ill-chosen or misinterpreted word could have destroyed everything. But they chose the right words and the night passed, catching them unawares.

They went to bed at dawn, exhausted, Mathieu huddling against his son's warm body and falling asleep at once, Rose overwhelmed at what she had confessed and what she'd learned, unable to get to sleep, hypnotized with fatigue but with her eyes wide open to what was shaping up to be a cold, grey Sunday.

Sébastien remained inconspicuous as long as he could; he even fixed breakfast all by himself – a bowl of cereal, a glass of juice – but around ten o'clock he'd had enough, and he jumped onto the living room sofa where his father was lying, singing the theme from "Passe-Partout."

Getting up was long and difficult. Mathieu felt as if he'd smoked too much, drunk too much. A full-fledged hangover with headache, upset stomach, the works . . . But Sébastien, rested and fresh as a newborn, a crayon in his fist and a smile on his lips, was demanding the attention he believed he was entitled to.

Rose got up around noon, dark rings around her eyes, which gleamed with a new light. They didn't talk about the night they'd just lived through – a certain shyness had returned – but each was aware that the secret bond that had been forged between them would be solid and durable, even if it wasn't always expressed aloud. Such privileged moments can't be summoned, they have to be simply allowed to come, and now they both knew it was possible.

The day passed then, between a boring movie on TV, some games with Sébastien that were sometimes enjoyable, sometimes not, reading the weekend papers, a long shared bath that filled the apartment with shouts and the bathroom with suds: Mathieu washed Sébastien's hair; Sébastien washed Mathieu's.

Rose took it all in with a look that was filled with satisfaction and emotion. After all, wasn't Mathieu's happiness more important than her prejudices? But there was an aftertaste, a hint of bitterness that spoiled the day for her a little: between comprehension and acceptance, there was one step she had yet to take, one that would probably be the hardest. Around five o'clock, when Mathieu and Sébastien were about to leave, she took Mathieu aside and said:

"Don't ask me to meet him right away . . . I'll need time."

He held her very tight, even rocking her a little, as if she were a big child.

"Let me know when you feel ready . . . Take as long as

you need . . . Even if it never happens, I won't hold it against you."

"It won't be never, but it may take a while . . . "

Sébastien demanded his share of hugs, the taxi came and they quickly took their leave.

Jean-Marc

All right, I admit it, I was bored!

The Saturday was fine; I listened to a lot of music – my new earphones are sensational – I moped around the house pretending to clean up, though all I did was move the dust around, I bought groceries at Lemercier's and a dozen magazines at the bookstore, a few local but mostly foreign, as behooves any good citizen of Outremont – I've just discovered the fashionable French weekly, *L'Evénement du jeudi*, which I'm hooked on – I even did a bit of work and enjoyed it a little, then I went up to have supper with Mélène and Jeanne, who were alone that evening, and who dished out the usual cracks about Saturday-night widowers. I reassured them by telling them Mathieu and Sébastien were "at the mother-in-law's." In all, a quiet day, fairly pleasant, that let me rediscover the enjoyment of looking after, by myself, those tedious little chores that for a few months now I'd got used to doing *à deux*.

I even treated myself to a bit of an outing: late Saturday night I went and checked out the bars. I had no intention of cheating on Mathieu, but I didn't feel like spending the rest of the evening in front of the TV set either. Depression and horror. Despite the forecast of freezing rain the boys were still wearing the tight little T-shirts I'd seen on them in August, still clutching the glass of warm beer. The place reeked of expensive perfume and poppers, the music nearly blasted you to the floor, the ultra-modern, super-sophisticated lighting had you reeling in three minutes, yet it was as sad and empty as the back side of the moon ... Let them call me neo-petit-bourgeois, intolerant, prematurely senile – I couldn't take it for more than half an hour. I didn't have the heart to go to the Paradise, I was afraid of running into Luc and "the others," the ones who'd been talking about me behind my back since August ... And with the cold and the slippery sidewalks, no way was I going to do Sainte-Catherine.

I walked to the Hotel Méridien where I had to wait a good twenty minutes for the 80 bus. I didn't want to take a taxi – although they were passing at the rate of three or four a minute – and I stood there freezing in my thin suede windbreaker, absolutely gorgeous but absolutely inappropriate for the unleashed elements that were raging about me. Then at the corner of Parc and Bernard, there wasn't a bus in sight, so I had to walk the rest of the way.

I was sneezing when I came home.

I'm so predictable, sometimes, it depresses me.

I went to bed feeling sorry for myself because I was afraid I'd caught the first cold of the season, because Mathieu wasn't there – suddenly the bed was so big! – and because (okay, it makes no sense, but that's me) I actually wouldn't have minded being wakened the next morning by a strident little voice asking me to come and play!

After freaking out for weeks at the thought of seeing the child again, here I was missing him! (Well, maybe "missing" is a bit strong, but let's say it would have been kind of nice to know he was asleep in my office, hugging his doggy.)

I was so annoyed with myself I pounded my pillow in disgust.

Sunday was a trial, painful and dragged out. I was sure I was coming down with something: my bones ached and I had trouble breathing, but the cold or flu or bronchitis hadn't actually set in and that made it worse. Several times I almost phoned Mathieu at his mother's place to ask him

178

and Sébastien to come over, but I restrained myself, saying we'll see in three weeks, maybe he'll get on your nerves again, maybe you don't really want to see him, it's just November and you've got the Sunday blues, or you want to be coddled because you're catching a cold . . .

I went up and played cards with Mélène. It was quite a performance: I cheated, I lost, I swore.

Then I treated myself to a solitary TV dinner, probably to crank up the suffering a little more, then flopped in front of the TV, where I submitted myself to an original drama that was highly pretentious and numbingly dull.

When Mathieu came home my sinuses were plugged, I had a fever, a cough, and a runny nose – and so did he!

What a wonderful week we spent! Sicks as dogs, both of us, but having the time of our lives: hardly getting out of bed, at least for the first two days, we ate whatever was around – mostly Campbell's Chicken Noodle soup which reminds me of my childhood and actually *tastes* of the flu because my mother poured so much into me when I was little – and watched whatever was on TV – American soaps in the daytime, Québécois *téléromans* at night, and old movies whenever they were on; we went into ecstasies over the incredible misogyny of "Benny Hill," the disconcerting vulgarity of Joan Rivers and the hilarious amateurism of "La Chance aux chansons" on channel 99 from France – we slept at weird times, often after eating too much, like puppies exhausted by the effort of their feeding. We were absolutely delighted at our joint illness and took advantage of it as if it were some unexpected, unplanned, improvised vacation. To hell with Eaton's and the CEGEP, up with the bedroom!

In fact we rarely left that room, which now smelled of Vicks, tiger balm and eucalyptus oil. Our pyjamas – I'd found two pairs at the back of a drawer – were rumpled, the bed was in a deplorable state, and we ourselves, from sweating and laughing and sleeping whenever we felt like it, were totally wasted as if we'd come through an American-style lost weekend. I didn't dare look in the bathroom mirror: I felt like the alcoholic version of myself. And Mathieu, though he was so handsome and usually so concerned about his appearance, let himself go too, his neglect surprising me a little but giving me something to laugh at as well: unshaven, with greasy, uncombed hair, he looked as if he'd just spent a month in a logging camp. I called him my "Canadien errant" or my "grubby lumberjack" which gave us both a giggle – an indication of how low our humour had sunk!

On the Thursday, around two a.m., as we were watching some sombre drama of which we'd missed the title, I told Mathieu, without thinking, that I hadn't felt so out of it since I'd had mononucleosis during Expo 67. Mathieu started.

"You were awfully young to have mono!"

"Not that young, I was twenty."

Mathieu propped himself up on one elbow.

"Weren't you born in 1950?"

"No, 45, like everybody else!"

Mathieu sat up in bed as if a spring had pinched him.

"The night we met you told me you were thirty-five! You're thirty-nine!"

I remembered our first conversation back in August, when I had indeed lied to Mathieu about my age – he'd even told me I didn't look thirty-five – and I started laughing like a lunatic, bent double in the bed, punching the mattress with both fists . . .

"You've been living with an old man for two months and you didn't even know it!"

Suddenly he didn't find it funny at all.

"I hate lies, Jean-Marc, I hate knowing you've been lying to me for months!"

"I lied to you once, Mathieu, one night when we didn't even know each other, and I did it because I was afraid you'd think I was too old ... And then I forgot about it, that's all ... If I hadn't I'd have rectified the situation, told you the truth, I'd have gladly told you how ancient I am ... "

"But the difference between us isn't just ten years, it's *fifteen*!"

"So what, Mathieu, what's the big deal?"

"The big deal is, when I'm forty you'll be *fifty-five*!"

It was the first time either of us had mentioned the future; Mathieu suddenly blushed red to the roots of his hair.

I took him in my arms.

"That's right, and when I'm sixty-five you'll be fifty, a famous actor – and supporting me ... When you retire I'll be so old, so crippled with arthritis and gaga from advanced Alzheimer's you'll leave me for a younger man ... some kid in his sixties ... "

He finally smiled. But he joined the game in a voice I hadn't heard before, in which I could detect enormous panic.

"When I'm eighty-five we'll celebrate your centenary at the French teachers' retirement home ... I'll bring my young seventy-year-old lover and you'll go wild with jealousy! The old men fight it out!"

He lay down again. He wasn't smiling now.

"I don't like talking about it, even as a joke. I'm so afraid of getting old!"

The night ended tenderly, with whispered confidences. My fears, his fears, my obsessions, his. Finally Mathieu said:

"Two exchanges of secrets in one week is a lot ... "

And then he told me about his night at his mother's.

And I realized that his mother was only five years older than I was.

And I got depressed.

Then I said fuck, life's too short, who cares, why not roll with the punches, tomorrow is another day, to hell with it ... but even inwardly I had trouble smiling.

The next day I decided to forget it all and pick up my flu where I'd left it.

Mathieu didn't bring up my age again, but he took a long bath, then a shower, and emerged from the bathroom as clean as a whistle and handsome as ever, his hair neatly combed, clean-shaven, shiny-eyed. He got back into bed with a little expression of disgust.

"Come on, Jean-Marc! Get up and get washed. We can be sick, but we don't have to be slobs. And while you make yourself beautiful I'll tidy up the bedroom."

December was quite a cheerful month. The first snow had arrived early, it was cold but not too damp, my students seemed fairly serious about preparing for their exams. Through patience, I'd managed a reconciliation with them and teaching had become bearable again. The days were shorter but not so gloomy as in November and I was no longer assailed by morbid thoughts when I left the CEGEP. The late afternoon sun, which came in the window of one of my classes, actually cheered me up.

Mathieu was working hard at Eaton's. It was the mad Christmas rush and the store was open late most nights.

I was expecting to spend the week between Christmas and New Year's in the Laurentians, at my brother Gaby's, whom I see once a year over the holidays and always have a falling-out with after a few days because we don't see eye-to-eye about a thing. Every year, in early December, when his wife calls with the invitation, I accept though I know it'll be just like the year before: a few days' respite with Gaby being a nice guy and carting me all over the Laurentians, driving like a madman because it's Christmas and he's with his little brother again and life is beautiful and we're going to have a *good* meal; and then Gaby the lush boozing it up on Christmas Eve – the first rows start when I reproach him – and then Gaby, who goes out of control on Boxing Day, calls me a goddamn faggot, first laughing, then more and more seriously, even bringing his two sons into it, telling them things like, he's fucking sick, there's nothing like a woman, and then, keep your hands off my kids and so forth. He's never accepted my homosexuality and it's the starting point for all our problems. We might be able to find some common ground about love, life, death, injustice, even just the status quo, but on that subject, never. Gaby thinks I'm sick and that's that.

But I was going to go back this year, and I knew I'd go back the next year too. Maybe because of Jeannine, who seems more and more defeated, who goes to so much trouble for nothing every year though no one but me even thanks her, her children, two big lumps the same age as Mathieu, taking for granted and as their due everything she does for them. They arrive with their wives and kids, they turn everything upside down, eat like pigs, belch – but maybe that's their form of thanks – unwrap their presents, then leave without a word. Or just about. It sometimes occurs to me that Gaby may be a little jealous of the life I lead ... I probably make more money than he does and I've got no responsibilities ... So he attacks ...

Anyway, I'd decided to bring Mathieu along this time, to see how my brother would react and in the hope that the presence of my boyfriend, the first one he'd met "officially," would keep him from making a fool of himself. It was risky but I'd talked to Jeannine about it, and to Mathieu, who was willing to go along.

So Christmas was approaching with its portion of joys and of problems. And Sébastien was phoning more and more often. I was getting used to his babble but I still couldn't understand a thing. No, that's wrong: a few frequently recurring words were much clearer than others, words like "presents," for instance, or "Santa Claus," or "Lego," or "He-Man," which sounded strangely like "hymen" in his mouth. Now that I was willing to spend more time listening to him, he'd talk to me on the phone as if we'd known each other forever, when we'd only met once. Obviously a lot was said about Christmas, which I thought was cute.

One Thursday night, around December 10, Louise called to ask if we'd keep Sébastien the next night and all day Saturday. She and Gaston wanted to do their Christmas shopping and Sébastien, who had given them a very complete list, would just get under foot, as her mother would say ... They'd come for him on Saturday night. Mathieu started to say he'd be working – which was true – and didn't want to leave Sébastien alone with me because we didn't know each other well enough and he was afraid Sébastien would be a nuisance, but without thinking, I offered to look after him, telling myself if ever there was a chance to test my ability to tolerate the kid, this is it. I regretted it at once but, strangely, when Mathieu asked if I was sure I could get through Saturday with my sanity intact, I said yes. When he hung up he gave me a funny look and he was right. I'd have given half my life for it to be two days later, but at the same time I was eager to see how things would develop.

Of course when they turned up around seven o'clock I was in the tub. With a towel around my waist I ran to open the door, thinking now I'm in for it, the hot water's going to freeze on my body and I'll be coughing my lungs out ... I was leaving long trails of soapy water on the fine wood in the hallway and I was sure I'd slip and fall on my way back to the bathroom.

Sébastien was all smiles, wearing an adorable sky blue parka that made him look like a little angel without wings.

"Gaston's got a new car!"

When Louise realized that I'd just got out of the bath she pushed Sébastien inside the hallway.

"Tell him about the car later, Sébastien, can't you see he's all wet ... "

She shut the door behind her.

"Hi, Jean-Marc. Finish your bath, I'll undress Sébastien ... "

But the child was already at the other end of the house.

"It's okay, I was just getting out ... "

Louise shouted, "Sébastien, your boots!" and a little voice replied, "I took them off!"

Indeed, two little boots were lying between us. We hadn't seen him take them off: he'd done it with dazzling speed.

Louise smiled.

"He can get undressed in a second when he wants to ... but if he doesn't ... "

An embarrassed little silence. Louise didn't dare look at me too long and I was squirming at being there in front of her half-naked. And freezing.

"Okay, I'll be going, Gaston's waiting ... Have a good weekend ... lots of luck ... And listen, thanks. This is a real favour ... "

A warm handshake that didn't quite connect. An exchange of ever so slightly frozen smiles.

I didn't hear her shut the door.

And fortunately, I didn't see Gaston's new car. I don't know a thing about cars, I don't care about them, and I wouldn't have had the faintest idea what to say. I'm always uncomfortable around people's new cars. All I can think of to say is, That's a fine-looking car, and every time, I get the feeling I'm insulting its owner.

I returned to the bathroom, trying to avoid the puddles. Sébastien, fully dressed, was sitting on the toilet waiting for me.

"Can I take my bath with you?"

"Haven't you had one?"

"Yes, but I want another one ... "

I assumed a "speaking-to-children" voice which I realized after three words was completely phony.

"You don't take two baths in a row just like that, Sébastien. You take a bath to get clean, not for fun. And anyway, I'm finished."

"You are not! If you were finished you wouldn't've been in the tub when we got here!"

So much for demagogy.

I was so cold I'd lowered myself into the warm water.

"See, you are not finished!"

"You're right, I'm not. Now go and get undressed while I wash, then I'll come to your bedroom ... "

Two minutes later he was back in the bathroom without a stitch on.

"This'll be fun, I brought my rubber ducky ... "

"Sébastien, I said no ... "

"How come? Daddy lets me."

"So would I, but you said you already had a bath ... "

"I forgot, I didn't really ... That was yesterday ... "

"Sébastien, don't make things worse by telling a lie!"

"It is not a lie!"

His chin was quivering. Tears welled up in his eyes. How could I resist?

"If you admit you told a lie I'll give you permission to get in the bath ... "

Instantaneously, a smile.

"It wasn't a lie ... it was a joke!"

We stayed in the bath a long time, playing with the ducky, making dancers out of washcloths, dissolving the soap by spinning it very fast between our hands. When it cooled off too much we ran more hot water, and when it was too hot we shrieked as if we'd been scalded.

We emerged from our bath exhausted and happy, with skin like prunes. Sébastien dried himself very seriously, telling me it's important in the winter so you won't catch cold. He showed me how you must dry the insides of your legs, the soles of your feet, your armpits. And then, just as seriously, he showed me his penis, telling me he'd just learned what it was called and saying you should never say "pecker" like Eric Boucher at nursery school, because it wasn't nice.

He got into his bunny-patterned pyjamas and, of course, asked about Goofus, casting greedy looks at the doggy.

When Mathieu came home from work Sébastien was already asleep and I had a sore throat.

"Goofus again?"

"What else . . . I think Sébastien's developing a fixation on that toy."

"You should've told him you can't play doggy every time he asks . . . "

"I did, but he pretends he doesn't understand . . . When it suits him he carries on as if he doesn't know that I'm the voice . . . "

We went to watch him sleep, crossing a good part of the house on tiptoe though it was totally unnecessary. He was lying on his stomach, one arm over the doggy's throat, who seemed to be choking, jaws open on his eternal rictus and lolling tongue.

We stood there for a good five minutes listening to

Sébastien's breathing, regular and almost inaudible. Mathieu put his arm around my waist.

"I love that child so much, Jean-Marc, it hurts. I love him more than anything in the world and I hardly ever see him ... "

I heard in that, not a threat, but a sort of warning, as if Mathieu were trying to tell me what would happen if I ever asked him to make a choice. Perhaps that was wrong, probably it was false, but I sensed the possibility of a rivalry and it saddened me. I was trying to prove my good faith, so why this remark? But no, surely it was just a declaration of love born of a genuine frustration that I, in my chronic egocentricity, interpreted otherwise. Or so I hoped.

Mathieu seemed preoccupied; he wanted to know everything that had happened during his absence, if Sébastien had been polite, a brat, tolerable, or a little monster; if he'd gone to bed willingly, if he'd brushed his teeth, if he'd gone peepee because sometimes, when he forgot, he still wet his bed, especially if he was very excited. I reassured him as best I could, even asked if he really trusted me.

"I'm not a fourteen-year-old babysitter, Mathieu. Maybe I've never looked after a child before, but I think I'm old enough to know pretty well what to do and what not to do ... We spent a very nice evening together, Sébastien went to bed a little late because I didn't want to be the heavy who put him to sleep the minute he got here, he turned in after one last session with Goofus ... And sure, maybe I shouldn't have because I know it gets him overexcited, but he asked so sweetly, you know him, you know how cute he can be, I couldn't resist ... "

We were flopped on the living room sofa in front of the inevitable Friday night movie. Mathieu turned to me, covered my mouth with his hand and looked me straight in the eye.

"Are you really sure this is how you want to spend your weekend? You aren't doing it just to make me happy?"
I vaguely heard laughter, I think I smelled bacon sizzling, and burnt toast. In my semi-conscious state I heard a silly nursery rhyme featuring blue bunnies and cows jumping over the moon, I'm sure I felt a kiss somewhere on my face and a voice saying softly: "Good morning anyway!" And another little voice: "Me too, I want a kiss!" And I prayed that I wouldn't end up on my hands and knees over the goddamn jigsaw puzzle.

I woke with a start at half-past ten. Sébastien was sitting on the floor beside the bed, surrounded by his own particular bric-à-brac: open books, an unfinished jigsaw (he'd fitted together twenty-three pieces and left out the other one, who knows why), He-Man's and She-Ra's, Goofus himself, who towered over these minuscule figures, a Lego set he'd brought from home . . .

As soon as he saw that my eyes were open he stood up, grinning.

"You sleep in on Saturday too, eh? Daddy told me this is Saturday. Gaston, when he sleeps in I'm not allowed to wake him up. I played while I was waiting for you; it was fun but I really really wanted you to wake up . . . "

A brief hesitation, then, timidly:

"And Goofus really really wanted . . . "

Strangely enough he didn't insist that I do the doggy's voice. His father must have given him a little sermon on the subject. Sébastien watched me eat my toast, he even "helped" me by dipping a cookie in my coffee. He grimaced to let me know what he thought of this barbaric adult drink and asked me to pour him some of that fruit-juice mixture arbitrarily called "punch," the mere colour of which makes me sick to my stomach. This one was pinkish-brown, it smelled just a little too strongly of cherries and it stained.

We watched the snow fall. It wasn't yet a storm, but a few gusts were strong enough to rattle the window-panes. Sébastien stood on tiptoe so he could see out. He pressed his mouth against the glass and blew, wiped away the condensation, then started again. His hands, unwashed since he'd left the kitchen, left disgusting little grease marks on the window.

I was explaining snowflakes to Sébastien, how they're formed, their velocity, the beauty of the crystals, how the motifs were repeated, when he interrupted me in mid-sentence:

"It's no fun when Daddy's away, is it?"

I confess I didn't complete my sentence.

I picked Sébastien up, then put him down on the floor. I was quite taken aback.

"Why isn't it fun?"

He sat on the floor and picked Goofus up by one paw.

"Daddy always plays with me."

There was no reproach in his voice; he was merely stating a rather obvious fact. I crouched beside him.

"I played with you too just now ... "

"Not very long though ... Daddy plays with me for a long long time ... "

I had nothing to say. But I couldn't see myself getting back on all fours to play bow-wow again, or running all over the house to hide while Sébastien counted to ten, invariably skipping the six and the eight ...

We stood there in silence for a few moments. Helpless, miserable, I looked at Sébastien who was amusing himself opening and closing his doggy's mouth. He spoke first. Looking me straight in the eye with his own big brown squirrel's eyes, he asked:

"Jean-Mak ... how come Daddy lives here?"

I thought okay, get ready, here it comes, the big scene, the explanations, the works ... How was I going to tell him?

What words would I use? Most important, how could I tell him without horrifying him? You try telling a four year old about the love between two men! I decided on the simple approach, hoping his questions wouldn't become more and more embarrassing. Or precise.

"Because Daddy and I love each other so we decided to live together . . . "

"Doesn't Daddy love Mummy?"

I felt as if I was walking with my eyes shut through a shop filled with crystal figurines.

"Of course he does . . . But they decided not to live in the same house any more."

"Why?"

There it was, the trap.

I must have stood there wide-eyed for quite a while, because Sébastien repeated his question.

"Why don't they live in the same house any more?"

"Because . . . they had a little fight . . . Not serious, but Daddy decided to move . . . It was a long time ago, when you were just a baby . . . "

"Did I use to live with them?"

"Yes . . . "

"I bet that was nice."

I seized this escape hatch that would let me make this final reply:

"Isn't it nice that Daddy lives with me and Mummy lives with Gaston? That makes lots of parents . . . "

"Yes, but I have to keep changing houses . . . And there's no mummy here . . . Why isn't there any mummy here?"

I took him in my arms. We made a fine trio, Goofus with his moony-eyed look like a satisfied lover, Sébastien with his embarrassing questions, and I afraid of not finding the right words to calm his fears.

"Do you think there always has to be a mummy?"

"Sure! I wish Mummy would come here with me . . . "

"But Mummy has to stay with Gaston . . . Do you understand that?"

He gave me a teary look that was devastating.

"No."

I hugged Sébastien and his doggy.

It was the only answer I could give him.

Eating at home was out of the question. The night before, when I'd put him to bed, I'd promised to take Sébastien to the movies, and he was already talking about it over breakfast, though the first show wasn't until one o'clock.

It's an understatement to say I had no appetite when we walked into the Laurier Bar-B-Q around noon.

Sébastien devoured part of his chicken leg and all his french fries while I sipped a coffee and looked around. The restaurant was nearly empty. On weekdays at this time, people are lined up, with waitresses constantly running from one side of the restaurant to the other, busboys wiping off tables, the whole hive, at the peak of productivity, buzzing, almost but not quite hysterical. The Laurier Bar-B-Q, one of the oldest and most celebrated establishments of the type in Montreal, since time immemorial the hangout for Outremont preppies who've made it their late-night headquarters for generations – the hot mocha with ice cream is an absolute must, they eat it, their children will eat it, I think it's a fine example of inherited traits – is also one of the fastest places in Montreal for a meal: if you've just got an hour, you can be sure you'll have a good thirty minutes left for prowling the boutiques on Laurier. Even if you have to wait in line, because everything's done very fast: the seating, the serving, and your consumption of the food.

That day, though, only a few elderly couples were occupying the plastic banquettes, a few single people too, who didn't feel like preparing Saturday lunch and were eating more slowly than they would during the week, their heads buried in *La Presse* or – it made a better impression – *Le Devoir*.

Sébastien wanted dessert but it was already past twelve-thirty. So I refused, but promised him popcorn at the movie. No, he wanted dessert. The waitress stood beside the table, smiling – what a cute little boy you've got – and seemed to be taking the kid's side, describing the pies, the cakes and the famous hot mocha with ice-cream ... I raised my voice a notch and slipped in a tiny hint of a threat: we'd be late for the movie, he'd miss the birth of Bambi, he wouldn't see him trying to stand up on the ice ... He didn't care about Bambi, he wanted a mocha with ice-cream. I raised my voice another notch, and then came the tears: big tears, copious and heavy, bathing his face and accompanied by kicks and screams.

I was petrified. The waitress wasn't laughing now, poor thing; she'd even backed away from the table a little, as if afraid Sébastien might hit her. She seemed to have no more experience with children than I did ... I rushed to pay and practically ran out of the restaurant holding Sébastien, still screaming, in my arms. I hailed a cab. (Going home was out of the question: I wanted to stay in a public place so I could call for help if he really got out of control.) The driver thought I was a child-batterer, I think, or a child-molester, but he cooled down a little when I gave him the address of the Cinéma Champlain. Sébastien, exhausted by his fit, fell asleep on the way there. Tears still stained his cheeks. I wiped his face with a Kleenex.

I had to wake him when we went into the theatre.

Bambi was a great moment in his life. He followed the fawn's life story with such intensity that I didn't look at the film at all; instead, I watched him react to it. He laughed (Thumper the rabbit delighted him), he was touched (the meeting of the two skunks drew some spinsterish sighs that surprised me), he was scared (the forest fire, the gunshots), he almost wept (the death of Bambi's mother, a very cruel scene for a children's film, one that had traumatized me when I was a youngster). He applauded the end of the movie, then demanded a second popcorn that I didn't dare refuse.

As he picked up his box of popcorn – I'd asked for the smallest size, but it was enormous – Sébastien asked casually:

"Why did Bambi's mother die?"

Good God!

We were slowly making our way towards the Papineau Métro station. The snow had already started to melt and we were floundering through some nasty icy slush. My feet were wet, but nothing in the world, not even double pleurisy, would have taken me back to the twenty-four-piece jigsaw puzzle and Goofus's vacant smile.

"How about a ride on the Métro, Sébastien?"

He had a mouth full of popcorn and a mustache of mock butter.

"Okay, a long one ... "

It was like an amusement park to him. Everything excited him: paying (honestly!), going down the escalators, watching for the train to arrive in what he called "the black hole," getting onto a car and, most exciting of all needless to say, zipping through the tunnel even though you could see nothing but electrical wires and small yellowish lights. He had knelt on me, pasted his nose against the glass and exclaimed every time we pulled into a station. At Lionel-Groulx, he wanted to get out.

"I was here before. I like it! It's big!"

We walked around the station several times. He ran ahead of me, playing cowboy or He-Man, who knows which, but

194

making plenty of noise, to the great pleasure of passersby who thought he was so cute and such a clever little boy. After twenty minutes I'd had enough and we got back on the subway heading in the opposite direction.

Christmas shoppers staggered joylessly under their packages, as if drained of energy. And there's no question that the fluorescent lights in the Montreal Métro are particularly cruel, making everybody look wan and depressed.

I was in no mood to go home. At the Peel station I asked Sébastien:

"How'd you like to visit Santa Claus at Eaton's? Then we could visit Daddy at work ... "

His "All right!" in perfect English brought a smile to every face in the car.

The line-up outside "Santa's Kingdom" was unbelievable. Some children, half-undressed, were stifling in their parents' arms, others, more foolhardy, were trying to elude adult vigilance and slip into the toy department, while others, especially the youngest, were content to weep bitterly. Through the shrieking and sobbing you could hear: "Michel, get over here! *Now*, I said!" or "Karine, Santa doesn't like little girls who ... !" or, again – the Dynasty influence – "Krystel, sweetheart, Mummy's going to be *very* cross ... "

A good-sized scoop of chocolate ice cream was melting in the middle of the carpet. Sébastien made a face.

"Yuck! That looks like doggy poop!"

We'd just arrived so we were at the end of the line. I knew we had a good half-hour's wait so I'd taken off Sébastien's parka and my own jacket. The heat was unbearable. The air was saturated with the sickly sweet odours of cheap perfume and candies, smells which made my head reel. Holiday crowds, compact, noisy and bustling, have always made me cranky: the usually peaceful Montrealers turn aggressive during the last weeks before Christmas. They rush at the department stores like well-trained cattle, persuaded by flashy advertising campaigns that it's time to spend all their money, down to the last cent, even go into debt to the eyeballs so they can buy useless and breathtakingly meaningless presents for their spoiled brats, and they all want to be served first; jostling, trading insults, sweating, often buying without thinking out of sheer exhaustion, they eventually go home in cars filled to the roof with boxes of every size, or on the crowded Métro where everybody crushes everybody else's packages, swearing as they do every year that never again . . .

"Are you sure you *absolutely* want to see Santa Claus? It's getting late and he may not be able to see all the children who're ahead of us . . . "

He leaned over and looked at the line that disappeared between the counters. His skin was damp. He'd already complained, on the escalator, that he felt sick to his stomach (probably from downing his popcorn too fast) and I was counting on that to get out of waiting in the line which already stretched out behind us.

"Daddy'll be finished work in fifteen minutes and we don't want to miss him . . . "

I tried to sound convincing without pushing it too hard. Sébastien seemed to think it over, then tugged on my sleeve and said:

"Anyway, Mummy said she'd take me to see Santa Claus . . . "

We'd come through the kingdom of schlock where red and green dominated, to a depressing brick-paper medieval castle, filled with smirking, felt-clad elves and a Star Fairy with crimson nails and bottle-thick glasses, and presided over by a skinny Santa Claus with undoubtedly suspect breath. I hoisted Sébastien onto my shoulders; he caught a glimpse of the jolly old man who was having his picture taken with a terrified child.

"He isn't a good Santa Claus ... I'll ask Mummy to take me to see a better one ... "

We went down to the men's clothing department.

"Do you still feel sick, Sébastien? Do you want to go to the bathroom?"

"Yes, I have to go peepee."

"Again! Are you sure?"

"Yes, and I want a drink."

Two very handsome young men were ostentatiously cruising each other in the second-floor bathroom. They were as subtle as two dogs who meet on the sidewalk. I knew one of them, who merely gave me a little nod that meant hello, but also meant don't talk to me, don't stick around, I'm onto a good one, and also: what the hell are you doing with that kid? He hesitated for a moment between curiosity to find out who Sébastien could be and the risky, even dangerous (part of their charm) delights promised by the good-looking guy at the next urinal. He opted for the latter and I left before Sébastien could ask why those two men were taking so long to make peepee.

Mathieu was waiting on a lady I could see from the back, with whom he seemed to be having an animated conversation. When he burst out laughing and laid a hand on her arm I realized that she wasn't a customer, that he was only pretending to serve her, and I felt an inexplicable lump of anxiety in my throat. And when Sébastien ran up to her shouting, "It's Granny Rose! It's Granny Rose!" I wanted to die.

I can't remember ever feeling so uncomfortable. Mathieu was almost trembling when he introduced us. I shook a hand made icy by nerves. She didn't dare look at me too closely and I merely nodded politely somewhere in the direction of her face. She leaned towards her son and I heard:

"Did you set this up, this little meeting?"

And Mathieu replied:

"Come on, Mamma, I didn't know he was coming to see me ... and he didn't know ... "

She quickly turned her attentions to her grandson, who was hopping up and down with excitement and tugging on her coat. She sat him on the counter. He kissed his father and immediately launched into the story of Bambi, starting with the first image in the first sequence.

Mathieu's mother and I were left stranded in the crowded aisle surrounded by jostling last-minute shoppers.

And the worst thing that could happen happened: a customer came looking for Mathieu. Rose appeared to feel faint. She leaned against the counter. Sébastien followed his father, asking where he was going with the man.

I decided there wasn't going to be any awkward silence, that the two of us weren't going to stand there like a pair of imbeciles, each pretending the other didn't exist, so I said without thinking:

"Why don't you come home for supper tonight, with Mathieu and Sébastien?"

I had risked her telling me to get lost or calling me every name in the book or simply walking away, but she turned her head towards me with the beginning of a smile.

"That's a good idea. Might as well take advantage ... A stroke of luck, you could say ... And I've got no plans for tonight."

I thought we were both very brave.

We'd kept the conversation going while Mathieu's customer tried on some trousers. Much was made of the early snow and the heat inside the store.

When Mathieu came back, frowning and wide-eyed, followed closely by Sébastien who seemed to be having the time of his life and to have forgotten all about feeling sick, we told him the news.

Sébastien let out an "All right!" throwing himself at his grandmother's legs; Mathieu leaned against the counter.

In the taxi I stole a look at her. She was trying to compose a mask of impassivity and, astoundingly, she actually succeeded, but something unguarded in the way she moved – her hand too busy on her cloth coat, her head turning too quickly when she'd finished talking – betrayed her ill-concealed nervousness.

She answered my questions succinctly, then immediately turned to Sébastien, who had started describing the rest of Bambi in minute detail.

Perhaps she regretted having accepted my invitation as much I regretted having issued it. To begin with, I didn't know if I had enough to feed four people, but that wasn't the real reason: the real reason was panic at the possibility of finding myself, after dessert, with three persons I'd have trouble talking to because of the embarrassment that would no doubt grow as the evening progressed. There's nothing grimmer than a silent dessert, and it seemed to me we were heading for precisely that.

"You'll see, Mamma, Jean-Marc's very impressive with his wok."

She looked around the kitchen.

"His what?"

Mathieu picked up the metal pan I'd just set on the stove and held it out to her.

"His wok . . . This . . . It's Chinese."

When he saw the wok Sébastien made a face. Smiling, I pinched his nose.

"You'll like it, Sébastien, it's shrimp again. Yesterday you told me you love shrimp ... In fact I bought them just for you."

Mathieu's mother, the expert cook, examined the wok.

"I remember, I've seen them in the stores ... And there's a Chinese fellow on the English channel that does demonstrations ... But he talks a mile a minute so I can't follow ... Is it good?"

I was about to launch into a full and detailed hymn of praise to the wok when Mathieu broke in. He was visibly nervous and so anxious for things go well that he was prepared to assume the burden of the conversation.

"At first, you'll see, it seems a little strange, but everything tastes so fresh ... It retains *all* the vitamins ... "

His mother gave him a strange look.

"You mean I skimped on your vitamins?"

"That's not what I meant, Mamma ... I just meant that when you cook with a wok everything retains *all* its vitamins ... "

I really wanted them out of my kitchen but I didn't dare say so. Sébastien's nose was a little too close to my knife – I was slicing lemons and he liked the smell – and Mathieu and his mother were sitting at the breakfast table, drinks in hand – beer for Rose, red wine for Mathieu.

"The doctor even said I was giving you too many vitamins! Come on, Mathieu, you were a healthy child because I always fed you properly, so don't start talking nonsense in front of other people ... "

I sliced my shallots amid relative silence, with only Sébastien speaking up now and then, asking me why I was doing this or that ... After his mother's little outburst, Mathieu had to find some harmless topic of conversation that would suit everybody, but I left him on his own, hoping he'd decide to move to the living room.

Rose got up and came over to me.

I was chopping ginger. Sébastien had just said that the

root looked like a little man and he'd given a disgusted "yuck" when I sliced off part of it.

"The little man lost his head!"

Rose came to look at the figure in question.

"That's ginger, eh? I see it at the Vietnamese woman's next door ... Smells good but I wouldn't know what to do with it ... "

I felt her growing impatient there on my left. She was shifting from one foot to the other, and running her hand over the electric stove which, to my great embarrassment, wasn't very clean. She was like someone who has something important to say and can't get it out.

"Well, it's a lovely house!"

"Thanks, I'm glad you like it ... "

I let her go on, unsure just what she wanted.

"Can I give you a hand?"

I should have thought of it. I realized she wasn't used to seeing a man cook while she has a drink and watches. And then I decided I was being unfair. And a boor. And macho. She was only a few years older than I, after all, and surely she was acting not out of some atavistic urge but out of simple kindness. (In fact Mathieu had often told me about his mother's regular bouts of feminism, her fierce struggle against the way women were treated at work, her union activity ...)

I replied without looking at her, I was so ashamed of myself.

"No, no thanks, it's all right ... I like chopping vegetables ... it's relaxing ... "

She bent over the wok, frowning slightly. For a moment she looked so much like Mathieu it disturbed me.

"You put in all that?"

"Yes, and it cooks in five minutes."

"That's long enough?"

"Don't worry, I won't feed you raw shrimp ... "

She laughed, but didn't seemed fully convinced.

"You're sure I can't give you a hand? I've finished my beer and I'd like to move around a little ... "

I gave in, telling myself she must be as uncomfortable as I was.

"If you really want ... I forgot to slice the mushrooms ... "

Sébastien tugged at his grandmother's skirt.

"Me can help too?"

He often used "me" instead of "I," I'd realized during that day, and it bothered me. I crouched beside him.

"*I* can help, Sébastien, not *me* ... "

Then I realized that I was the one who was behaving like a self-parody (my keen ear for grammatical errors is a particularly flagrant example) and I think I actually blushed.

"You can help your grandmother if you want ... "

"All right!"

I had to restrain myself from telling him that his "All right" in perfect English crept into his conversation a little too often ... The French teacher in me was too close to the surface, it must be nerves ...

Rose took Sébastien by the hand.

"Come here, sweetheart, granny's going to show you how to slice mushrooms ... You'll see, it's lots of fun ... "

She looked around the counter.

"Where's your knives?"

I took out the best one I own, a very long impressive implement, brand new, whose merits I'd been hearing for ages but which I'd seldom used, since I was used to my old nicked knives.

"Here, use this ... But I'll give you a smaller one, Sébastien ... " And to Mathieu's mother:

"You're so polite and formal, I keep expecting you to call me Sir. Let's make it Jean-Marc and Rose, okay?"

"Fine. Just call me Rose and stop saying Madame!"

Rose speared a shrimp with her fork and looked at it.

"Shrimp with lemon – it's different all right."

She tasted it reluctantly, then somewhat over-stated her appreciation of the dish.

"Mmm, it's delicious, really incredibly good ... I wasn't expecting this ... "

She chewed for a long time, watching each of the three of us in turn. Sébastien copied her, repeating his grandmother's remarks word-for-word.

I thought the game was won until Rose tasted a piece of broccoli. She couldn't conceal her surprise.

"Crisp, isn't it? It's ... It's practically raw ... "

I couldn't answer, it was true. I'd added the broccoli at the last minute and it was a little tough.

Mathieu sipped some wine, then wiped his mouth.

"Mamma always overcooks vegetables ... "

She leaned across the table and gave her son a little swat on the hand.

"You didn't always say that ... You used to think I was the best cook in the world, at least that's what you said ... "

We laughed.

I laid my napkin on the table.

"Would you like something else ... Or should we send out for barbecue?"

Rose protested: no, no, it's good, what are you talking about, it must have cost a fortune, all those shrimp ... As for Sébastien, he would have gladly eaten barbecued chicken. I could see my supper going down the drain and I felt pretty grim. Once again I'd put my foot in it and now I was floundering, trying to salvage something. But I'd been trying too hard; over the last miles my strength had run out: I felt like dumping it all in the garbage and going to bed. Especially because I thought my lemon shrimp was fantastic.

Mathieu suggested to Sébastien that he just eat what he

liked. The shrimps disappeared – fortunately! – but the vegetables sat there congealing in their lemon sauce.

As for Rose, she very politely ate everything. She even managed to say that you get used to undercooked vegetables, and that the lemon gave everything a piquant flavour that she liked . . . She must have read the helplessness in my eyes and was trying to patch things up a little, conciliatory and understanding, every bit the good Québécoise Mom.

Dessert, though – Queen Elizabeth cakes and ice cream from Bilboquet – was an unqualified success. Sébastien was awash in ice cream to his eyebrows, he asked for seconds, banging his spoon on his plate, to the dismay of his grandmother who considered the child's upbringing odd to say the least. But the atmosphere had relaxed; Rose proved to be a brilliant conversationalist, funny and quick at repartee. And best of all, a giggler. I saw in her some of the characteristics I was most fond of in Mathieu. She had brought him up alone and her influence was obvious. Mathieu too had become animated over dessert; he was less defensive and in the surreptitious glances he shot my way when Rose was talking with Sébastien I saw signs of encouragement that made me feel better: I was passing the test, everything was fine, I had nothing to worry about . . . Mathieu was getting to know me very well and he was quick to detect any moments of panic or doubt.

But from the look he gave his mother when Sébastien came to sit on my knees, I realized that he was playing a double game, reassuring his mother just as he'd reassured me. I nearly burst out laughing and disguised my guffaw as a loud smack on Sébastien's neck. He yawned with amazing intensity and rested his head on my chest, asking me to rub his belly as I'd done the night before. That was a trick my mother used to calm me when I was little: she'd put me on her lap, lean me against her vast bosom and rub my stomach very gently until I fell asleep. It was a privileged moment for both of us, one we were careful not to overdo: it served as a cement for our reconciliations after a squabble, or as an apotheosis to our ringing declarations of love.

Rose watched me with a strange expression. I felt obliged to tell her how this habit had come about, and slowly the conversation slid towards very general subjects – family, work (she was hostess in a big Montreal restaurant and very proud of it), likes and dislikes. She complained a little about her overheated apartment, expressed envy of the trees she'd seen outside my house, admitted her secret dream of one day buying a building in the Plateau Mont-Royal with six or seven flats, one of which she would live in, and which would pay for itself. It was low-key, warm and altogether agreeable. And when I deduced from Rose's voice, which became very quiet, that Sébastien had fallen asleep in my arms, relaxed and fragile, for a brief moment I felt intensely happy. These few minutes spent chatting softly over a cooling cup of coffee completely made up for the difficult day that was drawing to an end. This little person, all warm and trembling, who was entrusting to me utterly unconcerned his sleep, the most precarious state in which a human being can find himself, made me melt with gratitude and well-being.

It didn't last long.

Around eight o'clock the doorbell rang. Sébastien – was he actually asleep? – woke at once, exclaiming "It's Mummy! It's Mummy!" He ran through the house, followed by his father who was obviously overcome by the events. Rose had suddenly gone pale. She had brought her hand to her necklace and stiffened her neck as people do when they're expecting some imminent disaster. We'd stopped talking; we even avoided looking at one another. Something very delicate had just been broken, something it would be hard to reconstitute because we'd have to start from the very beginning: our first steps towards complicity had become utopian

205

now that a part of the former life of Mathieu and Rose had been introduced into the house.

I apologized and got up from the table.

"I'll go see what's going on. They weren't supposed to get here till much later ... "

Rose didn't move. I was sure she'd have given half her life to be somewhere else and I knew there was nothing I could do to help her.

Sébastien was in his mother's arms but he was holding out his own to Gaston, wanting a kiss. We said hello while the child was moving from one to the other with obvious delight. Embarrassed, Mathieu stood quite motionless in the doorway. I was the one who invited Louise and Gaston to come in.

As soon as Sebastien was on the floor again – Gaston wanted to take off his coat – Sébastien exclaimed:

"Granny Rose is here! Granny Rose is here!"

Louise was startled, but her lovely face was soon graced by a smile. I realized at once that the two women had loved each other very much and I was filled with a great sense of helplessness.

"She is? I'd love to see her – it's been so long."

Mathieu looked at me. I let him know that everything was all right. Unhesitatingly I took Sébastien's hand.

"Come on in, we're still eating ... "

Gaston was explaining their early arrival to Mathieu.

"We're early because I had another fight with my brother and my father ... In the middle of Da Giovanni, no less! I should've known better than to go Christmas shopping with the family ... It's hot, everybody gets on everybody else's nerves, nobody can decide what to buy the kids, the men get fed up before the women, and then all hell breaks loose ... We left the restaurant in the middle of supper."

At her end of the table, Rose had got to her feet. She was looking at Louise so intently, I felt as if the younger woman might fall, burned by her gaze. Louise walked around the table, hesitating slightly.

"Hello, Rose . . . It's so good to see you . . . This is my friend Gaston . . . Gaston, my mother-in-law . . . My former mother-in-law . . . "

Her voice was different; a tiny quaver made it almost guttural.

Rose ignored Gaston, not out of rudeness but because she couldn't take her eyes off Louise. They remained for a long moment, not touching. Years of affection, of complicity, of hope, in a simple and everyday world, in a life now distant and irretrievable, years of happiness that wasn't a prelude to any disaster but which a single disaster must have shattered in just a few hours, passed through the silent look which they exchanged. Never, I told myself, never will that woman look at me in such a way, and the thought broke my heart. I felt like an outsider in my own house, and I stepped back a few paces towards the kitchen.

Louise spoke first. I didn't hear what she was saying but it seemed to strike Rose full in the chest. Her head drooped; Louise took it in her hands and kissed the brow which I imagined to be hot with emotion. Rose burst into great, almost childish sobs and threw herself desperately into the arms of her former daughter-in-law.

Sébastien looked on in amazement.

We, the three men, not knowing what to do, escaped to the kitchen where we sat around the table, awkward and silent.

I wished I could reassure Mathieu – and myself – but Gaston's presence inhibited me and I think he felt ill at ease with us too. We didn't know him and there was a world of prejudice separating us. On both sides. Did we represent to him lousy faggots playing fast and loose with his happiness? I knew very well that to me, he represented the good guy who'll try to be understanding because he has to, but who'd much rather be somewhere else.

Mathieu scratched the edge of the table with his finger-nail.

"What do we think we're doing, in this day and age? What a turkey – one hint of trouble and I run!"

I moved my hand towards him but didn't dare to touch him.

"We didn't run, Mathieu . . . Anyway, it's better to leave them alone . . . Your mother's had quite a day . . . "

Gaston got to his feet as if to leave us to our conversation and leaned against the dishwasher. He lightly punched the arborite counter.

"I can't stand situations like this . . . I should've just ignored my brother's crap and finished my spaghetti!"

He looked at the refrigerator.

"Anything to drink? I could use a cold beer . . . "

I was in no mood to play host.

"Sure, help yourself . . . Sorry, I wasn't thinking."

Empty chatter, banalities, while just next door something was taking place that I sensed to be tragic and desperate. Of which I was partially the cause.

Sébastien swept into the kitchen.

"Why's Mummy and Granny Rose crying?"

Mathieu and I exchanged a look. Neither of us felt like embarking on a long and risky explanation. Mathieu took his son on his knees.

"They haven't seen each other for a long time . . . "

"Aren't they happy?"

"That's just it, they . . . they're too happy!"

"How can you be *too* happy?"

The mood of the evening was deteriorating into an uneasy tension that was, if not growing, then constant. For me anyway. Two or three times they mentioned leaving. We'd felt obliged to hold them back, they'd felt obliged to stay.

Rose and Louise were having a long talk: they were making up for lost time, huddled in an armchair, Rose seated comfortably, almost slumped against the cushions, while Louise was perched on the arm, which must have been very uncomfortable, to judge by the contortions it required. They were chatting like two little girls reunited after their holidays. Their heads were almost touching and, after the tears, now forgotten, came frequent bursts of laughter.

It was a little harder for us, the three men. Gaston had done his best to start a conversation about hockey, but in the face of our flagrant lack of interest, not to mention our total ignorance, he'd turned his attention to a second beer and fallen into a silence from which it was hard to extract him.

Sébastien was visibly delighted to see us all together and went from one of us to another, a gratified child who doesn't know how to thank his benefactors: he had kisses and cuddles for everyone, and affectionate words, and I really don't think that the prospect of Christmas presents provided any ulterior motive; he was just glad to have us all within reach and he was letting us know.

Mathieu was rather pale. He kept looking towards his mother and his former wife; I thought I could detect, not regret or nostalgia but a sort of guilt, perhaps at having come between two women who were so fond of each other, unintentionally causing them pain. He told me much later, when we were alone and exchanging our impressions of what had happened, that the deep understanding between Louise and Rose had been one of the only successes in his marriage and that witnessing it again had infuriated him. Just now, though, what I saw in him was very different from fury; instead, it seemed a sort of fatalism mixed with resignation.

As for me, I sometimes felt like a spectator at an event that had little to do with me, although it had actually been one of the most decisive days of my life. But I was so worn out from a variety of emotions, of exhausting efforts, of contradictory feelings, that I simply withdrew into myself and looked rather coolly at what was taking place in my own house, events that concerned some individuals I'd known for only a very short time. On the one hand my existence was at stake and I had an important choice to make, but on the other hand, it was hard to believe it was all really happening. To really take it in, I had to focus on Mathieu, on my great love for him. And then a certain sense of reality was restored, I felt a lump of emotion in my throat and I told myself yes, because of Mathieu I can accept it all, I must – the child, the mother-in-law, the ex-wife, the ex-wife's new boyfriend . . . But the confirmed bachelor in me was rebelling too, and it was time to kick over the traces.

One notion of freedom was disappearing from my life that evening, and I was aware of the sense of vertigo brought on by important choices.

Sébastien fell asleep all at once; he collapsed in his mother's arms after one last tickle, and that brought the evening to an end. Everyone seemed relieved to have found a reason to separate. Gaston offered Rose a lift and they left fairly quickly amid a rustle of winter coats, of new boots, of pecks on the cheek and awkward handshakes.

Immediately after they left Mathieu and I went to bed (it was only half-past ten) and after making love with newfound – or renewed – vigour, we talked. Till the small hours. He described his impressions, I told him mine, but in a much lighter tone than I would have expected. There wasn't a minute's heaviness and I was very relieved. Still, I concealed my existential anguish from him because I didn't want him to panic for nothing. And I'm pretty sure I fell asleep when he was in mid-sentence because I dreamed of a winged Santa Claus who went from house to house gathering loot, taking what was best from each of them instead of leaving presents under the chimney.

"You're snoring so loud Mélène just banged the floor!"

"Really?"

"Hardly. It's the witches downstairs, they just pounded the ceiling with their broomsticks."

"Really?"

"Jean-Marc, go back where you were . . . You left your brain behind . . . "

Louise and Gaston

"I know you think my friends are totally square . . . "
   "I never said that . . . "
"Maybe not, but I know what you're thinking!"
Gaston was fulminating. He'd controlled himself for too long and now he felt as if he might explode right in front of Sébastien, who had fallen asleep on his knees as soon as the car started up, after they'd left Rose, still visibly shaken, on her doorstep. But Sébastien had opened his eyes at the first angry word between them. They tried as much as possible not to quarrel in front of him, keeping for their bedroom or his absences any recriminations (which in fact were fairly rare), any fleeting coolness or childish sulking, which always ended in precise and passionate caresses.

Sébastien had never heard Gaston talk to his mother like this. He huddled inside his brand new parka, which was a little too big for him, pressing his nose against the zipper and nervously licking its little metal rings. He was hot and his nose was running.

Louise, who was driving with exaggerated caution because she too could feel the anger creeping up her spine, gestured to Gaston to keep his voice down, but he didn't notice, as he was busy trying to find words that wouldn't terrify Sébastien. He shifted the child, who had a tendency to let himself slip down too low on his knees.

"Sit still Sébastien, or you'll end up under the glove compartment!"
Sébastien wanted to laugh, but pretended to be asleep.

With an exasperated sigh, Gaston turned to Louise.

"Anyhow, my friends would never put on a scene like that ... I've never seen a bunch ... "

"A bunch of what? Eh? A bunch of what?"

Louise turned too abruptly onto Jean-Talon. Their bodies all tilted in the same direction. Gaston's seat belt was squeezing Sébastien, but he said nothing.

"I don't know ... I don't know how to say it because I've never seen it before! I'm trying to be more tolerant like you asked me, but Christ it's hard! I'm trying to accept things I never accepted before I knew you, but some of it's just too much! What the hell do you think we looked like tonight, eh? Tell me! Why didn't we just get the hell out of there? I haven't got anything to say to those guys and they don't give a shit about me ... It's normal, and there's no reason we have to go out of our way to see them for Christ's sake!"

Gaston was almost shouting. He felt Sébastien twitch. He looked down. The top part of a worried little face was staring at him. Sébastien had often seen his mother when she was worked up, usually because of him in fact, but this was the first time he'd heard Gaston raise his voice. It was a very nasty revelation, one that opened some disturbing prospects: until now, he'd always been able to run to Gaston when his mother was mad at him; he was the doting stepfather, the buffer, who could calm any anger with a hilarious joke or a soothing word, and now he was turning into a demon ...

"Gaston, are you mad?"

Louise furiously ground out her cigarette in the already-full ashtray.

"Of course not, Sébastien, Gaston isn't mad ... "

He unzipped the child's parka to get a better look at him.

"Yes I am, Sébastien. I'm mad, and here's what I look like when I'm mad. Not very nice, is it?"

"Noooo ... "

"But it won't last. Mummy and I'll have a talk and it'll pass ... "

"Don't talk so loud, it's scary."

Gaston hugged Sébastien against him.

"This time we might have to talk too loud ... Better plug your ears ... "

Louise had forgotten to close the venetian blind; the yellowish light from the street lamp just outside their window cast a patina of unreality over the room that unsettled Gaston: everything, including them, had turned yellow when he switched off the light and he thought if we're going to be up arguing half the night I don't want the room to look so depressing ... He got up, walked around the bed where Louise had just joined him, wearing the winter nightgown he'd laughed at when it first appeared in late November, and turned the plastic rod that controlled the movement of the vertical slats.

"What do we do when Sébastien starts with the embarrassing questions?"

He groped his way back to bed; Louise's voice was his only reference point, a precise location he could use as a guide.

"Answer them as honestly as we can, what else? Anyway, maybe those things won't be so important to Sébastien's generation ... "

Louise's naivety made his blood boil. He switched on his lamp in a fury that almost knocked it over.

"Louise, for God's sake! You think the whole world thinks like you? Most people think like me and you know it! And with everything you hear about murder and AIDS and sadism and masochism and old queens they don't even *try* to be tolerant! You saw at supper tonight, it's making serious problems with my family and I don't like it ... "

"What have your brilliant father and your genius brother

been telling you now? I was at the next table, talking with your mother, and we weren't paying attention to you ... You were so loud we didn't want people to know we were with you ... We thought you were fighting over some hockey game. Every table in Da Giovanni stopped eating so they could listen to you!"

"What it is, they're starting to talk ... Apparently my sister and Mum aren't taking it so hard, but the rest of them ... "

"Your brothers and your father are just a bunch of machos ... "

"That's right, they're flat-out macho and they've got big mouths, and you better believe it!"

Louise propped herself on one elbow, her head very close to Gaston's. Her lovely profile, that of a child who's grown too quickly, had always moved him. A wisp of hair had fallen on her forehead. He brushed it aside with a gesture so familiar that she felt as if she'd known Gaston forever. She pressed her nose against his shoulder. Made her voice more gentle.

"What're you trying to tell me?"

He put his arms around her and held her very tight; guessing that what he was about to say would be painful, she shut her eyes.

"Pa and my brothers, especially Paulot who didn't mince his words, they're trying to put it in my mother's head that it could be dangerous for Sébastien ... See, Jean-Marc's homosexual, and Sébastien's a little boy ... "

She sprang up as if he'd slapped her. She threw back the covers and leapt out of bed, then, realizing she couldn't tell him off while she was walking around the bed or pacing the floor and he was looking on from his pillows, she resumed her place, seething with fury.

"You pigs! Tell those brilliant brothers of yours, especially that genius Paulot, that if I had a little girl Sébastien's age I wouldn't let her near them – for the same goddamn reasons! They act a lot more like sex maniacs than Jean-Marc and Mathieu! Jean-Marc and Mathieu weren't slobbering over you or making vulgar remarks about your figure, but those brothers of yours, as soon as I walk into the room ... You nearly had a fight with Paulot over it once, remember ... But that, oh that's just fine, it's *normal*! They've got every right in the world because I'm a woman and they're straight men! They even make cracks about your little niece's breasts ... But that's not sexual I suppose. Or sick. By God, it makes me furious! I'm heterosexual too, but that doesn't mean I'm going to make a grab at Sébastien some day because I like men! You can tell them from me, there's things in life besides sex ... No, better not, they'll just laugh in your face ... "

They were silent for a while. Louise was afraid her argument hadn't been clear because she'd let herself get carried away; Gaston, on the other hand, could find nothing to say because all her arrows had struck home.

He'd been brought up, along with his brothers, with a horror of homosexuality, he'd made jokes about it all through his adolescence – his repertoire of fag stories was virtually unlimited – he'd occasionally even gone queer-bashing in Parc Lafontaine, which activity consisted of getting together with a bunch of guys to go and beat up the anonymous silhouettes who haunted the park at night. When he had to acknowledge to his family that his girlfriend's son had a homosexual father, then, it had been terrible: the male members of the clan had shrieked and talked about heredity, disease, deviation, danger; they couldn't understand why Louise even let Mathieu see Sébastien ...

This time it was he who approached her, very gently. He knew how she could be, he was afraid of being rejected with one of those cutting remarks that were her specialty, and that always left him totally defenseless.

"Don't take it out on them ... The family really likes Sébastien a lot, you know ... "

"They can damn well like him a little less and leave us alone! Do I interfere with their lives? Your sister-in-law Céline's always crying on my shoulder because Paulot's such an animal, but do you hear me giving her advice? I think we'd better go to sleep; we aren't going to settle anything tonight ... "

Docile, Gaston switched off his bedside lamp again, then snuggled against her.

"Louise ... "

She turned her head towards him, a vague smile drifting on her lips.

"When you use that voice I know you're going to ask me something important ... "

Once again she'd read him perfectly and he chose his words carefully.

"Maybe this is a bad time ... We've never talked about it before ... but ... I'd like us to have a baby ... "

And Louise was sure he'd been reading her mind, because she'd been obsessed by the thought for some time now, but she thought no, it's just coincidence, a lucky chance, we thought about it at the same time ...

"Okay!"

"Okay let's talk about it or okay let's do it?"

"Okay let's do it. Right now if you want. I didn't take my pill yet ... "

Gaston sat up in the bed, throwing back the covers.

"You mean, like, right *now*?"

Slowly she ran her hand over his stomach, lingering around his navel.

"It might be the best thing that could happen to us ...

I've actually been thinking about it too ... A baby, a little monster who'd have all the faults of both of us – wouldn't that be fantastic!"

She saw his head droop.

"Are you crying? My God, if the men in your family could see you now ... Where does that fit in with your simplistic ideas about humanity – a macho chauvinist who bursts into tears because his wife says sure, she wants to have a baby?"

"I'm not crying!"

She ruffled his hair, gave him a push, then started to tickle him, exclaiming:

"Honest to God, Gaston, you're hopeless!"

Sébastien was trying in vain to sink his Froot Loops. He'd seen a TV commercial that claimed nobody could do it: not children, not mummy or daddy. He'd been intrigued and asked his mother to buy a box, even though he didn't even like cereal that much. And yes, the Froot Loops were unsinkable: he'd tried with his fingers, with the back of his spoon, he'd tried blowing on them; they always rose to the surface of the milk, floating back and forth and forming concentric circles, like little wavelets, and it always made him laugh.

His mother told him for the fifth time not to play with his food. He gave her a look of feigned innocence.

"They do it on TV, the whole family, and they all have fun!"

Louise came over and tweaked his nose.

"On TV they're supposed to be selling Froot Loops; but you're supposed to be eating them ... Understand? If you keep pretending you *don't* understand I'll take them away and you'll have toast and jam for breakfast ... Gaston'll be glad to eat them, without trying to make them sink ... At least I hope he will ... "

He ate a few spoonfuls in silence, then with the same guileless look asked:

"Mummy . . . D'you know Jean-Mak and Daddy sleep in the same bed?"

Gaston looked at him over his *Journal de Montréal*. Louise leaned against the refrigerator door, which she'd just opened.

"Yes, I know. Why?"

She was sure her tone had been wrong, that Sébastien would guess how awkward she felt.

But he chewed his Froot Loops before he swallowed them, like a good little boy. His mother came and sat next to him, gesturing hopelessly to Gaston. He merely buried himself deeper in his newspaper. Sébastien looked at his mother, frowning.

"When you were little how many mummies and daddies did you have?"

"You know very well, Sébastien. I had one daddy and one mummy. You know them . . . "

"I know, Granny Simone and Grandpa Arthur. I bet you didn't have much fun."

"Of course I did . . . "

She didn't know exactly what he was getting at, if he wanted to talk about her and Mathieu's divorce, or about Mathieu's new life with Jean-Marc; she decided not to push things; she'd answer his questions as succinctly and clearly as she could, without provoking them. Gaston folded his paper and slipped into the living room as discreetly as possible, after giving Louise a look of encouragement. She was tempted to call him chicken, but restrained herself. She cleared the table and put the dirty dishes in the sink. Usually Sébastien vanished as soon as breakfast was over, for fear his mother might ask him to help her. But he sat there, watching her go back and forth in the kitchen, obviously upset about something.

Louise thought she couldn't leave him like that, in the middle of the questions he didn't dare, or didn't know, how to ask. She sat down across from him, nervous but determined to vanquish his concerns, whatever they might be. She'd take all the time they needed and Sébastien would emerge from this conversation as well-informed as a four-year-old can be. Then again, what exactly can you tell a four-year-old?

"Is something bothering you, Sébastien? You can tell mummy about it ... "

And the final blow came, in all innocence, the perfectly normal product of the mind of a child who is a member of a society with very definite rules and customs:

"Who's the mummy? Daddy or Jean-Mak?"

"I did my best to explain that every family doesn't necessarily have a mummy and a daddy, but I don't know if he really understood ... "

On the other end of the line, Mathieu was a little calmer now. He'd panicked when Louise first told him about the conversation with their son, because he'd intended to have the same one during Sébastien's next visit.

"Put him on ... I'll try and talk to him ... "

"Not on the phone ... Next time you see him you can tell him in your own words ... But try not to make your version too different from mine ... "

"No problem ... We'll decide what to tell him, and how ... But where did he come up with a question like that ... "

"I think it's mainly Gaston's brother Paulot that put it in his head ... "

"What the hell business is it of his? Can you reason with the guy, or do I have to push his face in?"

"I wouldn't try that if I were you ... "

"I can imagine: a borderline crazy with little pig eyes close together, right?"

"Sounds like you've met him . . . "

Sébastien swooped into the kitchen, a Transformer in each hand.

"Is it Daddy?"

Louise gave him the phone.

"Yes, want to give him a kiss?"

"Yay!"

Gaston was bouncing Sébastien on the end of his leg and singing the "William Tell Overture." The child howled with delight. When Gaston got tired he changed legs or begged for mercy, which Sébastien categorically refused.

"Oh *please*, let's play horsey again!"

After half an hour of these exhausting contortions, Gaston rolled on the floor and played dead. Sébastien jumped on him, expecting a tickling match. But Gaston caught him in his arms and asked:

"How'd you like to have a baby sister?"

Sébastien stopped in mid-rush and replied, precocious and imperturbable:

"Not particularly."

Jean-Marc

Mélène practically grabbed me by the scruff of the neck as I was on my way home from the CEGEP. I hadn't seen her for a long time and I was glad to be back in her granola kitchen, enveloped by her warmth – I'd missed her motherliness this past while – and the little barking laugh that had always been like a balm to my wounds.

She'd made a borscht that smelled wonderful and I ate it with genuine appetite. It was a real winter soup that reconciled you to life. Accompanied, though, by her inevitable six-grain bread, which I really loathe because you have to chew it for hours and always end up with seeds between your teeth. We talked about this and that, steering clear of sensitive subjects with a primness that was new to us. She watched me surreptitiously, the way I watched her when she got up to slice more bread or turn on the coffee-maker. I had no classes that afternoon and I'd intended to go and see one of the American blockbuster movies that start coming out around Christmas. But at Mélène's, time seemed suspended, the hours passed without our being aware of it and I realized I'd missed the first screening. I'd been there for more than two hours and we'd said nothing important, though we hadn't stopped talking. It was marvellous. I had the impression I was speaking more slowly than usual, I felt a sort of drowsiness, a paralyzing sense of well-being that cleared away all my recent problems, leaving only the fragility, the lightness of the present moment.

I got caught up on the entire family, even the witches

downstairs who still hadn't forgiven Mathieu, who'd even had the gall to complain about the noise Sébastien made when he ran through the house. (After *two* visits! What would it be like after months or years?) For a brief moment I felt nostalgic for the time, actually so recent although it felt so distant now, when I was the only man among these women whom I adored, protected from the ugliness I encountered during my nocturnal peregrinations by their healthiness, their level-headedness, their humour.

And then an image of making love with Mathieu appeared and washed away my nostalgia. I'd turned a corner, Mathieu was now my absolute priority, and I just needed to find a way to link these two poles of my life which, up till now, had merely grazed each other without really merging: the security of a family that we'd created ourselves, based on indissoluble friendships, and my life with Mathieu, a life that was more intimate and more exclusive.

I watched Mélène go back and forth in the kitchen she hated so much and my heart swelled with a love very different from the one I felt for Mathieu, but which was truly love, I was certain of that. I wished I could tell her, but how can you say "I love you" to a friend and not sound pompous or risk offending her sense of propriety – or your own? For a couple, love is declared with great exclamations and very specific acts; between friends, love is more delicate, something that with time may even become nebulous: one must learn to decode words and acts, while knowing that the other person is doing the same, and in the end everything becomes comfortable, taken for granted.

After my third coffee – and Mélène's coffee is closely related to dynamite – I couldn't sit still any longer; I'd progressed from the bland beatitude of the first hours to a kind of agitation I couldn't explain, and it made me do something that I knew was silly but still couldn't resist: how long has it been, I asked myself, since you've let Mélène know how much you love her? I felt at the same time like a total wimp and extremely perceptive. That is, my prudishness made me feel that telling her was a wimpish thing to do, but I felt perceptive too because I'd realized that Mélène probably needed this proof of affection as much as I did. So I didn't resist, the urge was too strong and any delay would have acted as a censor: when Mélène suggested that we continue the conversation in the living room I got up, took her in my arms and held her for a long time. And I told her. We stood there in the middle of the kitchen without talking. Tears weren't far away and I almost hoped that they'd come.

"It just takes a second, come up and give us a kiss . . . You always used to be around . . . too much, even . . . but now we never see you. I'm not criticizing, I'm just stating a fact . . . We understand what's happening, Jeanne and I, and we're very happy for you and Mathieu but . . . I don't know how to put it . . . "

"You feel abandoned?"

"We aren't on the verge of suicide but we miss you . . . And the others too. Our Saturday suppers aren't the same . . . We miss our favourite macho . . . "

I often used to put on a macho act when I'd had a bit to drink, to the delight of the ladies who found my imitation irresistible. They'd laugh at my vulgar jokes and call me "mon oncle Joe"; they'd throw paper napkins or launch a chorus of boos when I overdid it . . . I felt an aching urge to experience it all again. And I realized that the worst thing that could happen to me would be to have to make a final choice.

The pipes in our house are very dilapidated – another contentious subject between the clans: at the time, Mélène, Jeanne and I wanted to put in new plumbing next spring, but the two others preferred to save their money for a trip to

Europe, where they hadn't been for a year and a half, poor dears – and whenever anybody took a shower anywhere in the house, everybody knew it. My own shower emitted a long, spasmodic rumble, as if the pipes had a cold, which distinguished it from the other two; and so Mélène and I were somewhat taken aback when that very characteristic sound was heard in the midst of our effusions.

Mélène, who is terrified of burglars, screamed:

"There's somebody in your apartment!"

I quickly reassured her:

"Don't panic, burglars don't usually take showers ... Mathieu probably got off work early ... "

We'd obviously talked about Mathieu a lot. At least I had. In carefully chosen but very clear terms. Mélène now knew how truly important he was in my life and in a sense I'd given her permission to tell the rest of the family. As she'd got used to to having Mathieu around, it wasn't a major problem, although I sensed a hint not so much of jealousy but of disappointment, perhaps, as if she'd thought I was too old to fall in love again after the much desired break-up with Luc, and that situation had suited her fine. I don't think she'd consciously been aware of wanting me for herself; but sometimes I think that if Jeanne – though I adore her – were to disappear from Mélène's life it would be very hard for me to accept anyone who replaced her, no matter how beautiful, brilliant and kind she might be. Because it would change the equilibrium of a structure that had been built up with a lot of patience and a lot of care. In the end, bringing a new member into our closely united family was a bigger problem than the fact that I had a new lover.

Mélène invited Mathieu and me for supper; I said I'd check with him.

I found him emerging from the shower and as excited as a flea. Francine Beaupré, the secretary at the advertising agency, had taken him at his word: they were looking for someone to promote the virtues of milk in a huge advertising campaign, and his still-adolescent looks had attracted the sponsor's attention. It was a fabulous contract and if he got it he'd be able to quit Eaton's and devote all his time to acting.

"You know I'd never accept a job as the exclusive spokesman for a beer or a supermarket chain but milk . . . It's healthy, no side-effects. I know I'll get points if I land that contract . . . "

He'd often told me of his scruples about appearing in commercials. They paid very well but actors who do too many sometimes find their reputations tarnished, and Mathieu was terrified of ending up despised for making money too easily through the promotion of dubious wares. He still had everything to prove in his profession, and he didn't want to burn his bridges.

He set off for his audition in a feverish state that verged on hysteria. I understood: this opportunity was assuming the role of a deliverance. A few days of work would finally allow him to try his hand in a field he felt passionate about, one he was sure he was made for. No more men's suits, aggravating customers, and the uncomfortable feeling that he wasn't where he belonged but might have to stay there a long time anyway, because a job's a job . . .

As soon as he was out the door, the phone rang. Of course it was Mélène.

"I heard a bumpity-bump down the stairs just now so I looked out the window . . . He seemed to be in quite a state . . . I thought he'd pull the door right off the taxi – after he nearly twisted his foot on the bottom step . . . Is somebody sick? His son?"

The four of us ate a wonderful chicken dish, with ginger, honey and lemon, a specialty of Jeanne's that I've never made successfully because I always put in too much honey, so that the sauce hardens into a sweet glue that sinks to the bottom of your stomach. It was a delightful meal; Mathieu made us all laugh with his advertising agency anecdotes, miming the nonsense he'd been asked to perform or imitating the clients – arrogant pigs for whom nothing and no one was quite good enough.

The audition had gone very well; he thought he had a good chance of landing the contract. Mélène and Jeanne listened to him talk about himself with genuine pleasure. I felt a little as if they were seeing him for the first time, though they'd always been very cordial. He'd suddenly taken on a certain solidity in their eyes because he was opening up to them, talking about his hopes and his passions – movies, the theatre, his son . . . and me – about his problems being accepted in a closed circle where only the products of the theatre schools – and not just any theatre school – are even considered. He was self-taught and people like that are looked down on, rather like the amateurs in the days of Les Saltimbanques and Les Apprentis-Sorciers back in the sixties.

At dessert, between two bites of an apple pie that had a little too much cinnamon, Mélène said casually:

"Oh, I forget to tell you . . . Jeanne and I decided to have a Réveillon on Christmas Eve . . . Well, not a real one, but a supper . . . on the early side, so Sébastien can come . . . The family doesn't know him yet, it's about time we all met . . . We've been feeling you're afraid to introduce us . . . "

Sébastien

Eric Boucher had already punched Sébastien twice that morning. On account of a Transformer Sébastien wouldn't lend him. The first time Sébastien had cried, the second time he'd shot back with an insult – a little too energetically as it happens, because Eric, though he was the terror of the nursery school, had complained to the monitor, the gentle Mario who couldn't believe his ears. Mario had felt like congratulating Sébastien for putting the little monster in his place, but instead he'd just tried to make peace between them. A reconciliation between Eric and Sébastien was impossible; their mutual dislike went back to the beginning of September and they'd been squabbling ever since. The monitors had tried to analyze it; they had supervised both children closely, studying their behaviour, their personalities and tastes, and they'd discovered that Eric was a leader but vindictive, never forgiving anyone for anything, and he was often all alone, whereas Sébastien, though he was a leader too, was more flexible, more conciliatory – and much more popular. With jealousy added to their natural antipathy, the two children were constantly at war. Sébastien had a few of the boys and all the girls on his side, while Eric had to be content with the rest of the boys – the most aggressive ones, needless to say.

This social microcosm fascinated Mario. He'd have liked to know the backgrounds of these small creatures he adored, who were his responsibility for several hours a day, study their parents to see whether heredity played an important part in their behaviour: was Eric Boucher the offspring of some minor local dictator and Sébastien the child of a pacifist? Or was it the opposite, were the children reacting against their parents by developing a personality the very opposite of theirs? No, at four and five you're still subject to outside influences; Mario would have been happy to meet Sébastien's father, but not Eric's.

Meanwhile, Mario lay down beside Catherine: the little girl had been having trouble sleeping for a while now, and her mother had asked him to keep an eye on her. It was nap time and all the children were asleep. After the morning's hullabaloo – the noon hour agitation, the outing to the park which had been complicated by the fact that Catherine had lost a mitten and he'd had to go back through the slush to find it – Mario was very grateful for this half-hour of peace and quiet. The other two monitors had gone outside for a cigarette; today, it was his turn to take a nap with the children.

Catherine was moaning. He gently stroked the curve of her forehead with his fingertip, humming a tune she particularly liked. She huddled against his shoulder, sucking her thumb. Another one who needs more affection? Telling himself really, you ask too many questions, Mario rolled onto his back and fell asleep.

Mario's awakening was brutal; Eric Boucher flopped onto his stomach, shouting:

"Mario, I'm hungry!"

He thought that if Eric wakened his parents like this every morning, family breakfasts must be lively.

"Eric, you could have suffocated me! That hurt!"

Eric merely made a face.

One by one, the children woke up; conversations, often incomprehensible, resumed where they'd been broken off, and games did too. Groups re-formed automatically, as if the children all possessed magnets that attracted their friends and repelled the others.

It was time to fix their snack. Mario was on his way to tell his colleagues that nap-time was over when he saw Sébastien marching over to Eric Boucher. Anticipating another brawl he was about to intervene when he heard Sébastien say:

"I got something you haven't got!"

It was the worst insult you could offer Eric, who always wanted to be the one with the most – of everything. Accordingly he walked up to Sébastien, saying:

"You do not! I got more Transformers and I got more Schtroumpfs!"

"I don't mean that! I've got a mummy and *three* daddies!"

Silence. All heads turned towards Sébastien. Mario hid his surprise with a nervous giggle, and then, as he got the picture, thought he'd *really* like to meet Sébastien's father . . .

Meanwhile, Eric Boucher was standing stock-still in the middle of the playroom. His supporters stared at him wide-eyed, hoping he'd have some devastating reply to silence Sébastien. But nothing came; Eric couldn't beat Sébastien's trio of aces. He'd never been so humiliated: he began to howl. Fat tears poured down his cheeks, generous and inexhaustible, the genuinely sorrowful tears of an inconsolable child.

Sébastien was very proud of himself: he'd managed to make Eric Boucher cry without laying a hand on him.

He'd hesitated a long time before making his declaration. He'd been thinking about it since that morning but his discovery last weekend at Jean-Marc's had been so amazing that he'd wanted to keep it for himself a little longer, trying to comprehend it before he told anyone else . . . At nap time, then, he'd pretended to be asleep, the better to think. To his child's mind, something was awry: you could have two daddies and two mummies, like his cousin Karine, when your parents split up ... That was easy. But he wasn't quite sure about his own situation. How could he explain that Jean-Marc wasn't a mummy? His conversations with his mother and with Jean-Marc hadn't cleared matters up: their answers had been a little too complicated and he suspected they were just using fancy words to cover something deeper that they didn't want to talk about. He'd sensed their discomfort, but he couldn't explain that either: are there some things you really can't talk about? And what are they?

It was only when he thought about the obvious advantage that his special situation gave him over Eric Boucher that he'd decided to spill the beans. And he'd been right.

He went back to his own gang a good inch taller and pink with pleasure.

But the final blow came not from an enemy but from one of his greatest allies, Marie-Eve Quintal, though she was always discreet and looked at him with admiring eyes, and he could always wrap her around his little finger. Without looking up from her paintbrush she said mildly, as if it were the most normal thing in the word:

"*I*'ve got a daddy and *three* mummies ... "

The entire nursery school, even Eric Boucher, exclaimed: "Wow! Lucky you!"

Jean-Marc

Every Christmas cliché was there: the roast turkey and dressing, the pork *tourtières* with Heinz ketchup, the *cretons*, the pickles both sour and sweet – I hadn't seen mustard pickles with cauliflower and cucumber for years – the cranberry jelly, mashed potatoes, number two peas, doughnuts and doughnut holes, the apple pie, the *bûche de Noël*, and even, rarest treat of all, an old-fashioned lemon meringue pie and cream puffs filled with real whipped cream. Every mouthful home-made by an army of sprites who hadn't cooked so much for eons but had thrown themselves into it with surprising enjoyment and the requisite hilarity. Especially Mélène, who had feigned horror at the sight of all the poison invading her kitchen, hand on heart and eyes rolled back. (She'd even run to her bedroom when the pork was delivered, crying out: "*Vade retro Satanas!*")

I pitched in too, abandoning my wok for once to try my hand at my Aunt Jacqueline's cream puffs. The result looked awful and tasted delicious.

Jeanne was in charge of the kitchen and directed her crew quite masterfully. Each of us was assigned a role and a recipe: it might succeed or it might fail, but it had to be followed to the letter, regardless of the results. The kitchen and dining room had been subdivided into three command centres: for pastry, meat dishes and vegetables. (Michelle, as lazy as always, insisted on being responsible for the peas and potatoes, and at the last minute she forgot to open the can of cranberries!) All day, the house was a hive of activity, of songs from Abbé Gadbois' songbooks, of silly jokes and laughter and exclamations of disgust when a recipe didn't work out or of rapture when something exquisite emerged from the oven – the *tourtières* were a triumph: golden, aromatic, glistening with fat, everyone agreed they could make the cover of Madame Benoit's *Encyclopedia*. They were the work of Arielle, who was stunned at her accomplishment: she'd never made a *tourtière* in her life and was expecting to take from the oven some doughy, shapeless, probably foul-smelling masses, and here she'd produced a culinary triumph that brought her unanimous congratulations.

Mathieu amazed us all by producing, in our oven because Jeanne's was already over-burdened, the most gorgeous lemon pie we'd ever seen, even more spectacular than my mother's, which had always been my criterion. (I even caught myself thinking, to my great shame yet laughing up my sleeve, that Mathieu's pie would have seduced my mother . . .) Sébastien was terribly proud of his father and went around repeating: "My daddy makes the *goodest* pies!"

All this fuss was, in fact, because of Sébastien, on whose account we'd decided to celebrate Christmas five days early. We'd explained that he'd have two Christmases this year, one at home and one with us, two Christmas trees as well, two turkeys and, most of all, two sets of presents, and that put him in a trance. At this moment his presents were piled under the magnificent tree that Jeanne and Mélène had put up the night before, and Sébastien kept shaking them as he tried to guess their contents. His excitement mounted as the day progressed, his behaviour was very close to unbearable, but everyone still thought he was adorable, intelligent, cute and bright – and he was taking full advantage of it.

The presents were distributed just before dinner, under the mocking eye of Goofus whom Sébastien had set up beside him. Sébastien opened or, rather, bashed in his packages with cries of joy, shouting happily as he saw the toys the women had chosen, which were numerous and unusual: no He-Man's or Transformers but beautiful, educational, imaginative things that Sébastien hadn't even known existed, which thrilled him. He often asked: "What's this?" and listened attentively, despite his excitement, as the women explained. After ten minutes he had disappeared under a heap of wrapping paper, and Zouzou went to get her camera. Twice, Sébastien lost Goofus, and then when he found him again, showed him all the presents he'd missed while he was buried under the wrapping paper, talking to him as if he were a real person, to everyone's delight. Then he thanked each of my friends in turn, whom he was seeing for the first time; I caught glimpses of a few damp eyes and heard some envious sighs. Mathieu seemed very touched but sat silent in a corner, perhaps because his sense of propriety wouldn't let him show any emotional excess.

Supper itself was eaten amid a euphoria verging on hysteria. We'd decided to "act out" a typically Québécois meal and, aided by the wine, we'd got carried away a little, despite Sébastien's presence: the humour was rather rude, the laughter fairly crude, as each of us used his or her recollections of family Christmases, at which the liquor had flowed a little too freely, to bring out our imitations of Aunt Imelda or Uncle Edouard or Cousin Jeannine. We even had a singalong, featuring those old-fashioned songs with double or triple meanings, we were treated to misogynous tales that would make your hair stand on end – in the mouths of my women friends they became an extraordinary kind of release, their imitations of the men in their families being unusually nasty and unusually accurate – we heard some hilarious accounts of booze-induced behaviour, we had a mashed-potato fight that needless to say thrilled Sébastien, but worried me a little: in fact I felt obliged to explain to Sébastien several times that everybody was only fooling, this was the way grownups played and he mustn't ever act this way at home. And the worst thing was, he seemed to understand. He'd go from one person to the next, climbing into laps, singing, kissing the cheeks that were offered to him. The girls fussed over him, tickling him, raving over his complexion and his gorgeous eyes; he had the time of his life and took in all the attention as if he'd been born to it, dragging along a new plush toy that I had a hunch was going to give Goofus some competition . . .

He fell asleep, exhausted, just after his father's lemon pie had made its second triumphant round of the table. We put him in Jeanne and Mélène's bed where he slept like a log, despite the racket we continued to make long into the night.

The party for the child was gradually transformed into one of those family reunions we'd all been feeling the need of; the impersonations stopped, towards the end voices were muffled, damp effusions were exchanged, Mathieu was even solemnly admitted to the bosom of the family, a proof of affection and confidence that touched me deeply.

The Réveillon ended amid a comforting warmth, around one final cognac, a rare and delicious one that Jeanne had unearthed somewhere in the depths of Ontario, from a supplier who'd been holding on to his bottles for years without realizing their value. We took our leave of one another happy, some of us slightly tipsy and some of us more, swearing all sorts of things we'd, fortunately, forget the next day. Mathieu wrapped Sébastien in a blanket; I carried the presents – it took two trips, rather giddy ones as it happens, with the stairs dancing under my feet and the walls dangerously tossing and heaving.

Mélène and Jeanne held me in a long embrace, wishing me all those things that people who've had too much to drink wish to someone they suspect is very happy. The puzzle was finally complete, or so I thought at any rate: the last two pieces, Mathieu and Sébastien, were finally in place.

Sébastien had been with us for three days. The nursery school was closed, I was on vacation and Mathieu came home right after work; we were experiencing something that resembled a family life and I was finding it quite enjoyable. Sébastien no longer frightened me as he had during his first few visits; I knew now that I didn't have to keep an eye on him every minute, that he could amuse himself perfectly well, especially with all the new toys he'd piled up around his bed and wouldn't be separated from. In the afternoons we went to the movies or I rented videos. I saw Walt Disney's "Pinocchio" again with delight but I hated "Alice in Wonderland," which I thought was too complicated for children and, especially, too Americanized. Sébastien much preferred contemporary animation films, those hideous monstrosities made to instill and develop in children an instinct for war, competition, hostility (oh yes, I was becoming every inch the concerned parent).

It was now the day before Christmas Eve and I'd promised Louise I'd take Sébastien home that afternoon. The three of them were going to spend a week with her parents, who now lived somewhere in Charlevoix County.

Just before we got into the bathtub the phone rang. It was Mathieu, breathless as if he'd run two miles through every department in Eaton's, calling to say he'd got the contract for the milk commercial.

"They phoned me here, I left this number ... I'm so wound up I don't know how I'll make it through the day ... Do you realize what this means? Freedom! No more department store! I was on the verge of saying to hell with it anyway ... I can't take them any more, any of them! Salesmen or customers ... Wow! Imagine Sébastien when he sees the billboards in the Métro . . . And the TV commercials . . . You know it's going to be a closeup, with the big grin, the milk mustache – the works . . . I'll be making money like I've never made before . . . Enough to start my courses again . . . and I'll have enough time to look for real acting jobs! I know I'm naive, it'll be rough, but at least I've got a chance! Wow! You think it'll hurt me? You think producers won't want me because I'll be the guy with milk on his face? I hadn't thought of that . . . Listen, sorry, I better go, my boss is breathing down my neck . . . "

I hadn't been able to get two words in. I told Sébastien we'd be seeing his father on television, but he didn't seem to understand. I wasn't sure how I felt about seeing my lover's face plastered all over town, but it was a fantastic break for him. Here I was with another actor! Assuming that one advertising campaign can make an actor, of course . . . And I could already see the expression on Luc's face the first time he saw Mathieu's billboards . . .

There was water all over the bathroom. Mélène had given Sébastien, among other things, a rubber duck that spat a powerful stream of water from its beak, and we'd been trying it out. Sébastien was sitting on my folded knees, attempting to keep his balance while he splashed warm soapy water in my face. I was about to say enough, we've been in the tub so long our skin's going to shrink, when he asked me with utter candour, between two bursts of laughter:

"Jean-Mak . . . what does 'touch' mean?"

The question threw me completely. Normally a child his age would know the word. I reached out my hand towards his face and pressed the tip of his nose.

"There, I just touched you . . . "

Serious, concentrating, he filled his duck with water.

"I know about that . . . But the other day my Uncle Paulot asked me if you ever touched me . . . I said yes and he looked mad . . . Does it mean hit me? You don't hit me, do you?"

I thought I'd sink to the bottom of the tub. The significance hit me like a ton of bricks. I began by reassuring Sébastien with banalities like, No, I don't hit you and I never will, get that out of your head and never mind what Uncle Paulot said . . . but as I spoke I felt choked by the other implications of the word: somewhere, someone thought that because I was homosexual I was a danger to the child! I wanted to scream, to storm out of the tub and kill that son of a bitch who, on top of everything else, had had the gall to make such allusions to a four-year-old!

Sébastien was aware of my discomfort.

"Are you sick, Jean-Mak?"

"No, I'm not sick . . . but we're getting out of the bathtub, I have to take you to Mummy's . . . "

I packed his suitcase like a zombie. I'm sure I forgot half the things I should have put in. I was furious and at the same time I felt abandoned, as you do after a separation. Something had just broken in me, I didn't yet know what, but a muted pain had me almost bent double. Maybe it was my disappointment at seeing everything crumple all at once after so much effort . . . I'd wanted to love that child, in fact I was beginning to, and now with a single word some son of a bitch was destroying everything!

Would I have to struggle against accusations like that as long as I kept seeing Sébastien? And where would they come from? Would everybody suddenly start asking these questions? Paranoia wasn't far away.

Sébastien was quiet. I'm sure he thought I was mad at him, but I couldn't find a way to reassure him as I'd always done before: I was imprisoned by a pain that prevented me from thinking, from acting rationally. I started going around the house in circles, as if I were looking for something. I think I was afraid.

I cried my eyes out in Mathieu's arms. It was the first time I'd broken down before someone with such *generous* abandon, if I can put it that way. I'd suffered attacks of jealousy before, of course, I'd even come crawling to Luc when I found out I was the biggest cuckold in Montreal, but I'd never let myself go before another person to express my pain with such rage and despair. Not even Mélène, though I told her everything. (Especially not Mélène, because with her I've always tended to laugh at my troubles, not make a big deal of them ...)

There was absolutely nothing I could do to resolve the problem that had overwhelmed me, nothing but wait. But how can you wait when you're furious?

After I'd calmed down a little I managed to talk. For once, though, talking was more difficult than crying. Mathieu listened, motionless; I was sure his right arm, which I was resting on, must be numb, but he was silent and out of sheer apathy I didn't move. I was at the bottom of a slimy pond, something very ugly was prowling around me and I was totally unable to react. I wanted to stay there and smother in convulsions of rage, to watch myself, in a sense, disappear or vanish or merge into the mud. People often say that you have to touch bottom before you can gather the necessary energy for the leap to the surface, but strangely enough, this plunge into despair had left me rather lethargic. Even though, as far as I know, rage and lethargy are totally unrelated.

"I feel so old all of a sudden! So helpless! I don't know if I've got the courage to go through with it! I only want the good parts, can you understand? The good parts I've just discovered after months of worry! Why does this have to land on me now when I've stopped being afraid of him? I know it's selfish, but I don't want any of the problems Sébastien might ... might cause us. Especially not that kind! I couldn't live with that constant threat ... You're the one I love, Mathieu, not him! I'm not putting this very well ... You're the one who taught me how to love, but if you left tomorrow morning, if we split up, I'm not sure if I'd miss Sébastien – that makes me feel like a monster! I mean, I'm not going to ask you to see him somewhere else or not see him at all!"

Mathieu had wiped my forehead on a corner of the sheet. I was sweating. He obviously had no idea what to say. He saw the problem as I did, and he must have been as frightened as I was of the day of reckoning that lay before us.

"If you give in like that you'll freak out for sure, you won't make it ... "

I broke in:

"I know you're going to tell me that time will heal everything ... But I'm panicking *right now*, Mathieu, it's *right now* that somebody's accusing me of being a criminal! I don't give a damn if it'll be easier tomorrow, it's today that's hard! It's today that hurts! It's today that I'm totally fucking furious! I don't even know if I'll be able to look Sébastien in the eye when I see him again just because of his asshole uncle's insinuations! Maybe it's childish, but I can't just forget it, pretend it was never said! It's as if all this has ... broken my relationship with Sébastien in two ... On the one hand there's my discovery of the child, something I never expected, something that could very well transform my life, make me more responsible, and on the other hand there's that ... monstrous things we might have to contend with as long as Sébastien's still a minor, and that terrifies me ... After Paulot, who will it be? The people next door? And then the rest of the neighbourhood? When they see the three of us walking along Bernard next summer, what are the

Outremont preppies on the terrace of Bilboquet and their parents on the terrace of La Moulerie, what're they going to say?"

The idiocy of my last remarks made Mathieu smile and I shut up. If I was going to bring up such totally irrelevant issues, I'd be better off silent.

For a long time neither of us said anything. I wished the world could henceforth be limited to this bed, which I never wanted to leave. Two bodies welded together in a heap of rumpled sheets, with nothing around them.

I may have slept. When Mathieu spoke we still hadn't moved and, out of pity for his poor arm, I slipped my head onto his stomach.

"If I didn't love you so much I'd leave right now, Jean-Marc. Pack my bags without a word, get in a cab and go and hide out at my mother's, as usual. It would hurt, but the pain would go away eventually. Like it always does. A visit to hell, a visit to limbo, then back to the world ... We've all been there and we've all got over it. Never unscathed, but never too badly messed up either. But I don't want to go. I do not want to get over you. If it's courage you need, I've got enough for two. If you want I can let you have some ... "

I heard his voice resonate inside his body and for a brief moment I felt that I *was* Mathieu. And I knew that whatever happened, he was part of me forever. And I of him. The choice had been disconcertingly easy. A great warmth had opened up, like a flower unfolding. I'd discovered how to make that leap that would bring me back to the surface.

It was Sébastien who said hello.

"How come you answered the phone? I thought your mother didn't let you ... "

"Who is this?"

"It's Jean-Marc."

"Hi Jean-Mak!"

"Hi yourself. You didn't answer my question, Sébastien ... "

"Mummy's on the toilet!"

I heard Louise's voice in the distance (she must have opened the bathroom door to hear what her son was saying).

"Sébastien, for heaven's sake! I told you to say I was busy!"

"She's busy!"

"Anyway, you're the one I wanted to talk to ... "

"Really?"

His tone was rather cautious. I'd never called him before and he must have thought he was in for a scolding.

"Listen carefully to what I'm going to tell you, okay?"

"Okay ... "

His voice was even fainter now. I spoke quickly, to reassure him.

"If your Uncle Paulot ever talks about me again ... Now are you listening?"

"Yes ... "

"If your Uncle Paulot ever talks about me to you again, you have my permission to tell him he's a horse's ass."

A brief silence.

"Did you hear that, Sébastien?"

"Yes ... but Mummy won't let me ... "

"She'll let you ... You tell her to call me, we've got something to talk about, okay?"

Another brief silence, then very loudly into the phone: "Mummy, Jean-Mak says I can tell Uncle Paulot he's a horse's ass! Can I *really*?"

Mathieu

It wasn't true that he had enough courage for two. He'd rarely felt so fragile, so vulnerable. And yet he'd come to that crossroads he'd dreamed of so often. (The crossroads reminded him of his father's old religious books he'd leafed through as a child, that so often showed a family facing a crucifixion scene at a crossroads, and he smiled at the thought. But this time the family was a little complicated, because all its members were men and the choices represented by the two roads had nothing to do with the good and evil of the bygone world of his father.)

His decision to put it all on the line, to use the milk commercial as a launching pad for a career in the Montreal theatre scene terrified him, because he knew just how naive it was. But he also sensed it was his only chance and if he let it pass he'd be a menswear salesman forever, and the mere thought of a lifetime sentence behind the counter at Eaton's made him dizzy.

But did he have the courage to go knocking on the doors of Radio-Canada producers, to experience the humiliation of being told that his CV wasn't very impressive (one season of children's shows and a ton of film and television walk-ons wasn't a very solid basis for a young actor's reputation, even if it did gain him entry to the artist's union) and that he was very pretentious to turn up so ill-prepared? And then the audition scenes he'd have to work up (and with what actress as his partner?) before confronting the theatre directors ... He was sure he had talent – his teacher, one of the best and strictest in town, had been encouraging him to try his luck for a year now – but not so sure of his ability to persuade anybody to listen to his sales pitch. The hardest thing to do in this profession, he knew it, was to sell yourself ... He was giving himself two years then – the duration of the contract – to make his breakthrough, otherwise ...

Jean-Marc was snoring loudly that night. Mathieu had pushed him gently, then harder, so he'd change position. Half-awake, Jean-Marc apologized, went back to sleep – and started up again.

Mathieu lit a cigarette. He hated smoking in bed but he didn't feel like getting up. With the ashtray on his stomach and his arm outside the bed, he watched the smoke rise to the ceiling.

Helping Jean-Marc through this business wouldn't be easy either, he knew that. The second choice he'd made, to stay with him regardless of the difficulties, filled him with satisfaction and relief, because he really did love Jean-Marc very much – even though he'd almost left him, thinking I'll get over him, nobody's irreplaceable, why put myself through all that? – but still he refused to impose anything on Jean-Marc, either his concerns about the new job with all the unpleasant memories of Luc it could stir up, or about his son who, for the moment, represented more trouble than joy for both of them. Of course they'd talked a lot about it in recent days, with Jean-Marc agreeing about everything, but still Mathieu sensed a hesitation in him that he couldn't quite define, despite all their conversations: was Jean-Marc simply afraid of the problems created by Sébastien's visits as he claimed, or was he terrified of embarking on what seemed to be turning into a drama that might last a long time? Wasn't Sébastien, finally, merely a pretext by a confirmed bachelor to get around an awkward situation?

As if he'd been reading his mind, Jean-Marc woke up completely.

"Can't you sleep?"

"No."

"Still the same goddamn things bugging you?"

"That's it. Original, eh? I wish I had a collection of complicated problems so I could move the pain around, but where my problems are concerned I'm steady ... "

Jean-Marc pressed himself against him.

"I think this might help ... There's something I forgot to tell you tonight ... I called Sébastien before you came home ... I gave him permission to tell Paulot he's a horse's ass the first chance he gets ... And if Paulot comes to dump on us, which Louise said he's quite capable of doing, you know what? I'll french-kiss him!"

The roar of laughter that rose in the bedroom startled Mélène and Jeanne upstairs.

Jeanne gave her lover a disappointed look.

"We haven't laughed like that for ages."

Mélène slapped her rear affectionately.

"We're an old couple, sweetheart. Our problems are too boring to make us laugh or cry ... "

"That's not very romantic!"

"Make me unhappy, you'll see how romantic I can be!"

Now it was Jean-Marc and Mathieu's turn to be startled.

Mathieu looked up at the ceiling, after butting out his cigarette in the ashtray.

"That's really something, eh, to laugh like that, at this hour of the night, after so many years together ... "

Sébastien

Sébastien was wildly excited about going back to nursery school. He kept asking his mother how many days were left. Louise wanted to know why he was so eager; he just said that he wanted to see his friends. Still, he had fun playing with his toys, he went skating in the park with Gaston almost every afternoon – double-bladed skates, a gift from Gaston's parents, had thrilled him, though he still couldn't skate very well, merely standing in the middle of the ice, unable to take more than a couple of steps without falling, and he watched countless movies on his mother's brand-new VCR.

Louise and Gaston were on vacation. Originally they'd planned a trip to the Laurentians, but they soon realized they didn't have enough money and would have to stay in Montreal. They let the days pass slowly, fussing in the kitchen, entertaining friends, visiting others, making love frequently just in case, as Gaston said, "the baby didn't take the first time ... " It was all the more frustrating, then, to hear Sébastien constantly asking when the holidays would be over.

During the first week in January it became quite unbearable, so that to restore a semblance of peace, Louise made a week-long calendar from which Sébastien could tear off a leaf every morning, counting the ones that were left. And still he answered her questions evasively: Yes, he was enjoying his vacation, no he wasn't bored with her and Gaston, yes he liked spending weekends with his father and Jean-

nober. Nachw. v. G. R. Kaiser. 306 [2] – dazu *Erl. und Dok.* Hrsg. von G. R. Kaiser. 8172 [2] – *Kreisleriana.* Hrsg. von H. Castein. 5623 [2] – *Das Majorat.* 32 – *Meister Floh.* Hrsg. von W. Segebrecht. 365 [3] – *Meister Martin, der Küfner und seine Gesellen.* 52 – *Nußknacker und Mausekönig.* 1400 – *Prinzessin Brambilla.* 8 Kupfer nach Callotschen Originalblättern. Hrsg. von W. Nehring. 7953 [2] – *Rat Krespel. Die Fermate. Don Juan.* Nachw. von J. Kunz. 5274 – *Der Sandmann. Das öde Haus. Nachtstücke.* Hrsg. von M. Wacker. 230 – *Des Vetters Eckfenster.* Nachw. und Anm. von G. Kozielek. 231

Kleist, Heinrich v.: *Die Marquise von O... Das Erdbeben in Chili.* Nachw. von Ch. Wagenknecht. 8002 – *Michael Kohlhaas.* Nachw. von P.-W. Lützeler. 218 – dazu *Erl. und Dok.* Hrsg. von G. Hagedorn. 8106 – *Sämtliche Erzählungen.* Nachw. von W. Müller-Seidel. 8232 [3] – *Die Verlobung in St. Domingo. Das Bettelweib von Locarno. Der Findling.* 8003 – *Der Zweikampf. Die heilige Cäcilie. Sämtliche Anekdoten. Über das Marionettentheater und andere Prosa.* 8004

Novalis: *Heinrich von Ofterdingen.* Textrev. und Nachw. von W. Frühwald. 8939 [2]

Schlegel, Friedrich: *Lucinde.* Hrsg. von K. K. Polheim. 320 [2]

Tieck, Ludwig: *Die beiden merkwürdigsten Tage aus Siegmunds Leben. Fermer, der Geniale.* Hrsg. von W. Biesterfeld. 7822 – *Der blonde Eckbert. Der Runenberg. Die Elfen.* Nachw. von K. Nussbächer. 7732 – zu: Der blonde Eckbert. Der Runenberg *Erl. und Dok.* Hrsg. von H. Castein. 8178 – *Franz Sternbalds Wanderungen.* Studienausg. 16 Abb. Hrsg. von A. Anger. 8715 [5] – *Der Hexensabbat.* Hrsg. von W. Münz. 8478 [4] auch geb. – *Des Lebens Überfluß.* Nachw. von H. Bachmaier. 1925 – *Liebesgeschichte der schönen Magelone und des Grafen Peter von Provence.* Nachw. von E. Mornin. 731 – *Vittoria Accorombona.* Hrsg. von W. J. Lillyman. 9458 [6] – *William Lovell.* Hrsg. von W. Münz. 8328 [8]

Philipp Reclam jun. Stuttgart

E. T. A. Hoffmann

IN RECLAMS UNIVERSAL-BIBLIOTHEK

Philipp Reclam jun. Stuttgart

Marc, no he hadn't had any fights with the neighbourhood kids . . .

On the eve of his return to nursery school, before he went to sleep, as Louise was reading to him from *Winnie the Pooh* (which he wasn't listening to), he confessed to his mother:

"I can't wait to see Marie-Eve Quintal!"

Marie-Eve Quintal had arrived late, to the great dismay of Sébastien who'd been watching for her since he got off the bus. All the children were concentrating on their glue and cut paper when the door opened to let in Marie-Eve, pretty and tanned after a week in Florida with her grandparents, and more in love with Sébastien than ever. She'd made a beeline for him, before she even took off her snowsuit, and planted on his cheek a wet kiss that still smelled of chocolate milk. He kissed her in turn – a drier, more discreet embrace – and told her excitedly, holding out both arms towards her, all his fingers wide apart:

"Know how many mummies I've got? Lots and lots and lots. *That* many!"